THE ANIMUS CHRONICLES

INCUBUS
THE DESCENT

Christian Francis

Encyclopocalypse Publications
www.encyclopocalypse.com

Always for you, Vicky...
xxx

CONTENTS

PART 1
The Prophecy

"The fearefull aboundinge at this time in this countrie, of these detestable slaves of the Devil, the Witches or enchaunters, hath moved me (beloved reader) to dispatch in post, this following treatise of mine to resolve the doubting both that such assaults of Satan are most certainly practised and that the instrument thereof merits most severely to be punished."

King James I - Daemonologie, 1597

The Offer

Ferenc knew he had no other choice.

He had to stop Elizabeth.

For the sake of all that was good in the lands that he ruled, he knew he had to wipe this scourge clean from the existence of man. For too long a shadow had fallen over the kingdom and blotted its soul with a horrific stain.

He could have claimed ignorance of what was happening, of what his wife had become— But that would be a lie. He knew she was no longer the joyous love of his life. He knew that the people she ruled over now feared her. He knew that she was responsible for the deaths of scores of his beloved people. But he could not admit it to himself until now. He had blocked it all out of his mind and whisked himself away to foreign lands, leading his armies for years at a time. Leaving her alone to her ways. Her evil ways. Far away from him. Too far away to be stopped.

But all things must come to pass. He finally had to face up to the naked truth of what was happening. In the midst of clearing out an Ottoman stronghold after a lengthy and bloody battle, he had received a missive from the proctor of his affairs; detailing how Elizabeth's 'passions' had gone too far— And how children had begun to go missing from the surrounding villages.

With a heavy heart and the truth being accepted, he left the battlefield and returned home to Castle Sárvár to face her. To make his amends.

History had a way of distorting reality to a point where it was no longer even a reflection of the truth, but instead a grotesquery of the writer's fevered mind. With regard to Ferenc, his history was to be rewritten by King Matthias. In wishing to extinguish the rumors of Elizabeth and Ferenc, Matthias' revisionism slowly became the truth over the following years – extinguishing the reality. This new history would say that he was complicit with his wife's actions, that he would die of a mysterious illness on the battlefield. That he had two living children who would be banished from the Castle after his death. That he impaled his enemies like his friend Vlad Tepes. These were all tales that over the coming weeks, Ferenc would not care about if he happened to have advance warning of. He would appreciate the talk of his death, as he would need the anonymity. What life held in store for him was something which could not be recorded. But for now, as Ferenc rode back to the Castle, this revisionism was not yet in the mind of the soon-to-be plotting King.

Out of a small stained-glass window on one side of the Castle's chapel, the darkness from the nighttime had settled in like a slumbering giant, stretching a calmness out over this troubled land. This calmness, though, did not affect the mind of Ferenc, which was anything but calm; rather a hive of dread.

Having now arrived back from the bloody fields of battle, he kneeled at the altar in the chapel, praying to any God that might choose to listen to his words.

In his mid-40s, Ferenc's slim physique belied his strength. Dressed in meticulously decorated leather garments, he looked every part the soldier he had grown up to be. His face haggard and weather-beaten, his beard's gray hair now winning the battle over the darker hairs of his youth.

"Please… If there is any God in these heavens. Give me strength. Steel my hand. Steady my nerves." He spoke under his breath, ending his prayers. Prayers he knew would be fruitless. Prayer was alien to him. He had never even been in this chapel during his adult life. His only memories of this room were being dragged here as a child, forced into praising his parents' God. The teachers his parents forced on him were the same. They were strict and pious men, expelling rants of the fire and the brimstone awaiting his soul if he did not live a God-fearing life. Maybe they were right.

Maybe he was damned. He had long believed that any God in heaven was either evil, a fiction or was absent, because the rampage of evil throughout the world could not exist under the watch of a real and present benevolent deity. Today, though, with what he had tasked himself to do, he had to ensure that *if* there was a God, that He was on his side and would hold him up if he started to fall. Even the help of a God he did not praise would be appreciated, as nothing could afford to fail in this endeavor.

Standing up from the altar, he picked up his sheathed sword, propped against the altar's stone leg. Strapping its large black belt around his waist, he glanced out of the window, out across the silent darkness, hoping in vain to himself. Wishing to one day again meet the sunrise with a smile on his face. A wish he knew was most likely but a foolish dream.

From the chapel, he walked down a high-ceilinged stone passageway; its walls flanked with flaming torches held firmly in ornate clasps. Ferenc took the first one he came to and held it ahead of him – lighting his way as he walked through the doorway leading to a narrow stone staircase.

His mind wandered to thoughts of his child; the baby born to him and Elizabeth. Hanna. She had breathed for but a day before a cruel act of nature extinguished her light. Taken away in her sleep whilst he battled in another Empire. His greatest regret was not being able to look into her eyes before she closed them forever. Maybe if there was a God, He'd decided to steal her away, knowing what Elizabeth was becoming. He thought Hanna's arrival in her belly and her grand entrance 9 months later could have taken the darkness from his wife's soul – after all, she *was* suddenly happy when her condition became clear. She became attentive to the child inside of her. This, though, did not last beyond the birth. As soon as Hanna was taken away into the depths of death and he returned home from battle, her demeanor was thrown back to where it was before. No emotions about what befell their child; just a cold look to any and every one. Even when Ferenc sobbed in front of her as he spoke of their loss, she just smiled and said, "She is in a better place than the hell you trap me in," then walked away to find fleeting pleasures with her chosen courtesan. Even in her time of grief, she ran between the legs of another person.

His foot trembled in its leather-clad boot as he slowly took his first step upwards. These were the steps leading to Elizabeth's room – the place he had chosen for this confrontation. The grit beneath his boot scraped as each labored step lifted him closer to what he had denied would ever happen.

In his hand the torch threw dancing yellow and orange lights around, illuminating the stone walls around him. His forlorn face glanced downward as he took each pained step.

A seemingly endless ascent was soon brought to a close as he took his last step, bringing him to the hall in the Castle's tower.

"Ferenc," was the hushed greeting of the guard who waited for him at the top of the staircase. More than just a guard, this man was the

Proctor of the Castle in his absence. Someone who ran everything in his stead. A man who had witnessed what Ferenc had been avoiding. . . a large man in his 60s, called Janez. His advancing age had not withered his body, or his mind. He was an imposing figure with an expression of stone. And it was this man – aside from his wife – who was the only person who he permitted to call him by his first name. without any formality of titles.

Ferenc smiled weakly at his friend; then to the other man who stood beside him. Milo, Janez's brother. "My Lord," Milo whispered in traditional reverence.

"It's all prepared." Janez spoke, continuing the hushed tone, as he motioned to behind Milo, where a pile of stone and a few pails of mortar rested in the shadows. The reality of what was about to be done crept over Ferenc, his eyes slightly widened and filled with dread.

"We can..." Janez continued to speak softly. "We can handle this for you... We can end this forever without you even seeing her again."

"No," Ferenc answered kindly. "I could not ask that of any man. You should not be tainted with her blood. No, my friend. This is my duty."

Janez smiled at him and put a hand on his shoulder assuredly. "Then," he said, "and I know it will not bring you any comfort, but please... know you are not alone. Remember that God is with you every step of the way."

Ferenc paused for a moment, reflecting on how he wished he believed in any higher power. Though his friend was a good man and probably the only person who would tell him the unabashed truth, no matter the cost, he couldn't help but wonder whether his strong beliefs made him a fool.

"You are not to blame," Janez continued. "She is the scourge. Not you."

"If I stayed, I could have saved her soul… and my daughter's life… Instead… Instead, I slaughtered the Ottomans and Habsburg's bastard soldiers in a poor attempt at ignoring the very evils in my own home." His voice wavered as he struggled to keep his hushed tones through his emotion.

Janez continued his kind smile and his hand more reassuringly gripped Ferenc's shoulder. "Well, let us pray that God will look favorably on her punishment, then give us the chance to save what is left of her tarnished soul."

Ferenc swallowed hard and pushed any fears he may have had deep, deep down, to the same place he kept the tears that were aching to come out. He nodded to Janez, then to Milo and turned, starting the walk down the hallway, toward to the large set of double doors at the end.

Janez turned to Milo, then motioned to the bricks and mortar behind them. "We will have to work quickly and quietly, okay?"

Milo nodded. He would always do what his brother asked. He was – and always had been – his moral compass. Even as a young boy, Janez was the responsible one. The God-fearing one. The honest and good one. Even through his years being raised alongside him, Milo was far removed from his brother's goodness. It was only in recent years that he had asked his brother – as the proctor and de facto law maker for the Castle – for forgiveness and guidance for his past transgressions. The people he hurt, the things he stole, he now saw these sins of his as clear as day and was working for his brother to atone for his past. But now, he was tasked with something *as bad as*, if not worse than, his previous sins. He knew better than to question a man like Janez, but what he was about to do could not be considered a just action.

"Brother," Janez whispered with a concerned look on his face. "I know what thoughts are hanging heavily with you."

Milo didn't reply.

"Just know, this is God's work. Battling evil can never be done by half. It *has* to be actioned with a fist of stone, not dismissed with a cowardly smile."

Milo nodded slightly. "I know… I know."

The metal latches on the large set of wooden doors made an echoing, clacking sound as Ferenc lifted them, pushing open the entrance to the bedroom. Without even looking up, he walked in, then turned, closing the large doors behind him.

"Ferenc! You came home!"

With a small forced smile, he turned back into the room and saw an image that would cause many sleepless nights and force him onto a path of no return.

A grotesque scene stretched outward over this large stone-lined room. With the hand-carved four-poster bed at one end, it seemed to be the only part of the room which was not soaked in blood.

Around the room, embedded into the stone floor, were six large metal spikes. On each, the body of a naked young man was skewered and impaled onto it; in through the anus and out through their mouths. Their deceased and pained expressions were wide-eyed and tormented. The blood from each of them had pooled onto the floor, down tiny crevasses carved into the stone which the spikes were fixed into. All these crevasses fed the blood across the floor, leading to a ten-foot wide circular bathing pool, directly in the middle of the room. One which had not been there when Ferenc last left the Castle.

Within this newly built stone bath was the deepest red liquid. The blood of many innocents had flowed from the spikes and collected below into this congealing swamp. Floating within this thick scarlet water, bobbed carved off human body parts: breasts, genitals, hearts, heads, of at least 12 different victims.

Bathing in the middle of this abomination, with a wide grin on her face, was Elizabeth. With blood covering every inch of her, her eyes and teeth shone out as their whiteness contrasted with the deep murky reddish colors surrounding them.

"You like what I have done with the place?" she smiled nonchalantly.

Ferenc stood aghast. If he hadn't witnessed the constant horrors of war, he might have vomited at the stench of decay and split open bowels – let alone the vision of butchery which he now saw.

"I presume you are here to kill me?" Elizabeth chuckled, as she saw Ferenc's attempt to not lose the contents of his stomach, sickened by the vision of what she had created in the room.

"You need absolution... This is... Evil," he uttered, trying to meet her gaze, whilst blocking out the vile images of murder around her.

Her head tilted to one side as she displayed a mock-questioning look. "Absolution? From whom? You have no God to absolve me."

"Whichever God will have you. For you are possessed by something ungodly." He tried not to breathe the sickening smell in too much.

"Oh, I have *my* Gods and they are more than happy with me." She spoke as she caressed some of the blood she bathed in, over her neck and up her face.

"Please, Elizabeth..." he pleaded.

"Take me..." she interjected as she dropped her hand from her face back into the blood. "Right now. Just come over here and ravish me."

"What?" He did not know this woman in front of him. When they married she had been a picture of innocence. A paragon of virtue. And their conjoining was a saving grace for both of them. She would be raised up to a position far above what her family had previously achieved and in return he would have an heir. Someone to carry on his bloodline. But that was where the relationship ended.

"I'll even let you take me like a man, as that *is* what you prefer, after all."

He did not reply, and instead just nodded to himself. Convincing himself that there was no return for her. She was beyond any help anything except death could provide.

"No? You disappoint me. Now what do you want to do? Kill me? Burn me? Quarter me? Hang me?" she asked as she glanced down and in the water in front of her, noticed a heart float by. She picked it up in her hand gently.

"I am sorry, Elizabeth. I truly am," Ferenc said as he turned back to the door. "I must leave you here. Forever."

Elizabeth held the severed heart in her hand and squeezed it slowly. The thick blood oozing out, as her fingers dug in and split the muscle. "You are trapping me here? Is that the extent of your cruelty?"

"Goodbye Elizabeth. May a God save your soul from the fires," he said meekly, walking away.

"I welcome the fires." She spoke still looking at the heart in her hand, as she suddenly changed tack. "Oh, husband?" she called out.

Ferenc stopped before opening the door, choosing not to turn around. Though the image of that room would forever be burned into his memory, he never wanted to see it, or his wife again.

"I shall hunt you down. You *do* know that, don't you?"

"Forgive me," he proffered weakly as he reached out and lifted the latch to the door.

"A simple warning then: Hide from the shadows. Because I will be there. Waiting. And when you peer into that darkness, I will turn your whole life into a whore's ruined cunt. I will flay you and display you for the world to see..."

And those were the last words he heard before he opened the door. Instead of a clear path to the hallway, Janez and Milo were laying the stones and mortar high, blocking up the room. Ferenc clambered over the half-built wall and into the hallway. Janez then, without looking inside, pulled the door closed, knowing never to look into the eye of evil.

"Poor, poor Ferenc. You know not what you do," Elizabeth called out from the closed room, as she happily lay back into the blood pool. Her head rested on the stone behind her as she dropped the heart and moved her hand downwards, into the murky depths towards her groin.

In the hallway, Ferenc was composing himself from the horror he'd witnessed, taking breaths of unpolluted air as deeply as he could. Janez and Milo had now finished building the wall which trapped Elizabeth inside. The stones they lifted were large and needed two hands to move them. When the mortar dried, the wall would be impossible for Elizabeth to knock down.

"What now?" Janez asked whilst placing the final stone. Milo then handed him a pail of mortar, which he took with a polite smile.

"Now we punish those who helped her," Ferenc said as he looked out of the window, "and banish this evil." He did not know how many guards she had. Janez, Milo and himself had already disposed of the four that guarded her tower, but there were surely more in wait.

"And what then?" Janez asked, as he started to fill in the gaps between the stones with more mortar.

Ferenc thought for a moment. "Then, my friend, you will have the Castle to do with as you please." He knew as soon as he saw what Elizabeth had done, that he could never live as the Count, or within this Castle, ever again.

Janez had sent him many letters during his time away, apprising Ferenc of the gossip around Elizabeth. The hushed rumors that she was the Devil's whore, luring innocents to her bed, innocents who were never seen or heard of again. Tales that Ferenc and Janez had initially dismissed as gossip. It was only the last letter sent that had convinced Ferenc to return to his homeland, to face whatever truths were in his writing. A letter which detailed the disappearance of seven newborn babies from the village and of the mothers that had petitioned Janez to find them. It spoke forlornly of his investigations which led to straight to Elizabeth's doorstep. She had had her guards steal these innocents, and had them brought to her bedroom. He did not know for what, nor did he want to know. He only knew that she had murdered them; she admitted as much to him when he confronted her. It was in this last letter that Janez pleaded for Ferenc to return, for she had stopped working her evil in the dark and started to air her murderousness in the light of day.

When Ferenc returned, he was met with the truth of her butchery in an instant. The path up from the village to the Castle was lined with impaled 'criminals', murdered on spikes like the ones in her bedroom. These were all people who acted against her; Men, women, children, young, old… It didn't matter. Those who uttered a word of displeasure or fear, even those who wanted to escape the village – all were met with the punishment of impalement. Over the course of a couple of months, the once happy village became a tormented and violent place.

Janez turned to Ferenc, handing the nearly empty pail of mortar back to Milo. "You are not planning on staying?"

"No." He turned to Janez. "When we finish here, I cannot remain. Her name and all her past *must* be extinguished, myself included."

"What do you plan to do?" Janez asked with some sadness to his tone.

Ferenc looked directly at him and softly replied. "Atone."

Janez smirked in confusion "What for? For punishing the wicked?"

"Her sins… They would never have existed had it not been for me. My absence and cowardice enabled this to happen. And I should have been strong enough to take her life, but I could not."

"You cannot blame yourself," Janez said as he took a step closer. "Her blasphemy is on *her* soul alone. And this punishment is as good as the death which she shall receive soon enough."

"Whether that is true, I cannot say. But all I know is that the moral balance must be restored," Ferenc said, with each determined word laced with a conviction which he had not spoken with in a long time. "For every drop of innocence that she has destroyed. I, in turn, must destroy something evil."

Toil & Trouble

The mist fell over itself as it crept over the dirt-laden ground, billowing up into thick white plumes as it silently danced, the breeze taking it in gusts upon its journey.

The darkness clung to the surrounding trees like a newborn at its mother's teat, refusing to let go as it consumed the surrounding light. Only the trees at the front of this forest could be seen at all, the rest hidden amongst the blanket of the consuming night. The visible trees formed a semicircle around three figures. Figures who stood around a large metal cauldron, their large black cloaks concealed their faces from view.

The figure in the middle of the trio, tall and broad, had her aged hand held outward, protruding from her cloak, holding a large stick which stirred the liquid contents of the cauldron, the surface of which glistened in the dulled moonlight high from above the trees. Bones and eyeballs floated in the steaming murky liquid as this large female figure stirred it slowly. Purposefully.

The skin on her hand had a greenish tint to it. A skin full of scars and boils reaching up her forearm and into her cloaked sleeve. The nails at the end of each of these fingers were blackened from dirt and cracked with age.

This tall figure turned to the others. "Thrice the branded cat hath mew'd!" She spoke in a rasping, broken voice.

"Thrice and twice the hedge-pig whin'd!" the second figure said.

The first looked upwards, as the moonlight caught her face. Gnarled and twisted. Her nose was hooked and large. Her eyes blind and milky. Her skin wrinkled and sagging as if she had lived hundreds of years.

The third figure leaned forward, the moonlight illuminating her face, which was eerily similar to the others. "Harper cries 'Tis time, 'tis time!'" she exclaimed.

The second figure cackled upward as her face became visible through the hood. All three figures were identical, in their grotesque and ancient visage. Only their body sizes showed any differentiation between them.

The first figure leaned over the cauldron and breathed in its stench. "Round about the cauldron go; In the poison'd entrails throw. Toad, that under cold stone days and nights has thirty-one swelter'd venom sleeping got, boil thou first i' the charmed pot." She spoke joyously under her breath.

These figures then all spoke in unison, "Double, double toil and trouble; Fire burn and cauldron bubble."

An hour later, the stage where the forest stood, had now been changed to a Castle exterior and was brightly illuminated with all the surrounding stage and house lights. The audience who had just watched this performance now stood on their feet in rapturous applause. The three figures – or more correctly, the three witches – all took their bows amongst the rest of the cast of *Macbeth*, each of them smiling and thankful as they completed yet another night's performance.

Walking back to their dressing rooms, the three witches looked exhausted. Their hoods now pushed back, displaying the full extent of their stage makeup. The one in front – the first witch – walked into the dressing room off the side of the corridor. On the door to this room was a printout saying *The Witches Coven, Do Not Enter Without Knocking, Lest Thee Be Cursed.*

Inside sat three chairs in front of three large makeup stations. Behind them, on the other side of the room sat a large sofa, strewn with clothing.

The first of them sat in the far chair with an exhausted sigh. This was Rebecca Hopkins. In her late thirties, but feeling like she was 60. Standing at six foot four, she was an imposing figure, especially next to the other two witches who were barely past five feet tall each.

"This doesn't get any fucking easier, does it?" Rebecca said, turning to the second witch, her voice laced with a soft and gentle London accent. The second witch, named Janine, slumped herself down in the chair next to Rebecca and with a strong tug, ripped off her fake nose, exposing her real, more petite nose underneath. "No, it fucking does not." Her Brooklyn accent was strong and loud.

"They're gonna be pissed at you for that," The third witch, Sarah said, motioning to the ripped-off prosthetic as she too took a seat in front of her makeup station.

"I *am* pissed at you!" echoed a voice from outside of the room, as the makeup artist for the show, Dominique, walked in. "I told you to stop doing that," she said pointedly to Janine, as she walked straight past her to stand behind Rebecca's chair.

"You love me really." Janine spoke with a smile that illuminated her heavily made-up face, turning the grotesque witch's makeup into a pleasant sight.

"You at least not fuck it up with your nails?" Dominique asked as she looked at the ripped-off witch's nose, which now lay on the makeup counter in front of Janine. Complete with obvious gouges from her nails along the latex, from where she'd grabbed it.

Janine shrugged.

"Bitch," Dominique replied with a smile. "Good thing you're pretty." She grabbed a bottle of liquid and a brush, then started her process to remove the latex appliances from Rebecca's face. "And just for that, you can be last tonight."

"Aw that's unfair!" Janine mock-complained and crossed her arms in a fake tantrum.

"Well, be a cunt get treated like a cunt," Sarah laughed as she picked up an old can of lemonade from in front of her, and with her mouth on the straw sticking out of the top, took a slurp.

"You know the rules!" Dominique scolded as she removed Rebecca's fake ears.

"Yeah, yeah," Sarah said dismissively.

Through the removed appliance, Rebecca's blonde hair could be seen behind her real ears.

"Sarah, you know full well. No cunts allowed in here!" Janine smirked.

"Exactly. None except you, my dear Janine." Quipped Dominique.

Rebecca burst out laughing at this. Her deep laugh so contagious it made everyone smile.

"Oh, the great Rebecca Hopkins finds that funny, does she?" Janine grinned at her.

"Miss. Hopkins," Sarah said in a fake male timbre. "Is it true that after your successful Hollywood career, you slummed it, acting alongside a small cunt from Queens?"

"Hey, less of the small!" Janine said, turning to face Sarah.

"Less of the small, more of the cunt. Got it..." Sarah replied in the same male voice, sending the witches into loud hysterics.

"All of you! Stop it! I'm trying to work here!" Dominique said as she peeled the witch's face from Rebecca, exposing her real features.

"Fine!" Janine exclaimed. "Besides, I AM a cunt. Why? 'cos tonight, I fucking said it again! You all hear it this time?"

"You said 'twice' again?" Dominique asked, badly masking a smile.

"Can't fucking shake it!" Janine exclaimed turning to her "Thrice and once the hedge-pig whin'd? Thrice and twice rhymes and sounds better. Shakespeare didn't know what the fuck he was writing!"

"Fucking Shakespeare!" Rebecca grinned. "Didn't know a fucking thing, right?"

"That's what I'm saying!" replied Janine. "Old limey bastard."

Dominique rolled her eyes. This wasn't the first time she'd had to endure Janine's humor. "Less of the Limey, you Yankee!"

"Less of the limey, more of the cunt?" Sara enquired.

"I'm fine with that!" Rebecca smiled.

"Oh we *know*," Dominique said softly, as she removed some remnants of latex from Rebecca's temples.

"Hey everyone, this is supposed to be about me. Now all of you tell me how amazing I was, tonight!" Janine said, giggling.

"Apologies, you were as good as I was in my films," Rebecca smirked.

Janine's head shot around in an instant. Her shock-filled expression bursting through her makeup, straight at Rebecca. "How… Fucking… *DARE*… you," sending the whole room into fits of laughter.

Later that night, in the alleyway behind the theater, the stage door opened, the London nighttime breeze spilling inwards. This night was unseasonably warm for the time of year, as Rebecca felt as she walked out of the theater with a small rucksack slung over her shoulder. Dressed in old black jeans and a checked lumberjack shirt, she ran her fingers through her shoulder-length platinum-blonde hair, breathing in the city air. She glanced down the alleyway, glad there were no throngs of waiting fans like there had been on her first week here. No autograph hunters lying in wait for her to give them free eBay stock. Now she was old news. No one really cared that she was there anymore. And that was *exactly* how she wanted it.

Janine followed out of the backstage door, stunningly beautiful in her early 20s, with , black, straight hair, wearing a short skirt and a crop top. Not the kind of clothes most would wear at this time of night, especially at this time of year – but Janine lived in her own world. A world of happiness and revealing clothing.

As she saw Rebecca, she reached into her handbag, bringing out a well-read paperback. "I forgot to return this to you."

With a smile, Rebecca took the book from her hands. A book about outcasts and acceptance. Though a violent horror, it was – to her anyway – an important tale.

"I couldn't finish it," Janine said with an apologetic shrug.

"What? Really? How come?" Rebecca asked as she took back the book.

"It's so gross! You said it was a nice story!"

"It is!" Rebecca replied in surprise.

"Well anyway. Thank you. Just not my bag, baby!" She smiled at Rebecca before continuing. "You're out tomorrow, right?"

"Hopefully," Rebecca replied, as Janine turned and walked away happily.

"No hopefully about it, Definitely! You still gotta show me how you English have fun!" she said as she walked with a skip past where Rebecca was standing toward the mouth of the alleyway, leading into the main city streets.

"Fine. Definitely!" Rebecca called out.

"That's my girl!" Janine shouted back as she continued her journey.

"Oh, I fucking wish," Rebecca said under her breath as she watched this vision of beauty walk away. "Damnit," she continued as she turned to walk further into the alley.

That had been the second time she had lent this book to anyone. Both times to women she had felt attraction for, and both had said the same thing. It was too violent and they just couldn't read it. As if that is all they could see in the words. They could not recognise the beauty amongst the horror. This book in question was called *The Changeling* by Deacon Sorbic, her favourite author, and the only man she thought truly understood her soul, with the main characters thinking exactly as she did. Doing exactly what she would. And her wanting others to read it was maybe a subconscious test for them. Maybe this was her showing the worst of herself, so when someone finally liked it, she knew she had found a perfect partner. Or maybe she was just a fan of horror books and read too much into it.

Shrugging it off she shut her eyes for a moment as she muttered, "She's too young for you, anyway… Much too fucking young."

No sooner had she finished speaking than she opened her eyes to be met with a short old lady standing in the middle of the alley, directly in her path, staring up at her with an intent smile.

How the hell did I not see her before? Rebecca thought to herself as this old lady's smile remained unchanged on her face.

"I had to meet you," she said weakly as she took a step closer to Rebecca, who was now trying to hide her shock with a small smile. Fans did this kind of stuff all the time and she had never got used to it.

"Hello, did you want an autograph?" Rebecca asked as she reached for the pen which held permanent residence in her back pocket, for this very reason. "I think I have a spare headshot in my bag."

"Oh no, no, no dear," The old lady said, shaking her head.

Reaching forward, she grabbed Rebecca's hand, her cold leathery grip sending a shiver down Rebecca's spine. "I just want to be in your grace," she continued. "For when it all ends."

"Grace?" Rebecca asked as she moved backwards slightly, loosening the old lady's grip from her, causing her to retract it. "I'm sorry, what do you mean?"

The old lady bent down, picked up an ornate framed painting, which had been resting against her leg. "Oh, please forgive me… Here." She held up the painting to Rebecca. "Have a look."

Holding it outward, the old lady peered over the frame with a smile. "And then it can begin, you see? As was *foretold*. You can become your fate."

Rebecca stared at the painting. It depicted a woman (who looked a lot like Rebecca) standing on a hill, dressed in ornate armor – holding the severed head of Jesus, complete with halo. Around her, up the sides of the hill, demons and monsters all lay prostrate, in subjugation to this person. Rebecca stared, taking in as much as she could, as if the painting was demanding her attention more than was natural. Her eyes moved to focus on the image's background, where clouds made up the form of a leviathan resembling the traditional image of the horned devil. "I… Did you paint this?" she asked, not knowing what to make of anything. "Who even *are* you?" She turned her gaze from the canvas back to the old lady.

"My name is Phyllis, little bird," she said, still with a smile.

Little bird? How did she know that name? Little bird was something she'd never heard from anyone except one person – her mother. It was the name she called her affectionately. A name no one else should have known.

"Do you know me?" Rebecca asked, hoping the reply would be something that would quell her rising worry.

Phyllis shook her head slightly. "No. But I ask that you do. I ask that when the time comes, you let my blood be your baptism wine!"

And there we have it, Rebecca thought to herself. *Another fucking mental fan. Painted a picture, then made it really weird. Standard.*

Ever since the Oscar, her fans had turned into something different; from nice people to lunatics. The exact reason she'd left the business and took bit parts in the theater instead. And the reason she would never do events again. No conventions. No meet and greets. Because of *this* kind of thing. *These* kinds of fans.

Shaking her head and choosing not to engage, Rebecca just walked past Phyllis toward the end of the unlit alley, where her car was parked within the thick shadows. This was the one perk she was given for taking a small role in the show. Even the actor playing Macbeth himself would not be allowed to park here.

After Rebecca walked away, Phyllis, thankfully, did not follow. Instead she placed the painting beside herself again and called out, "It shall all come to pass little bird! And you shall hold the souls of the sanctimonious, then crush them in your hands!"

Getting into her car and slamming its door behind her, Rebecca turned the headlights on and looked ahead. Tonight had been ruined for her, because of this one fan. They always had a way of doing that. She understood the adulation of those with fame, but sometimes they took it all too far and placed their insanity directly in her path. But now, looking ahead, she saw that the alley was empty. Phyllis – the mad old woman – had gone.

Vanished in a single moment. She was nowhere in sight.

"Fucking nutters…" she muttered under her breath as she closed her eyes for a second and put her hand to the ignition key.

"You shall see!" Phyllis spoke loudly appearing outside the driver's side window from nowhere.

"Fuck!" a shocked Rebecca exclaimed loudly, as she turned and saw the old grinning lady outside of her car.

Not wanting to engage more, she turned on the engine and left this insanity behind her, driving away at speed. Leaving the theatre for two days. At least this show's run was nearly over.

The front door to her house opened. The wind was picking up outside and gusted in, billowing up the coats that hung on hooks in the entrance hallway. Rebecca removed her key from the door lock and closed it behind her, shutting out the night-time.

"I'm home," she called out. Her voice reflected the exhaustion that her body felt. She loved the theater. She loved the anonymity of her part. She loved that it was a tiny role she was playing, but it was every night and had been for weeks. She was entitled to days off, but felt like she had something to prove, so would push through and see if she could do the whole 3 month run of performances, and only taking days off where the show didn't run. There was an understudy at hand for when it was required, but she hoped she could do this all on her own. It was not like she needed the money from it. Her acting career had afforded her a significant amount of wealth, but she was the kind of person where you could never tell. Her car was second-hand. Her house was a small maisonette. She never wore expensive clothes. Didn't own a single piece of jewelry. Not through any frugalness, she just didn't feel the need. She just had to prove to herself that she could do this one thing. A small part. A small show. And now, finally, two days off. She had forgotten what that felt like. But she had plans. She would not rest. Tomorrow, she would meet Ian for coffee, then in the evening go out with Janine. Perfect. She could sleep when she was dead.

Taking her coat off, she hung it on an already full clothes hook, on top of many other coats, and threw her handbag onto the floor beside her small collection of shoes.

Shutting her eyes for a moment, she wallowed in the stillness of the house, and took a breath.

"That you, sweetie?" came a female voice from the living room.

"No, it's a burglar. I'm here to murder you and take all the valuables," Rebecca replied, deadpan, as she walked into where the voice had come from. This small room was her sanctum, where she spent most of her time off. Complete with a huge collection of vinyl on built-in shelves, a centerpiece record player and a large overstuffed sofa at the other end. There was no television; a strange omission from this room and strange for anyone in this day and age. Not in this room or even in the house. She avoided them as much as she avoided newspapers and the internet. She had an old mobile phone, one which only her family, friends and agent could call her on – and that was good enough. Despite her agent's best efforts for her to at least get email, she never would.

Sitting on the sofa with a book on her lap and a cup of tea on the table in front of her, was Leanne, Rebecca's mother. In her late sixties, she had an air of kindness and joy about her. Her gray hair was fashioned into a neat bob which sat perfectly on her head; the kind of woman who took great care in her appearance – not through vanity, but because she believed that one should always look presentable, whether alone or in public.

"Murder me? You read too many of those books," she said, wafting her hand at the collection of horror novels on the shelves above the vinyl. "You should read some nice romance ones!"

"Ha-ha. Yeah, that will happen. Anyway, who did you think it was?" Rebecca asked, as she walked in and leaned down, kissing her mother on her cheek.

"Good night tonight?" Leanne said after taking another sip of tea. "Was my little witch a smash hit success?"

"I'm just tired," Rebecca replied as she walked over to a small desk by the entrance to the kitchen. "How's dog?"

"Your cat is a cat, not a dog. Anyway she is fine. All fed and asleep on your bed."

"Dog is a cat, we've talked about this... It's her name"

"I really don't understand why you feel the need to confuse matters. Can't you call her Mittens, or Whiskers?"

"She wants to be called Dog. She told me." She pulled out the chair from underneath the desk.

Leanne rolled her eyes, smiling. "Fine."

"On the plus side, though…" Rebecca said as she took a seat, "I have a new psycho fan."

Leanne took a sip of her tea and shook her head. "What is it about these horny little shits wanting you to sign their bits?"

"Their bits?!" Rebecca laughed. "I'd have preferred one of *those* perverts to what I got!"

Leanne looked surprised at Rebecca. "Not a pervert then?" she asked.

Over the past 5 years, most of her fans had been men – mainly young – all trying it on with her. Play one superhero and your fan-base changes and not for the better. For a family friendly genre, the fans were handsy and demanding. As if they owned you. As if you were there only to be the version of the character that they saw fit.

Leanne continued. "Who was it then?"

"An old woman with a painting. Wanted me to drink her blood or something," Rebecca said, as she stood up again and walked into the adjoining kitchen, where she made a bee-line for the fridge. "It was so weird. Creeped me out," she continued as she opened the fridge door and took out a can of Coke. Inside, on one of the shelves, she noticed a sandwich on a plate. “Whose sandwich is this?” she called out.

“The burglars; made it especially for them,” came the reply from the living room.

“Awesome,” Rebecca muttered as she picked up one half of it and took a bite.

“Why did she have a painting?” Leanne asked, now standing at the entrance to the kitchen.

“Dunno,” Rebecca replied with a mouthful of food.

“Swallow first, my dear,” Leanne said with a disappointed stare. “It’s not—”

“Becoming of a lady, yeah I know,” Rebecca interrupted as she took another bite. No matter how many times her mother said that, she would never remember. Some part of her brain always made her forget to swallow first then speak. And Leanne knew this. It was expected and something between them that was a constant. Finishing her mouthful, Rebecca continued. “It was freaky, though. Looked like it was of me and there were lots of monsters around.” Leanne looked back stone-faced at this – she had no reply. “...and I swear she called me Little Bird,” Rebecca continued and looked at her mother,. “I thought she may have known you?”

Taking another sip of tea, Leanne then smiled reassuringly. “I’m sure you were mistaken.”

“Called herself Phyllis. You know anyone called that?”

Leanne shook her head, “Afraid I do not.” She then walked over to the sink, poured the remnants of her tea away and ran her cup under the warm water tap, washing it for a few moments before placing it in the washbowl in the sink. "It's over now, though," she said as she turned to Rebecca. "Mad fan gone for good. No need to worry about silly people and their silly paintings. Now will I see you tomorrow?"

"You're not staying?" Rebecca asked as she cracked open her can of Coke and took a swig.

"Not tonight. Have some errands to run early. Anyway, you rest and have a nice sleep. Stop thinking about the crazies." Leanne walked over to Rebecca and gave her a quick hug. "Love you, little bird," she spoke softly.

"Love you too, Mum"

Outside a few minutes later, Leanne sat in her small car, parked on the street outside her daughter's house. She was tired; something that she would never let Rebecca see. Coming over every day to feed her cat was a small favor. But at her age, even doing this every day was wearing. Especially as she also had many other things to do. This was just another thing on her already full plate – but she would never complain, nor say no. This was Rebecca. And she was more than happy to help. She would just be happier when the play ended and things could go back to normal. But at the moment, things were far from normal.

Starting her car, she reversed off the driveway and into the empty street.

Her phone sat attached by a magnet to the dashboard. Before driving off, she scrolled on her contact list to "Office" and pressed to call. The ring came through the car speakers.

The car pulled away as it rang. "Hello?" a female voice answered.

"Helen? It's Leanne." She spoke out loud as she drove through the London streets.

"Yes ma'am, how can I help you?" Her demeanor sounded attentive and with slight trepidation, like there was some fear in her toward Leanne.

"Can I ask… Did you know that Phyllis showed Rebecca the *Mater Tenebris*?" She spoke with a calm smile.

"Uhhh… I…"

"No, well, she did. And the fact I didn't get a call from you or anyone else telling me that it was missing… Well that has to be addressed." Her demeanor suddenly shifted to very stern. "Find that bitch." Her smile dropped off her lips as fast as gravity would allow "And keep her there till I get there."

"Phyllis? Are you sure her?" Helen asked. "She's—"

"Of course, I'm *sure*," Leanne interrupted. "Are you calling me a liar?"

"No, of course not." Helen started to sound panicked, angering Leanne. "When do you—?"

"Tonight, are you fucking deaf *and* stupid? Just fucking *do it*!"

"I'm sorry." And this was why Helen was wary of Leanne. She had experience of her inclination to shift emotions on a dime. One moment laughing. The next in a rage. "I will find her for you."

"Make sure the congregation is there. They have to be. They all need to witness. And do not let *her* or *anyone* know why. Just call them all in and keep *her* there at all costs." Leanne then hung up the call without another word.

As she drove faster, her face sneered. "Bastards," she uttered as she carried on into the night. Her mind raced, but she couldn't let her anger get the better of her "Keep calm, Leanne. Just relax." She spoke to herself, calming her voice and forcing a smile. "Just a mistake... easily fixable."

By Royal Decree

Ferenc walked down the cobbled London streets. He had come to this city before, as a child. It had been a much smaller place back then. Now it seemed to be a never-ending labyrinth of streets and houses unlike anything from his homeland. Not that he had been to his homeland for the past few years. Ever since his farewell with his wife, he had left Hungary and traveled country to country, town to town, looking for ways he could right any wrongs. His guilt over his wife hung as heavy as ever and he had been forcing himself into the underbellies of society, hunting for the darkness – and then vanquishing it as best he could. And this had been done with modest success. He was still standing, and he had sent many enemies to their graves.

His journey started through the Ottoman territory where, without his armor or inscribed sword, he could pass as a wandering mercenary, looking for work. No one cared where he was from as long as he showed no enemy allegiance – which he never did. He knew enough about all the neighboring countries to say the right thing at the right time and he knew enough languages to pretend to be from somewhere else.

This journey was not an easy one, though. He did not look to fight the usual fights a mercenary traditionally would. He would look for the *real* darkness. The darkness like Elizabeth spoke of. He wanted to peer behind the curtain and kill the monsters that fed on humanity. And that is what he had been doing. Exacting revenge for his wife's soul and to pay penance for the souls that she had stolen. It was in this darkness that he had found terrifying monsters, but more surprisingly, good monsters. He was shocked to find out that in the dark, there were monsters of good *and* evil, as in life both coexisted. He was educated enough to know to not take his vengeance out on those who were good, regardless of any external monstrosity they might exhibit.

From the swamp creatures of the Czersk marshlands, to the baby-eating forest of Linz, he had removed many things from existence that should not be. Evil things, whose very knowledge of would blacken any normal person's soul with fear. Not that he wasn't afraid, he was. But this was now his cause. What he had to do. And for once he understood what faith was. Not in a religious sense, but before his quest he had never understood why anyone would believe something that they had no proof of. He had always been a man of facts and figures. But after what he had experienced, he knew. He *knew* without *any* doubt, that Elizabeth – somehow – was not dead, and what he was doing here was a preamble to whatever was to come. He had unwavering faith in that, it was probably the only thing he had ever truly believed in. He saw evil all around now, hiding in plain sight. And his mind always went back to that night. It was not just her in the blood, but everything within that damned room. The air stank of it – not just filth and rot – but evil. And he believed that Elizabeth, *his* Elizabeth, had gone many years previously. As for the woman in the blood pool – her eyes were like pits to a bottomless well of power older than both of them. He felt her evil was something that took her. Something that would not let her just die behind a wall. Though her remains had been found, he still could not believe something so evil could die so willingly.

But in London, he had a particular mission; this was not a visit of pleasure. He was on the trail of a creature that dwelled in the sewers of cities. A creature of pure fury who had left a trail of death in its wake all down the country. Blubbery and grotesque, this creature had a vertical mouth of serrated teeth along its engorged naked stomach. Only attacking at night, it would emerge from below and hunt for its next kill – its food of choice being of the human variety and its selection was indiscriminate; his food just needed to be living and afraid.

Human remains had been found scattered along riverbanks, or next to other bodies of water; remains with huge bite marks gouged right though them. This trail led to London, where he had not found it yet, but he was hot on its trail. The police of each constituency, naturally, had no leads of what this could be and chalked it down to wild animal attacks, which they were in part correct. But for those people who dwelled amongst the fringes of humanity, they knew *exactly* what it was. It was a creature called the Moogle. An embodiment of chaos from the Far East. Talked of only in hushed whispers – few had seen one, let along fought one and lived. Ferenc had though. He had met this particular one in Valence, on the banks of the Rhône. It was a battle he had nearly lost, had he not been able to land a striking blow with his dagger into the Moogle's eye socket. Though unable to see the creature's actual eyes, due to how far back they were set within its nose-less face, he felt contact with his blade as it was rammed in deep, as if something was pierced and then hit bone. The gargantuan monster roared in fury and flung Ferenc back with a mighty backhand. Losing consciousness, he awoke a few hours later, complete with cracked ribs and a concussion. He did not know why the Moogle left him alive, he would not have done the same if he was in his attacker's shoes. But he followed the blood trail in pursuit.

Standing on the cobbled streets of this city, his ribs still gave him a dull ache, but nothing that would stop this mission. He would find this creature and kill it. Anything so monstrous did not deserve to live in this world. But at this moment he was not on the hunt.; he stood holding a small scroll of parchment – a missive left at the inn where he was residing. It read: *Count Ferenc, please venture to the Nevermore Chambers on Wood Streete. Noon, today.*

He had no clue as to the origin of this note, but he knew enough that he could not ignore it. Not only did the author know where he was staying, but he knew who he was.

He had not been a Count for three years now. That was how long he had been on this crusade. King Matthias had already concocted the story of his death by disease in the battlefield against the Turks – and this was the story that everyone had believed. This King had already taken over the Castle and imprisoned any sympathizers. He had found the bricked-up bedroom in the tower, and gasped at the sight of all the decayed bodies strewn across the stone floors and walls. He had found the remains of Elizabeth, who was found in her bed, sitting cross-legged, facing the door with what appeared to be a smile on her heavily decaying face. Even in death, she was waiting and amused at the fear she instilled. The only people who knew that he was alive and knew of his location, were Janez and his brother Milo – the former keeping him abreast of all the happenings in the homeland. Janez was kept on in the Castle as proctor, looking after the Castle for the King, who would never return. After seeing Elizabeth in the room, he vowed to himself that it was unholy ground.

Whoever had written this note had either got their information of his living status from Janez or Milo – not that they knew where he was staying in England – or they had seen him around town and recognized him from the past; though he did not look the same anymore. His beard was now longer and grayer. His hair shorn and kept shaved, his leather clothes unmarked by symbols of allegiances or family lines. Like any other person wishing to do their work away from humanity, deep in the shadows, he was anonymous in name and being. No one could have recognized him. So, he had no choice but to find these chambers and confront the note's author.

Stopping for a moment, Ferenc looked around at the buildings on either side of the cobbles, hoping to see a street name, or a sign. Anything.

"You lost, mister?" came a small voice from behind him. Turning, he saw a young boy, no more than 10 years old. Filthy and in rags. Perched on a cracked wooden box, which was sat against the wall of a closed barber shop. This child – with eyes so bright and sad – made a good living as a beggar, these eyes his main weapon to procure coin from any passer-by with a heart. This boy knew the power his sad face had over some wealthy people, predominantly women from high society who ventured past. This time, though, he was looking at a different way to earn.

"Yes, I am lost, it seems." Ferenc's English was rusty, but coming back to him. He much preferred speaking it to the other languages he'd had to use recently, as he found English the easiest to speak and be understood, even with a thick accent.

"It's a shillin' if you wanna know where to go," the boy said with a smirk on his face. He knew his marks. Even at his young age, he knew the demeanor he needed to have for each person. And he knew there was no point lying to a man like this, as he would not fall for a sad tale of lies and misdirection.

"Excuse me? A shilling? For what? Directions?" Ferenc smiled at the boy, impressed.

"It's what it'll cost ya. Not much really, when ya fink of the time you'll gain getting' there sooner." Ferenc was surprised at the eloquence of this child, despite the pronunciations, he spoke like a man double his age.

"But I could ask anyone else I pass, and get the information for *free*. So, tell me, boy, why should I pay you for something I don't have to pay for?"

"Why shouldn't you pay me? Where's the harm? And besides. Information purchased is more reliable than information freely given." The boy spoke as he scratched his cheek.

Ferenc couldn't fault the boy's bluster and self-confidence. Reaching into his pocket he brought out a shilling, paused for a moment, then pulled out another. "Then I need to pay you two shillings. As I need two pieces of information."

The boy's eyes widened. *Was this man stupid, or just stupidly rich,* he thought.

"First. Where is Nevermore Chambers?" he asked.

"Really?" The boy looked confused. "Why there?"

"Yes. Really and why not?"

"Nuffin' there. No one's been livin' there for years" The boy pointed behind Ferenc. "It's right behind ya. Under that 'ouse."

Ferenc turned and saw the building being pointed to. It had an etched sign above the door saying "*God Begot House*"

"You sure? I see no signs for these chambers."

"Oh, it's there…" the boy said. "Now, the 'uver shillin'?"

Ferenc looked back at the boy, and held the two shillings up to him in his gloved hand. "What is your name?"

"William, why?" the boy replied curiously.

"Well, William. That is the second piece of information I required. Pleasure to make your acquaintance." He tossed the coins over to the boy, who caught them with a surprised smile. "I hope you have a wonderful day, William."

"You too," the boy said as he watched this strange man walk over to the house. Normally a man offering money so freely wanted something he wasn't willing to give. But this was a first. A man who just gave him money without the pauper act, or out of need? It was refreshing.

Ferenc turned back to the boy and called out, "Is there a back door, do you know?"

The boy smiled. "Don't think so, never seen one before… I'll give you that information for free."

Pushing open the metal gate to God Begot House, Ferenc walked in. The weeds in the courtyard were so overgrown, they had taken over the place. They entwined and suffocated the other plants, consuming the metal railings like snakes coiling around their prey. He had to break through the many knotted branches that stood between him and the entrance to that building.

Standing in a small clearing, he glanced around. The windows and the large wooden front door had all been boarded up long ago. He was about to walk back to the boy and get back his shilling, when he saw a door to one side, a door which was open. And from inside, a dull flickering light could be seen. Walking closer, he saw a small carving in the arch above the door; *Nevermore Chambers*. Barely legible. *What kind of place was this?* He was used to clandestine meetings, but not like this. He'd broken through the weeds to get in, so if anyone else was here – how did they get in? The boy outside said there was no back door. But, of course, the boy could easily be lying.

In the doorway, Ferenc peered into the building. He saw a lantern hanging off a hook on the wall. Drawing his sword silently, he took the lantern and took a moment's pause to think. This could easily be a trap by King Matthias, or by someone else wishing to hide the truth. But he had to know, and his curiosity could easily become his downfall.

Footstep by footstep he walked down the stone corridor. The flame from inside of the lantern cast its yellow-orange glow across the aged stone walls and arched ceiling.

Ahead of him, the stone floor turned into steps leading downwards into the darkness. Swallowing cautiously, he lifted his sword higher and took his first tentative steps downward. Trying to make each step as quiet as possible, he trod lightly, but the dirt under each foot cracked against the stone and echoed downwards to whatever was waiting for him.

At the base of the steps, the stone floor had turned into dirt. Well-worn and very old. The walls were no longer of the same clean brickwork as the hallway above, but were now rough and dirty, with weeds growing out of the cracks in abundance.

Lifting the lantern, he stopped for a moment, listening for any audible sign of another person or persons. Anyone who may be down there with him. But there was nothing except the sound of the breeze from above, whistling down to where he was.

He decided there was no use in hiding from this anymore.

"Hello?" he called out. "Is anybody here?"

Taking a step forward he continued, "I warn you; I will not hesitate to send you back to whatever Hell you crawled from."

The hallway ahead of him curved to the left, as he cautiously walked around it and another doorway came into view. Its large wooden double doors hung wide open. Ferenc could see more lanterns illuminating the darkness within.

His pace slowed as he entered this room and he saw a man standing in the center, facing him. This was a giant of a man, standing at least a foot taller than him. With a large scar from the base of his neck, running up over his head – creating an inch-wide hairless gap through his tight curly black hair – and down his forehead and over where his left eye used to be, ending parallel to his mouth. This was a man who knew pain and death well. A man who anyone would be a fool to stand against. This man was Gobolt. He stood next to two wooden chairs. On one rested a black sack, tied at one end, its contents hidden.

Ferenc raised his sword towards this man. "Tell me, friend. Do I need my blade towards you?"

"That depends," came Gobolt's rough voice. "What is your name?"

"My name is of no consequence," Ferenc said, standing in the doorway to the room, ready to escape should the need arise.

"That's a pity. I was waiting for the man who bricked up his bloodthirsty whore of a wife, leaving her to die the death she more than deserved. What was her name again? I forget."

"Her name…" Ferenc said through gritted teeth, "was Elizabeth." He gripped his sword tighter, holding his temper as he needed to know what this man wanted and how he knew of this.

"Apologies, friend," Gobolt said, and smiled. He enjoyed offending people. It brought their true selves to the surface and with this man, he could tell his true self was tempered rage. "I was waiting for you. That is if you are indeed the man who, for the past few years, has been cutting down the scum of this earth – creatures most don't even know exist."

"What do you know of me?" Ferenc asked as he took a step towards him, sword still held up defensively.

With a grin, Gobolt grabbed the sack from the chair next to him, untied one end and peered inside. "This should answer you well enough." He then hurled the contents of the sack toward Ferenc. It landed with a wet thud between them.

Wide-eyed, Ferenc took a couple of steps into the room, towards the severed head which Gobolt had thrown in front of him. It was a very familiar head, that of the Moogle, which he was hunting. Its damaged eye identifying it as the very monster he'd encountered. "I see you made him look like me," Gobolt said, motioning to his own destroyed eye.

Ferenc stared down at the monster's head. From its long lank ginger hair, to its ear to ear wide mouth full of serrated teeth, to its two gill-like holes which made up its nose and finally its deep eye sockets – it could never have been anything except a predator which needed to be put down.

He then looked up to Gobolt. "How did you—?"

"Kill it?" Gobolt spoke without breaking eye contact. "Wouldn't be the first Moogle I ran through, my friend."

"Moogle? That is its name?"

"Bloody ridiculous, don't ya think? Such a big scary demon, given a name that sounds like a young boy's name for his own cock."

"Any name could not justify what this thing was." He slowly lowered his sword, knowing if this stranger had indeed killed the Moogle alone, then he was a formidable fighter who would have killed him already, if he had indeed wanted him dead. "So, what is the name of the one who killed this thing?"

"Gobolt,." came the man's reply, as he dropped the empty sack to the floor.

"Gobolt? Sounds like a young boy's name for his own cock." Ferenc spoke with a smile, causing Gobolt to laugh a deep bellowing laugh.

"Then I must ask. Why does Gobolt claim to know my life, then kill the demons I hunt?"

"Me? I'm just a soldier who knows things about things... You're here to see the man who wrote to you. Myself, I cannot say I even know how to write. And besides, I would've just walked up to you in the street and spoken to you, man to man."

"So, who wanted me here?" Ferenc asked sheathing his sword.

"Gobolt, I have heard enough," came the voice from of the darkened end of the room. A double set of doors opened fully and a man in his forties, dressed in a regal tunic, flanked by two guardsmen in red armor, walked in. "This is who we seek."

This man walking towards him was King James 1st. Ferenc had never met him, but knew enough to know who he was by sight. Immediately he dropped to his knee and bowed his head toward the king.

"Forgive me, your majesty."

"Stand up," Gobolt said, mocking him. "He's not your fuckin' king, ya foreign bastard."

The king now stood next to Gobolt, and put his hand on his shoulder. "It's okay, my friend. He is just following custom. Unlike some I know."

"Oh lick my balls, Sir King of Assholes," Gobolt grumbled. The King smirked and turned to Ferenc. "Thank you for coming to see me, under these… conditions."

Ferenc looked up and saw the king motion him to stand. "Apologies, your majesty."

"James. Please. Call me James. Anyone's position and titles mean nothing here."

Ferenc slowly stood up, wary of this situation.

"Count Ferenc, welcome to England," the king exclaimed.

"I… I am not him anymore… Just Ferenc is my name now. That other man died in Hungary."

"Of a disease. I heard. My condolences to your former self." He motioned to Gobolt, who picked up a chair and placed it opposite the other one. "Please, Ferenc. Please sit." He motioned to the opposite chair as he himself sat down.

Gobolt walked over beside the king and spoke in a bassy monotone. "I'll be outside with the men." The King nodded to confirm. Gobolt walked over to where the guards stood, and they followed him out of the doorway, deeper into the chambers.

King James waited until the doors were closed then turned back to Ferenc. “I’m sure you are wondering what this is, so I shall get to the point. I’m sure I will be able to answer all your questions.”

Ferenc sat on the chair placed opposite the King. “Many questions.” he confirmed.

“Well, I shall be as forthcoming as I can. This, Ferenc, is a time of great evils. As you well know.”

Ferenc nodded.

“I know all about you; your battles across various kingdoms and the demons you’ve dispatched. The rights you have wronged. And stating it plainly, I wish for you to join us.”

“Who is us?” Ferenc asked.

“We have no name. But we are a group of men like you. We believe in ridding evil from humanity’s soul.”

“And you want me to join you?”

“Why *wouldn’t* we? As you can imagine there are few people who can do what you do. And we are more effective as an army than alone. You see I have many fighters, but not many who can lead.”

Ferenc glanced down at the floor where the Moogle’s severed head sat, then back to the King. “I presume this is not sanctioned? As we are meeting here... And not in the palace. So, needs to be secret.” He was being polite, but could not think of a good reason he would accept this offer. Even an offer from a king.

"There are no official positions, no. We cannot have the populous seeing that evils are indeed manifest. Some will, of course, know the truth by happenstance, but if the country as a whole saw the extent of what is out there... I dread to think what panic and chaos would ensue. I want you to join the cause as you have faced pure evil and you didn't blink – instead you devoted yourself you this holy war. God smiles upon you. And so do I... Though I am aware of your lack of belief."

"I do not think your God looks too kindly on people like me," Ferenc replied.

"I think your proclivities are none of anyone's business. And as you were created by Our Lord, He would not disown you for what He made. That would make Him fallible. He created you as you are, and that is a blessed creation."

Ferenc looked taken aback at his words.

"I am of the belief that the church is corrupt and a very dangerous force in our times. They have decreed laws which are against the very word of God Himself. Even Jesus Christ spoke out against the concept of churches, yet *still* they exist, wielding such wealth and power that a king like me is a mere pauper in comparison to the Vatican. So, no, I put no stock in what they deem to be deviant or corrupt. God is love and purity. And whether you see it or not, you *are* in God's favor. And this place..." he said, motioning to his surroundings. "...is yours to do with as you will."

"So, not only do you want me in your holy militia; you offer me a room?" Ferenc said plainly.

"Not meaning to sound ungrateful for the offer, of course."

"No, of course not. But this is not just a house with a basement. It is a building that has access to tunnels that leads to my chambers at the palace. And can be a base for your operations."

"I see" Ferenc said, and nodded.

"Yet, you are not convinced… Well I have one more thing to offer. What if I could tell you that you are indeed correct and your wife is still… well I hesitate to say alive, so will instead say 'present'? Your wife Elizabeth, is indeed, still present"

God Begot

God Begot House had seen worse days. For hundreds of years this house had existed in various forms. Whether a fire, a refurbishment, or a renovation – it had been rebuilt inside and out time and time again. No matter what the condition, though, since 1752 it had belonged to the same people. Not by familial ties, but bequeathed by the owner to a successor. There was only one constant; they were always female. The latest rebuild of the house was to mimic the original Baroque style, in a tribute to the building's origins, from the days when it was taken from a king and given to the darkness.

Imposing to all the other buildings in the street, this house was a large eight-bedroomed structure. The gardens that were once overgrown and unkempt, were now pristine and very fertile.

Unlocking the gate, Leanne walked through and let it swing shut behind her. After a few more steps, she stood still for a moment, listening whilst looking forwards. Waiting for a loud click of the gate automatically locking to emanate from its internal mechanisms. When it did, she smiled to herself and walked up the path to the front door.

Her earlier phone call with Helen had angered her, but now, she seemed happy and over any negative emotions.

As she got to the front door, she looked to the right, towards the Nevermore Chambers – which were the only part of the house not renovated. The door was the same as it was when Ferenc had walked through it, complete with the chambers name carved above it, barely legible.

The large wooden front door to the house opened and Leanne walked in, closing it behind her. Taking her coat off, she hung it on a coat rack to the left of the door – keeping her handbag with her. The rest of the room looked reminiscent of a hotel lobby. It was big with 15-foot-high ceilings, black and white marble floors and a reception area at the other side of the room. Behind this reception desk, a split staircase running up each side of the walls. The décor was accented with golden motifs and adorned with few but still impressive furnishings; vases worth more than the most expensive cars, thought-lost paintings from some of the masters, even the ashtray on the reception desk was worth a yearly wage – not that Leanne would ever allow smoking in her house.

From a side door, a flustered woman in her 40s hurried in. She carried a notepad and a pen in one hand and a cup of tea in the other. This was Helen – Assistant to Leanne, and a very much brow-beaten woman. She handed the tea up to Leanne, who didn't thank or even acknowledge her assistant. She just took the tea and sipped it as she checked the time on her watch.

"Everyone is below," Helen said with a smile, trying to make sure she did what was asked at all times.

"Phyllis?" Leanne asked, deadpan, taking another sip of her tea.

"Down there too," Helen said, all too happy to confirm. "I told them that it was a last-minute meeting about the fundraiser, so no suspicions were aroused."

Leanne looked up at Helen with a genuine smile, breaking the tenseness that Helen felt. "That was a great cover story, my dear. Well done."

Helen looked genuinely relieved. Despite the occasional abuse, she idolized Leanne and took all the barbs as justified because of her own failings. "I hope you don't mind me asking, but did she *really* show Rebecca?"

"You didn't notice it was gone?" Leanne asked genuinely. "You are down there *all the time*."

"I went back down as soon as you called; it was there hanging where it should be, just as it was when I was down there earlier. I could have only been away from there for 90 minutes at most. I am really sorry if—"

"Oh, I am not blaming *you*," Leanne interrupted, "This is on *her*. It has hung there for decades, safe and sound, never a problem… Now, speaking of her… Where *was* she when you found her?"

Helen shrugged and looked confused. "It was weird. She was just praying beside the painting. Acting as if nothing happened."

"Poor woman. Her faith is too blind to the rules that need to be followed. She sees what is to come in a singularity and that…" Leanne took another sip. "…will be her undoing."

Deep in Nevermore Chambers – the same room which once was host to a meeting with King James 1st – a group of women now sat on pews at the front of an altar. Aged between 16 and 90, these two dozen women were of varying classes and ethnicities and all sat talking amongst themselves quietly. They were in wait of their leader, Leanne. Waiting for her to address them.

The altar at the end of the room in front of them, was not made of stone or wood, but was constructed of dozens upon dozens of individually etched human bones, tied together with chains and rope. From afar, it looked impressive with the edges of the tibia, fibula, femur and radius bones used, all working as patterned framing devices for the many curved spines. Each of which, were placed together in the middle on every side of the altar, each making a differing large spiral pattern. It was only when someone would get closer and recognize what this altar was made out of, did the realization of its evil become clear.

On the wall behind the altar hung the *Mater Tenebris* painting. Lording over the proceedings as decoration of upmost importance.

In the front pew, staring at the painting with an eerie smile, sat Phyllis,. Slightly rocking back and forth. In her own world. Oblivious to those chatting loudly all around her about the most banal of topics.

"I can't believe he was voted off!" squawked one of the women sitting directly behind her. "I know, right? He was such a fit bloke. Really nice too." Loudly proclaimed another. On any other day, Phyllis would try to include herself in the conversations. She adored to be involved. A solitary person – not by choice – she had always been a quiet outsider, without enough personality to be memorable. But she had a heart that loved everyone. She craved inclusion and only wanted to have her place in the world have a purpose greater than what she had now. And Rebecca *was* her purpose – it was *all* their purposes. For the past 57 years, she had been part of this coven by design, and had witnessed many strange and beautiful things, all in the lead-up to the prophecy unfurling its purpose. The prophecy which would, as she interpreted it, bring balance to all chaotic worlds. To clean the slate by extreme means. To prepare all for what was to come. Of course, the methodology this was to follow was abhorrent to her, but she knew that if something is broken, sometimes it is best to destroy it completely, then start over. Good and evil were vague constructs, determined by the masses. They were not real or quantifiable. After all, if one could kill a person for the right reasons, for the greater good, then the whole viewpoint that killing is wrong is proven incorrect. But killing is only a sin to those who cherish all life and cannot see past their own morality and mortality. And despite the death, there was a grand design in all this. And it was such a beautiful design..

Despite its meagre appearance and the few people sitting in this room, one could assume that this coven was insignificant – at best an unsuccessful cult – but that would be an incorrect and deadly assumption. For this coven was one of many – and the small numbers here were entirely intentional to keep all branches of the group a secret he sole reason of which was to hide from view. For this group was not in the minority in all the places they existed, but had to remain hidden until the time came. Until the call came. Of course, from an outsider this would all seem a bit ridiculous. Why hide at all? But theirs was not to question why. Theirs was to follow the edict handed down to them by their creator, a very powerful woman. Labeled a witch, she carried great power, but a witch was too simplistic a description – a more appropriate label she would prefer would be a Goddess. And to her followers, this was exactly what she was. These followers were here to prepare for a new reality for their Goddess. And Phyllis would do anything to ensure her Goddess and her compatriots saw her as an integral member.

From the back of the room, Leanne entered, striding purposefully, smiling to everyone as she walked up to the altar, Phyllis included. Helen trailed behind with her clipboard in hand. She tried her best to avoid the gaze of the congregation. She would have preferred to remain upstairs for this, but Leanne made it her duty to be there to assist. As they walked by the seated women, they all fell silent, leaving their banal conversations in the wind.

At the altar, Leanne placed her handbag onto its bone top. Helen walked up and stood next to her obediently.

"Now then," Leanne began as she turned to address her audience. "I hope you all had a pleasant evening and I didn't ruin any plans by calling you all here? Sorry it's so late."

Those she spoke to, smiled, none more so than Phyllis. She adulated Leanne, saw her as equal to the Goddess, herself.

"We are here tonight, as there has been some… miscommunication." Her demeanor was calm and happy, she was speaking as if reading a bedtime story for a nervous child. "Sisters, I called you in because of something that was brought to my attention tonight. Something concerning."

Turning around, she motioned to the painting on the wall. "Mater Tenebris… The prophecy. We all know it well," she said, and turned with a smile. "Correct?"

Her audience nodded, some saying '*yes*' in hushed tones. "Now what does the prophecy say?"

With that, Phyllis' hand darted up in the air with passion. She knew. She knew all too well. And Leanne saw this.

"My dear…" she said, and motioned to Phyllis. "What does it say?"

Phyllis' smile somehow was bigger now she was singled out. "It says *'The chosen shalt become Mater Tenebris.'*"

Leanne smiled. "Indeed it does. Yet some have taken this prophecy and read too much into it. It is merely our celebration of the end goal – not for anyone else. Not like her seeing this painting will suddenly make the prophecy happen," Leanne said as she noticed Phyllis' smile drop as she listened the words telling her that what she thought was incorrect. "We are here at the behest of the Goddess. Preparing her vessel for her life. The life as depicted within the painting, of course… But this…" She pointed to the painting, "this painting is *just* a painting. And one that is *only* for us. You may ask why do we even have this? Well every reality needs it anchor to the purpose. A guiding point. And this is ours. Each rotation getting closer and closer. Until only the Goddess herself declares our purpose complete. Am I making sense?"

The congregation understood. All but Phyllis, who looked a bit confused.

"Now there is someone here, who took this painting off of the wall, where it had hung on for many years, then took it across the city…"

A few of the congregation looked shocked at this revelation.

"… Where to, you ask? Well, only to the chosen one. And showed it right to her. Expecting it to begin something magical. Expecting to fall in her graces."

Phyllis looked sheepish and worried.

"My dear Phyllis?" Leanne spoke softly and kindly. "Come up here for a moment."

"M.. Me?" Phyllis stuttered. She was in trouble. She did something wrong. This was a nightmare for her. She was terrified of not doing the right thing. Her mind already began punishing her for her supposed wrongdoing. "I thought… I thought I did good."

"Oh, you silly ninny. All is ok. Just come up beside me and I can teach you."

Slowly, Phyllis stood up. The other members were looking at her; she could feel their disappointment, she thought.

"I just wanted her to see…" Phyllis said as she walked to Leanne. "I'm sorry. I didn't know…"

"It's okay," Leanne said reassuringly. "I have something for you which may help you. A gift. One you have long deserved."

Phyllis suddenly looked touched by this "You do? A gift?"

"Yes."

Phyllis was now at the altar in front of Leanne. "Turn and face your sisters," Leanne said to her. "It's a surprise, you see?"

Phyllis, in all her 78 years, had never been given anything. She had no family. No friends, bar those sisters here in this room. And she spent every waking moment either praying to her Goddess, or cleaning her house. So, to be singled out and told she was getting a gift? That Leanne cared enough to teach her anything…was a huge deal.

Now, facing her sisters, she smiled happily. They though, saw what Phyllis did not; Leanne taking out a butcher's cleaver from her handbag.

And they all looked on quietly, obediently and attentively.

Leanne placed one hand on Phyllis' shoulder. The cleaver in her other, raised high, unseen to her intended victim. She still spoke kindly despite the words uttered being threatening. "I did not gestate our salvation for you to set your own fucking timetable, now did I?"

Phyllis' expression of joy slightly slipped. "Excuse me?"

"The Goddess demands *obedience*! We are not ready for the end yet. We have had no call by Her. We have, as far as we know, hundreds of lifetimes to go to fulfill what the Goddess demands." And with that the cleaver came down and embedded in Phyllis' thin neck. Leanne's other hand prevented her victim from falling.

Lifting the cleaver up again, Leanne then slammed its blade deeper into the now-gaping neck wound, causing the blood to jet out, spraying outwards for a few feet. Phyllis' face expressed pain and shock, but her voice could only gurgle as she tried to scream or breathe.

Hacking at her again, Phyllis' legs buckled and her small body slumped to the floor. As she did, Leanne was on her in a second. Hacking at her neck over and over. Each time the cleaver hit her open wound, it burrowed in deeper into her throat, severing her windpipe, her breath spluttering out of the hole with a jet of crimson. Again and again. Deeper and deeper. Phyllis was still alive as the blade severed her spine and her head separated from her body. Separated without breath and without a heartbeat. Her eyes remained open. Her brain functioned for a few moments more, as Leanne held her head up by its hair as she stood up. Holding her up towards the congregation. Her last moments of consciousness was of her seeing her fellow coven looking at her and laughing at her demise. If she could, she would have cried. Not because her life was taken. Not from the insurmountable pain and fear she felt. But because her only family laughed. Her only friends mocked her demise.

"And this my beautiful ones…" Leanne began as she showed them all her handiwork, holding up Phyllis' head to them. "…this was long overdue." She then dropped the head to the floor, where it hit with a wet thud – then rolled to look upwards at her.

Leanne noticed this and with her foot, nudged the head to turn away, before looking back up to her congregation. "I think all is okay though." She looked as if she was convincing herself. "But we must face the potential outcome..." She handed the bloody cleaver to Helen who took it from her obediently. "Our hand may be forced. If she enquires more and the reality starts to unravel, then we will need a reset. I have prayed to our Goddess for guidance. But with this world being what it is – with fate being what it is – we must be prepared for every eventuality."

Glancing down at the corpse of Phyllis, Leanne smiled. "This should all give us pause for thought…" She looked back up to the others with a smile. “Now go in the grace of our infernal majesty.”

“The blood purifies,” they replied in unison.

“Feel free to take a piece of her flesh, should you desire?” she offered with a grin.

And they desired.

They *all* desired.

And then, they *all* fed.

Deciding Factors

"You're looking at this like you're one of *them*. You left that primordial privy that humanity shits into as soon as you peeked your beady little eyes behind the curtain, and decided that your blade would readdress the evils infecting our lands." Gobolt was a brute of a man. A man with no desire to temper his language. A man who suffered no fools. A man who was fighting the good fight and would give his life for it.

"So, I'm not a human?" Ferenc asked him with a smile. On his walk through the city streets – towards the Inn where he was staying – Gobolt had accompanied him to collect his possessions in order to bring them back to God Begot House, his new residence as general in a holy war for the king.

"Well, humans are dumb cunts. The lot of them. No exceptions. And as soon as you see the truth of the world, you are no longer part of their bullshit," He said as they walked through a street market full of people buying fruit and vegetables from various shady street sellers. Gobolt then stopped with his arms outstretched, motioning to the surrounding people milling around him. "Look at them! Dumb, dumb cunts. One and all."

A woman passing looked at Gobolt in shock. He noticed her expression and gave her a wink. "No offense, beautiful." She looked more offended and walked on. He laughed to himself at this, then glanced to Ferenc. "See?"

"She didn't like your language. And that makes her something less in your eyes?"

"No. You're not seeing it. She was offended because she judged me based on what I said. I called them "dumb cunts", then I am struck off in their minds. They're a race of cunts, who are at their very core incapable of seeing anything beneath their own surface."

Ferenc, amused at this tirade, glanced around at the passers-by. "You think they are bad because they don't know the truth? But up until a few years ago, I didn't know the truth. In fact now, I know very little of the truth." He looked squarely at Gobolt. "So, what did that make me, and what does that make me now?"

"A dumb cunt. Obviously," came the reply.

Ferenc smirked and they continued walking through the crowded market. "I prefer to think of them as lucky."

"Lucky? How are these fucks lucky?" Gobolt asked as he caught up with Ferenc's brisk pace through the throng of people.

"Because they don't see the truth. That's lucky," Ferenc said across the line of people between them. Their pace was slowed down by the pedestrians in their path. He continued, "They get to live their lives without seeing what is really in the shadows. They don't see the monsters waiting to eat them—"

Without noticing, Ferenc had said this as he slowly passed a small boy who had now heard the last sentence uttered – This boy looked up to him wide eyed and afraid. Noticing, Ferenc smiled at the boy and lied. "Just a joke. They wouldn't eat you."

Gobolt, sidling up to Ferenc, also addressed the boy. "This man speaks the truth… They wouldn't eat you. They would first fuck you whilst you slept." He laughed as he strode on, leaving Ferenc in this embarrassing situation.

It would take a lot for Ferenc to get accustomed to Gobolt's rude brashness, but he could see that this was a good man at heart.

"What makes you the authority on humans?" Ferenc asked as they broke through the marketplace and onto a less populated street, lined with only a handful of pedestrians and beggars. "You judge their lack of knowledge, which is not their fault as no one is telling them the truth... Besides, you were in the shadows once too."

Coming to a halt, Gobolt put his arm out and motioned for Ferenc to stop. "Let me be clear," he said as he looked quickly up and down the street, glancing at all the people he could for a brief moment. "Okay. What do you see, Count?"

Ferenc, looking confused looked around him, trying to see what Gobolt had. "Are you going to say dumb cunts?"

"No. Well they are, but more. What do you *see?*"

Ferenc looks around and shrugged "I… I do not know what you want me to say. People? A street? London?"

Gobolt put his hands on Ferenc's shoulders, then looked intently into his eyes. "I'll make it easy on you. That poor wretch begging behind me? *What. Do. You. See?*"

Ferenc's attention turned to the old woman Gobolt mentioned, wrapped head to foot in a shawl, only her face and hands visible. Sat on the side of the pebbled pavement, with a small clay bowl in front of her, hoping to get any generosity from a passerby. But her bowl was empty. The people ignored her. The shawl she dressed herself in was dirty, discolored and frayed. Her skin was leathery, weather-beaten and wrinkled beyond its years. Her eyes were milky and pale from blindness.

"Spare some kindness," she said, soft and broken. She was starving and cold – But despite her pleas, no pedestrian saw her.

"I see a woman. Begging for money," Ferenc said as he looked at her, feeling great pangs of sympathy.

"Beyond that. That is an effect, not what is really there."

He looked again. "I… I'm not sure what you mean."

Gobolt gripped his shoulder tight. "And that is my point. No one sees. No one chooses to see. No one wants to know… So, with all you've seen. The demons, the witches, the monsters. The knowledge that there is a world that exists within this world.

One you have to look deeper to see. So, please, just look again. Open the curtain."

Ferenc took another look at the woman. Studying her. Almost imperceptible, a small tentacle fell down from her hairline over her forehead. Within a second it had retreated back. His eyes widened in surprise as he saw it.

"Ah. You see it," Gobolt said with a smile as he slapped where he let go of Ferenc's shoulder. "And that's why humanity is a rancid nest of dumb cunts. The truth's there for all to see. But they don't *look*. They choose to not know *how* to look."

"What is she?" Ferenc asked softly, before turning his gaze back to Gobolt.

"Her?" Gobolt glanced at her "She's from a race called the Poda. From the sea." He turned back to finish his answer. "When they get too old, they come to land, to ease the burden on their communities. They sacrifice themselves. And always end up on the streets, begging, until they starve and dry up, leaving a husk that turns to dust if touched."

"She's not dangerous?" To Ferenc, that was a valid question, yet was met with a look of scorn.

"And what about what I have just told you makes you think this poor thing would hurt a soul?"

"I didn't mean to offend. I just have not seen this kind before…"

Reaching into his tunic, Gobolt brought out a leather purse of money. Opening it up, he reached in and took out a couple of golden coins, before returning the purse to where it was previously held. Then turning, he walked over to the old lady beggar and crouched down beside her. Gently, he lifted up her hand and placed the coins in them, then closed her fist over them. He leaned in and whispered something in her ear. Her eyes welled with tears as she smiled kindly at him, touched by his words and generosity. With one hand, he cradled her face for a moment. "Take care of yourself, my dear." She nodded gratefully at him as he stood back up and returned to Ferenc, continuing his conversation.

"Both the monsters and humans are equally full of good and evil, both capable of ending us all. And all sides are in constant battle for superiority. But now the balance between good and evil is in danger as those big bastard scales are tipping in the favor of evil. It's why James needs you and others to join. Why he wanted you in particular. He needs a leader to head what there is of an army. You saw the truth and didn't run. You ran at it with your sword out and a battle scream in your heart. But not only that. Not only did you leave a trail of dead evil behind, you recognized that there were good beings who were not human. Ones more delicate and fragile than even the youngest of human babies. And not to mention you have led many armies into battle before."

"How do you know what I have done? How do any of you?" Ferenc asked. The king also spoke of things that he thought no one could have known, but had brushed over any explanations.

"Your actions have not been silent for those people who pay an arse hair of attention to the reality of the worlds. I know you saved more than you destroyed. You may not know it, but you have been a champion for the good in all realms and they do not forget. And you may have only met a fraction of the kinds of beings out there. But you *will* meet more. So many more. And you will see. You will see it *all*. And we will get revenge for all the good ones and the dumb cunt humans out there. Anyone who cannot fight for themselves."

He smiled at Ferenc, who weakly smiled back. He had no idea what he was letting himself in for, but he knew he could not have said no.

They both continued down the cobbled street. At the end stood the Willow Tree Inn, the building where Ferenc was currently residing.

"You really hate your own kind, don't you?" Ferenc enquired. "You speak as though humans are the ones we vanquish."

"Didn't James tell you?" Gobolt replied with a laugh. "I'm not human, my friend. Not by a long shot."

And he was not.

And never had been.

Since time began, tribes have told fables to their children. Fables meant to make them understand the dangers of the world in relatable ways. One of these tales was the tale of the boy and the Black Witch.

Witches were not the same creatures as modern day sees them, but instead were creatures with twisted and gnarled bodies and a blood thirst for innocence, which fueled their lifespan and enhanced their power. Born in-between realms, they could manipulate reality to be obscured within their victim's eyes. They could, in order to hide their grotesque appearance, make themselves appear as anyone – or anything – they so wished. They could also use this illusionary skill to manifest their thoughts as a temporary reality to those who witnessed it. But all their parlor tricks were just that. Tricks. Illusions. Things with no real substance in themselves. But still, they had real destructive effect on the victims. What they created was incorporeal in nature, with no physical substance to them. If a witch imagined a knife being thrown at you, there would not be a real knife there, but it would still be fatal. The effect of a human witnessing these illusions was, in many cases, deathly. The illusion itself was like a virus. Proximity to it would eat through the victim's consciousness and cause them to not only *believe* what they saw was true, but take an active unconscious role in making the illusion true. Seeing that imaginary knife being thrown at them wouldn't hurt them, but from the virus' effect, they would instead stab themselves in the face with their own knife – and still believe it was the imaginary knife the witch threw, that was the thing that hit them.

These creatures came to this reality and hid as females – though they themselves were hermaphroditic, they chose to align themselves as female as they could incubate a life, though it was not possible for to them to breed amongst themselves – only with other species. Coupling with another witch could not result in a child, as their kind could not produce living sperm. This meant that their existence as a pure form was finite. They *could* live eternally with the right supply of innocence to consume, but without any, they would wither and die. Nevertheless, if they did happen to mother a child, then that child would only be carrying half of their genetics, so would not be afforded all the powers that came with being a pure witch – and the half of the genetics it *did* carry would be poison to the other half, which it would naturally try to consume, and this would result in the child's life expectancy being less than a day. No baby could survive it. Which never stopped them trying to sire progeny with all manner of other species.

Witches could also possess and inhabit bodies like parasites. They could overtake a whole mind, or just infect it. And live incorporeally in another flesh.

The Black Witch was one of the deadliest of these creatures to exist, mainly due to the scale on which she would feed. Unlike others of her kind, who would feed on a couple of people a few times a year, she would feed once every couple of decades – which enabled her continued survival and anonymity wherever she chose to call home. She would choose bigger targets than other witches and watch the horror she had wrought from nearby, waiting for them to end themselves so she could consume them. She had little fear when it came to procuring the innocence she needed to feast on. She would traditionally enter villages disguised as an injured old woman who told a story of being attacked nearby and her family had been taken or were dying – She needed help! The story she would weave would normally involve a trap of sorts, maybe she was traveling across the land in a cart, her whole family moving en masse to a better future in unknown lands, when all of a sudden, they were set upon. What attacked them would change from village to village and was whatever or whomever the village's mortal enemies happened to be. Be it indigenous people, bears, wolves, a neighboring village . . . Anything to get the biggest and bravest men to go and help her. She would, of course, disguised as this old woman - be too weak to go with them, but she would give them plenty of directions. The strongest of the village would be incensed to help, find this old woman's family and right the wrong brought on by whatever evils had befallen them. Her performance was of such intensity, that she was always left with a village of the weak and innocent. This was not done because she feared the strong ones in the villages, but she wanted to watch their lives be destroyed after they saw what she had done upon their return.

When they had left in a furor of anger and demanding justice for this injured visitor and when she knew they would not hear any screams, she would shed the skin of the old woman and reveal her true, twisted form. She would show an illusion to the whole village of darkness and blood. She would make them believe themselves blind, then hear screams of offered assistance beckoning them. They would try to run, find help. Unable to hear the same screams of the people next to them going through the same panic. A grand illusion of desperation and fear.

One by one they would stumble their way to where the Black Witch stood. Crying and screaming, their arms outstretched as they would try to find light in their darkness. And no sooner had they arrived, than the Black Witch's mouth would open to such a wide degree, that she could and would lunge forwards and bite through the head of the blinded victim – her mouth over the top half of the skull. For a few moments she would feast on the blood jetting out of their cracked cranium, the victim's mouth still on show, still screaming about being blind, not knowing the pain they were actually in. Not seeing the elongated neck of the witch above them, undulating as she drank them dry. When finished, she would drop the dry husk of a body to the floor, complete with the top half of their heads crumpled in from the bite.

One by one the whole village would suffer the same fate, staggering blinded to her, with no idea that they were being guided to the same place to die. And this would happen until there were dozens of bodies – of all ages – piled up in one single part of town.

She would then hide from sight and wait for the men to return empty-handed. It would normally be the next day, due to the distance they had to travel. But they always returned despondent and exhausted. Then they would find all their loved ones, brutalized and deceased. Their anguish was then far from over, as she would show them visions of these dead coming back to life, returning as bloodthirsty creatures, all wishing to kill these men. The men would imagine these undead running at them and clawing them to death with nails, teeth, anything. They would see the vision of these cannibalistic undead demons eating them – whereas in reality and from the witch's virus effect, they would in fact be clawing *themselves* to death. Eating themselves. Ripping out their own eyes and tongues with their own hands. Reaching down and ripping off their own genitalia, clawing at their own chest to get to their heart. Biting the flesh from their own arms. And whilst this was happening, the Black Witch would be in the shadows, hidden, masturbating to this horror.

In the end, they too would be dead and all that would be left for the Black Witch was to feed on the final morsels. The sick and the very young, who could not walk in the blind panic to suffer the first round of deaths.

Slowed down from the sheer amount of food she had eaten, the Black Witch would slump around the village slowly, leaving a trail of semen and vaginal arousal fluid behind her as she went, both of her sets of genitals having been spent from her excitement. And though too full to eat more, she would find the space to pick off the infirm and the too young – a dessert to her huge meal.

Then she, with her body engorged to breaking point, like an overfull water skin made of rubber, would shuffle off into the wilderness. After arriving as a tiny woman, she left as a mountainous, bloated creature. Then she would not appear again for many years, where she would be in another part of the world, at the doors of another village. Small in stature once more. Empty of Food. Hungry for death.

She never left a soul alive in all of her centuries of feeding. From the days of the cavemen, she had effectively wiped out entire tribes and no one outside of the circle of those who knew what witches were, had a single clue as to the cause of these massacres. The name, the Black Witch, was not one the Witch gave herself, for all pureblood witches had no actual names. They had no need for them. They were solitary apart from when they fed. They lived alone. They ate alone. There were no covens. No groups of three around a cauldron saying "Hubble bubble toil and trouble". Those were their acolytes who took the mantle Witch erroneously. They were normally soulless humans or demons in disguise, acting on behalf of the real Witch.

Humans were a Witch's only target. Those who dwelled in the shadows were safe from their feeding maw – as witches only ate humans and could not digest other beings – despite this, those hidden people were still terrified of a Witch and none so much as the Witch dressed in the black cloak.

But there was one who had escaped her. A child. A child born of two Lycan Skinwalkers. Deep in the valleys of Wales, sat the village of Mythur Standing. A small farming community of less than

100 people – all salt of the earth and hardworking. An idyllic life that would soon be extinguished.

Whilst cutting wood in the forest, one of the villagers happened upon a howling wolf, in pain and yelping as she was giving birth. Due to complications that were too foreign to this woodcutter, he had no idea how to save her from what was to come as he saw her through the trees, splayed on the ground in a clearing, howling in agony. His scent soon reached her nose, alerting her – and her gaze darted to his. Normally the wild wolf would attack the man and there would be a bloody battle. But not today. Today, she looked at him in pain, , begging for any kindness. And against all of his best instincts, the woodcutter approached the wolf in her time of need, comforted her as her impending delivery ended her life. As he cradled the wolf's head on his lap, she glanced up at him one final time before the darkness stole her away. She wanted to say thank you to him. Thank you for not leaving her alone.

After she passed, the woodcutter saw that there was still movement within the belly of the wolf. The baby was still living. And to his shock, after cutting open her belly fur, found the cub inside was in fact, human. A boy.

The woodcutter knew what this was. He had heard the tales of Lycan shapeshifters. Werewolves, but looking at this baby's eyes, the eyes just like its mother's, he knew he would not be able to do what he knew he should. And as he lived alone on the edge of town – decided to take the child back as his own.

He did not want a son. But over the years that was what he got. The village believed it was his nephew, given to him after his estranged sister died – not that he ever had a sister. But the village never questioned this. And welcomed the new addition.

Knowing what was to come, the woodcutter built a lockable pit under his house where his boy could be safe when the moon was full. Once a month he would buy a lamb from a neighboring farm and lock it in the pit with the boy during his change. Even as a newborn, this baby would best the lamb and feed on it, as its Lycan side demanded. Then, the day after the moon had left, the boy would be a boy again and for a month he would have his son. His son whom he named after his own father – Gobolt.

And when, on his 7th birthday, the Black Witch arrived at the village gates, Gobolt's life would be forever changed and placed on a path of revenge.

The Witch did as she usually did. The strongest of the men went away, including his father. She cast her spell over the rest and they made their way to the center of the village to be massacred. But her spells did not work on young Gobolt. He watched from his kitchen window as the village was decimated. He watched as the men came back and he saw his father tear out his own heart and, in the last few seconds of his life, take a bite from it.

Terrified, young Gobolt hid under the table. Crying uncontrollably – Until eventually, hours later, the door opened, and the Black Witch stood there. She could smell this boy hiding from the other side of the village.

Smashing her way in, without any fight from the boy – who was paralyzed with fear – she picked him up and took a bite of the side of his head, through his eye and over his fragile skull. Not knowing what he really was, as she had never smelled a Lycan before, she could only recognize the smell of the boy's innocence.

His screams then, were only eclipsed by her own, as his Lycan blood burned like acid in her mouth. In pain, she dropped his bleeding body to the floor. Within a few moments, she had slouched away – full of the flesh of the village and with a mouth on fire from the boy's blood.

A normal child would have died, but this boy did not. He ran away to the woods., his brain exposed from the bite, and the boy's anguish and pain forced the wolf out of him. This wolf stayed in the forefront until he was fully healed physically – but that took many years.

During those years and every day without fail, the wolf sat on the hill overlooking the village. He watched as the massacre was discovered by a band of nomadic travelers. He watched as the village was cleared and eventually demolished. He watched as holy men blessed the area, as they had now deemed it poisoned by the devil. He watched as a single chapel was built on this site; a holy place to try to counteract the evil of what had occurred here. A place with lodgings for people traveling through – as the village was on a trade route for other villages. The priest who lived at this chapel had seen the wolf every day watching from the tree-line and took to always leaving food out for him. Welcoming even the wild animals to the grace of his God's kindness. In any other wolf, the Lycan side would have normally ripped the priest limb from limb upon first sight – but the boy inside, though weak and healing, somehow had moral control. And from the moment of the Black Witch's attack on him, he always would have. Whether it was from the extensive damage to the boy's brain, or the amount of death he already seen, the Lycan side was never going to be the indiscriminate killer it had once been.

But still… this boy, Gobolt, was far from human.

For the many years leading up to his adulthood, and his meeting with a Hungarian Count called Ferenc, he had kept the wolf locked away; never let it run free. He knew that as a boy he controlled the beast, but there was no guaranteeing that it would be a continual fixture when he transformed into a larger, more adult beast. So he continued to lock himself in a cage every time the nighttime celestial satellite was in full bloom. He knew the wolf had once obeyed him. But that was then, not now. He never wanted to know what the monster inside him was capable of, as the monster stole all memories during his transformation hours. He may still have had moral control during the change, but he had no way to know, and he never wanted to find out that the monster ever gained the upper hand over his goodness.

And So… It Began

"Here we are…" Ian said with a smirk on his face as he read from the newspaper in his hands. "Rebecca Hopkins, the sexless actress... Wow." His eyes widened with surprise, before continuing. "That's how they start the review?"

Across the table from him sat Rebecca, whose face was now dripping with annoyance. "Well, that's bloody great…" she began. "Sexless? They gotta keep banging that goddamn drum, don't they? Is it all like that?"

The reviews Rebecca got were always a sore point for her. The critics always loved her performance, never criticized her acting ability. But always – ALWAYS – mentioned her lack of femininity, or called her 'mannish' 'butch' 'plain' – and now 'sexless'. She knew she should not ever take these things to heart. She knew she should never read her reviews – and over the past few years, she had managed to successfully evade the entirety of the internet's opinion and all the press about her – she only ever heard the highlights of important bits from Ian; the one person she trusted outside of her own family. Now, though, she thought it may have been different. Now, she was in the theater and only had a small role amongst what she saw as much better actors. This is why she'd thought she would be safe in demanding Ian read her the latest review aloud.

The coffee shop was bustling around them as Ian held the newspaper open in front of him, reading the rest of the review to himself, then glancing up at Rebecca, wondering to himself whether he should tell her every word. He had known her for nearly 30 years. Been with her every step of the way during her career. Been her closest friend and confidante since kindergarten. Kept her away from the online trolling about her. Tried to only show her the good press - But now she wanted to hear all of this review. As if this one local paper was the summation of her whole career. Not just this one hack's prejudice and ignorant opinions.

"Go on... I may as well know," Rebecca said with a smile. "What's the worst it can say?"

"Are you sure?" he asked as a waitress swung by and picked up his empty coffee cup. "Thank you" he said softly to her, as she then smiled automatically before walking away. He then turned his attention back to Rebecca, who was still cradling her half-filled cup of almost cold liquid. "It's the same old crap," he said.

"Then you shouldn't mind reading it," she retorted. "If you don't, I'll just take the paper off you and read it myself."

Several customers milled about the serving counter next to their table, waiting to procure their particular flavor of caffeine to start their day. As Rebecca was used to when in public spaces, a couple of the customers had noticed her. She had learned over the years to totally block out the whispers and the pictures people might take of her with their phones. All of them always tried to be subtle in this, but failed miserably each and every time. She found it best to only engage and pay them attention if they plucked up the nerve to come over for an autograph or a photo. Both her and Ian found it part of the routine, instead of an annoyance, but knew enough to keep most of it blocked out of their attention. Rebecca, though, could not wait for the day the attention faded to nothing. The glare of fame was too much for her to handle; the constant fake adulation from the producers, the cruelty of the critics, the merciless torment from the fans, not to mention the cult-like behavior from her peers.

Ian glanced up and noticed the couple of the fans at the counter, neither of whom plucked up the courage to come over to see Rebecca. He then looked to her and smiled. She wanted to know what the review said? *So be it.* Though if this was six months ago he would not have even told her there was a review, as the reviews on opening night were much, much worse.

"Fine…" Ian said as he looked back down at the newspaper. "...Rebecca Hopkins.. blah blah… Sexless actress… blah blah… Marked her stage debut in a minor role as one of Macbeth's witches last year. With the show coming to the end of its run this reviewer thought he would give it a second chance. But all the same problems remained. Hopkins was a curious choice to say the least. A major Hollywood actress suddenly evaporating out of the limelight. Canceling multi-million dollar deals, then escaping back to her country with her tail tucked between her legs – then making the decision to take a role so insignificant, in a production so bereft of any innovative presentation or worth, well, it begs the question – Why? When she could star in so many bigger and better productions? Utilizing her immense skill in something surpassing what was a banal waste of an evening. Be warned fans of Ms. Hopkins. For she has made such a bizarre choice for her stage debut. And over the months, the play has somehow become sloppier and bizarrely seeming more unrehearsed in regards to the main players. Hopkins is almost unrecognizable under a mountain of prosthetics, and appears only for a couple of measly scenes. It makes one suspect that the story of how she purposely fell into this theatrical mire of unexceptional tedium would make a much better show… The bard would not be impressed."

Ian stopped reading, closed the paper and looked at Rebecca with an "I told you so" look. "Happy now?" he asked. "Your life better for knowing this critic's bullshit?"

"That's the review of the whole show? Really? Just talks about me?" she asked as she then took the paper from Ian's hands, opening its pages to see for herself.

"You're surprised by that?" Ian replied. "You are not a small deal, you know?"

Rebecca found the page in question and scanned the review for herself. It was just as Ian read out.

"You're a fucking big star," he said as he motioned to her with both hands. "Rebecca Hopkins in *any* show will be the focus of the review. You know that. And you knew this show was not the best one out there."

Rebecca closed the paper with a sigh. "I hate this," she said softly. "I fucking hate it all."

"Well, it's not like it's ever been any different. They find you an enigma they *need* to understand. Like you're some kind of puzzle to be solved. Like they are scared by a woman who actually has a brain. And besides, you've got no one to blame but yourself. You're the one who decided to take this role for the pussy!"

"I did not!" she protested.

"Well, you and I can keep that secret then."

"Maybe I should just tell people why I quit it all?" she mumbled to herself looking down at the paper. "They're not going to stop with this crap."

"You'd be better off telling them you burned-out after spending all your money on heroine and prostitutes… Now stop being morose, you sexless beast and drink your fucking coffee."

Taking a sip, she grimaced at its coldness, then put the cup back on its saucer and pushed it slightly away from her. "Think I'm done."

Ian stood up from the table, picked up his denim jacket that was draped over the back of the chair and slung it over his shoulders – wearing it like a shawl. With his hand out to Rebecca, he motioned for her to take it.

"Now come on and stop being a whiney prick… We have a museum to go to!"

Smiling, she took his hand and stood up. She always appreciated his humor. It was the only way she could normalize the abnormality of the entertainment industry. He was her filter. Her protector. Her knight in shining armor. A knight who was a foot shorter than she was.

Since the day she'd moved to America, following her career where it would be most profitable – Los Angeles – he had been in tow. More than an assistant, he had the title of Llod – A title she made up – Meaning Last Line of Defence. L.L.O.D. And that was exactly what he was. All her decisions were sounded off him. All her projects were discussed with him. He was not controlling or guiding her, but she needed the person who had no bullshit ulterior motive. She needed someone who would tell her plainly when she was taking a crap role that her asshole agent forced upon her for his own gain. Though she didn't always listen to his advice, she knew he was telling her the truth as he saw it. And that was priceless.

As she stood up, she looked down at her cup, feeling relieved this was not LA and she *could* just leave the cup there, as England did not have the same fan –culture. In LA some over-ambitious fan would have most likely grabbed the cup after she left and sold it online, along with a blurry photo of her drinking from it.

Along the autumnal streets, the cold wind blew trash and leaves along the sidewalk as Ian and Rebecca walked with their arms linked. Around them, the city was going about its day: taxis honking each other in a futile fight to get to their destination 15 seconds faster. Commuters rushed about with their attention focussed solely on themselves. She was anonymous in this kind of environment. She felt herself in this place at this time.

"Why are you even worried at all?" Ian asked as he glanced into a passing shop window.

"I'm not worried," she said. "I just want to know what the fuck it's about."

"It's just a picture. Okay, fine. An old bat was creepy with it. And you look like the woman in it. So, what? I look like a bazillion other guys in the club trolling for cock. Everyone, my dear. Even *you*, are ten-a-penny. I could find a hundred paintings with either of us in it."

"But you *knew* this one… You say you saw it… Besides, have you got anything better to do?"

"Better? God no. This is the highlight of my week!" Ian's eyes glistened as he spoke. He relished these kinds of mysteries. "We get to go on an adventure!"

"Well, you could have lied and said you never knew the painting. Save us all the hassle of coming across town in rush hour," Rebecca smirked.

Ian shrugged. "I probably don't know," he said, which resulted in Rebecca rolling her eyes at him. Smiling, he continued. "Worst case scenario.

The painting I'm thinking of is not the same one, so there are two ones with someone like you on them. So, if so, you can get twice as upset about it all."

"If there's another one, I'll hold you personally responsible." She put on a mock-fierce expression toward him, before it broke into a smile, looking forward as they continued to walk.

"You think I control painters? Painters that have been dead for centuries" Ian asked mockingly.

"You, my dear are capable of anything," she began. "There is nothing you are not capable of.... Except pleasing a woman."

"And it is the thing I am most proud of," he asserted.

"You please me, though."

"Rebecca Vagina Hopkins. *How dare you*!" His face fell into a mock-shocked expression as he spoke.

She turned her look toward him and spoke with narrow threatening eyes. "You please my naked body."

Ian stopped in his tracks, breaking free of her linked arm. Moving his hands up to his cheeks, he opened his mouth, his face now horrified "Wash your fucking mouth out and take that back!"

Rebecca took a step toward him with a seductive glare. "I'd touch myself as well... slowly."

His jaw was almost on the floor with mock offense. He slowly spoke as if reciting Shakespeare, rolling his r's and projecting as if on stage "Rebecca... Tabitha... Hopkins."

The seductive look now fallen into quizzical "Tabitha? I thought my middle name was Vagina, according to you?"

"Shh…" Ian hushed her, breaking his character, before jumping back in. "Rebecca Tabitha Hopkins... You keep your *grotty vaginal threats* to yourself."

A family of fat American tourists passed. This stereotypical family with their 2.4 children, complete with phones in their hands as they took pictures of everything they happened across. They cemented their tourist status by wearing matching *I Love London* t-shirts. The parents had heard Ian's outburst and look horrified at him as they passed; the children smiling at the strange swearing Englishman.

Ian smiled at them as they hurried past – totally oblivious to Rebecca standing there, just offended by *him*. "Welcome to London!" he called out after them. "Steer clear of the vaginas!"

The Westmore Art Gallery & Museum was a large building spread over three floors. Once a factory, it had become a museum in the late 1800s – and along with the Natural History Museum (which opened in the same year) it had gone from strength to strength and become a staple of London tourism, showcasing an ever-rotating selection of paintings and sculptures by the masters. Half of the pieces on display from its expansive archive, the other half on loan from other museums and private collections.

Ian strode into the building alongside Rebecca, leading them across the marble slab floors, through the throng of tourists gawking at the high ceilings, over to the customer service desk.

A young woman, barely aged 18, sat on the other side of the counter. Her heavy build almost broke through the sides of her blue uniform suit. She looked bored. Very bored. And it was obvious how much she hated this job. The contempt she felt would almost be as evident if she wore a sign saying *'Leave me the fuck alone'* written on it.

Getting to the counter, with Rebecca stood behind him, Ian greeted this young woman with a wide genuine smile. He then glanced at her name badge – which stated *'Hello! I'm Aednat – Ask me anything',* then back at her.

"Hello… Aaaay.. Umm Adenat? Aaaeeeydnat?" He struggled. "I'm sorry, how do you pronounce your name?"

"You say it Ey-nit." She spoke in her strong Irish brogue, complete with her stone-faced bored look. "How can I help today, sir?"

"Well, awesome, Aednat." His smile was still wide and welcoming. "Wondering if you can help? Now, it's a weird request I have."

"You don't say?" Her expression not changed one bit.

"I do indeed," Ian said, ignoring her tone. He was not the kind of man who was oblivious to others, he knew exactly what this girl was thinking. That she was looking at him as if he were dirt. He just didn't care. "Well… I came here in in the early 90s. Before you were born. Uhhh..." he continued as her expression was still unchanged by any of his words. "And there was a religious exhibition or something on. So, we are trying to find one of the paintings from there."

"We don't do time machines. Try the Tate," she replied blankly, hoping this annoyance would leave her alone. Just like all the annoyances who bugged her all-day long.

"No? Damn. That's just what I wanted!" Ian said genuinely, which did not elicit even as much as a smile from this miserable girl. "Are there any listings of old shows? Old brochures? Something? Someone who has been alive longer than a week, who may still work here?" His insult totally flew over the head of Aednat, who turned, got off her stool and muttered to herself, "Never a normal fucking question."

She waddled over to the desk behind her and picked up the phone.

From behind, Rebecca stepped up to Ian. "Anything?" she asked in a whisper.

His reply was intentionally loud enough for Aednat to hear over her call. "This *charming* young lady is calling someone now to help us in our mission."

Aednat glanced at him coldly as she continued her call. Rebecca met her gaze and smiled back.

If they were any closer to her, they would have seen the slight change in Aednat's expression as she recognized Rebecca – but both of them would have chalked it down to recognition of her movie star status.

That was not, though, what her recognition was.

Not at all.

Waiting in the curator's office was akin to being in a hospital waiting room. The whole room stank of bleach. The furniture was basic and functional. The floor was a beige linoleum. The bookshelves were neat and sterile in decoration. Each book the same size. The same color spine. No text on them describing the title. Just a roman numeral from I to XXXX.

The curator's desk was much the same; a notepad, placed precisely 5cm from the left and bottom edge of the desk. A 2B pencil – sharpened perfectly, 1cm horizontally to the top of the notepad. Placed on the opposite position to the notepad – to match its position to the millimeter on the other side – was an old rotary phone.

In his 70s, Chester Entwhistle was a figure of order and precision. His role as the curator was his life, and a role he had worked at since his late teens. More than programming the museum's collection, he managed the extensive archive which lay beneath the museum. Deep within a labyrinthine system of rooms; each housed a few dozen large, hermetically sealed chambers containing numerous priceless artworks.

Chester also knew something no one else did. Most of the art in the museum was fake; faked by his own very hand. A master at duplicating paint strokes, he had spent his life perfecting the great painters, whose original art the museum had in its vaults. As well as the curator, he was also the restorer for the pieces, under which guise he created these master fakes. His restoration studio was, in fact, a forger's lair. Complete with ancient oil paints, pastels, canvasses. Everything he would need to ensure the copy would be indistinguishable from the original. He had, on many occasions, got to the last stroke of a copy and painted a slight incorrect way compared to the original. To which, he would calmly remove the canvas and destroy it. He was a perfectionist who could not abide any disorder. His creations needed to be beyond reproach for his own needs; his own sexual needs.

When a forged copy was complete, he would – with the utmost care – remove the original from the vaults (or from display) and swap out the canvasses from their frames. Taking the original down to his lair, he would place it face-up on the floor. It was at this point that his decorum and order would abandon him, for he would strip naked, squat over the masterpiece and defecate and urinate onto it. Soon after this vulgar display, he would masturbate in a fury whilst smearing his own feces and urine over himself – writhing on the paining – then smearing his own excrement into the grooves of the painting itself, this whole ordeal ending in his ejaculation. From the excitement he had just endured, he would then sleep in his own filth, atop the canvas.

When awake, he would calmly shower himself then remove the soiled canvas to the furnace – wiping it from existence. He would then disinfect the studio with a methodical and meticulous routine.

This was his only passion.

This was his only joy.

He hated being human' but he still endured it for the greater purpose.

"May I be of assistance?" Chester asked as he walked into his office, greeting Rebecca and Ian, who were sat on the chairs in front of his desk.

He walked around them and sat down in his large leather throne-like chair. His thin smile and reptilian-esque face lent him an air of menace. At 6 foot 8, he towered over most people, and with his skeletal frame and fitted black suits, he was an imposing and unsettling figure. His hair was slicked back and dyed jet black, his eyes a piercing pale blue. His skin was clean-shaven, yet sagging and wrinkled from his advancing years.

"Yes," Rebecca began. "We are looking for a painting. A particular painting."

"Well…" Chester said, and smiled at her. "You have certainly come to the right place."

"I don't know the name. But I can describe it. And my friend here..." she said, motioning to Ian, who quickly raised his hand up in a wave to Chester, mouthing the word 'Hi'. "My friend thinks he saw it here in the 90s, at an exhibition."

"I can certainly try my best. I would have programmed any exhibition with relevant pieces, so I should be able to assist."

"It's got monsters in it, I think," she began, but Ian cut her off with "Jesus, woman, that's not how you describe it."

He turned to Chester with a smile. "Basically, the painting has her on a mount, holding a severed head whilst lots of demons bow to her. And the devil is in the clouds behind."

Chester smirked. "I was afraid it would be that one. Ah well. All good things, eh?"

Rebecca looked at Ian, confused, but he just shrugged at her.

"Please can you wait on the chairs outside in the hallway? I need to make a rather delicate phone call about this."

"Uhh, okay," Ian said, looking at Rebecca. "Guess we will wait outside, then. Not weird at all."

Chester was old. He felt older than he was. He was tired. Too tired for this. He had been through this many times before. For most this would be a surprising turn of events, but he knew what was to come. He had seen this and many other cities rise and fall. He had seen kings turn to dust. Now in this skin of an old man, his real older self – which hid underneath the skin – was resigned to the inevitable.

"Hello? Yes, it's Chester Entwhistle from the Westmore. I need to speak to Mrs. Hopkins." He sniffed as he waited on the line. He could see the silhouettes of his two visitors outside through the frosted glass. They knew something was amiss. And if it was even a decade before, he would have handled this turn of events differently. But he was tired with this rotation. It had gone on far too long.

As soon as he heard Leanne Hopkins' voice on the other end of the phone, he could tell she was on the same page as him. "Leanne? I think we need a reset. She came here again. Can it continue?"

Her silence on the other end of this phone conversation spoke louder than any of her words ever could. Leanne knew that her hopes of Rebecca dropping any thought of the painting was now too much to rely on. She knew Chester was right. She knew the Goddess would agree.

"She asked about it then?" she asked rhetorically.

"Naturally. As she always would. It's in her nature isn't it? Maybe we should accept that we need to change the path as she doesn't seem any more corrupt than the last dozen times." Chester spoke whilst opening up the desk drawer next to him. In the middle of an organized compartmental stationary drawer, sat a large serrated blade. "So, I can assume it will be brought forward?" he continued as he picked up the knife, placed it on the desk and shut the drawer.

In God Begot House, Leanne paused, her eyes closed for a moment. She knew hers was not to question why. This was the purpose. She was to get Rebecca to the brink… But this was far too early. She didn't want to say goodbye to what she had built. She didn't want to have to go back and start over. She did not, though, have a choice. She knew her purpose was not directed by her own want, but by a higher power.

"I shall ask Her first, but I think we have no choice but to put the call out…. So, I guess it has to begin now."

"I shall see you on the other side then, Mrs. Hopkins" he said, and sighed as he placed the phone back onto the receiver. He had seen these happen before. He didn't want to sit through the madness of this world's end all over again. He was tired. He was done with this one.

Picking up the knife and with no ceremony, no pause for thought, he ripped the serrated edge of the blade across his throat and started to saw into his own neck. Back and forth – with force and speed – he dragged the razor-sharp teeth of the knife across his throat. Deeper and deeper. His expression blank. Not feeling pain. Not looking in the slightest bit as any human would in this situation. But then, he wasn't human.

"This is stupid," Rebecca exclaimed as she stood up from the chair and turned to the Curator's office door. She glanced back to Ian quickly. "Let's just go. I can't be bothered. It's just a fucking painting."

Her hand turned the handle and she opened the frosted glass covered door.

Recoiling in terror and disgust, she couldn't find a voice to scream as she saw Chester over halfway through sawing into his own neck, blood jetting out from the wound, covering the desk and staining any other place it reached, his teeth now gritted and his eyes wide – determined to finish the job. He choked as he gasped for his next breath. A breath that would not come.

His last few sawing attempts were weak and fumbled, as he then slumped into his chair. His head tipped backwards, exposing the cavernous wound that he had just caused; the blood still arcing upwards in bursts as his heartbeat thumped its last beats.

Backing out of the office, Rebecca closed her eyes for a second. This couldn't be real.

Ian was now beside her, fighting back the vomit. "Oh, fuck no," he managed to utter in-between retching.

Running was all they could think of doing.

They tore out into the foyer where dozens of people were queued for their visit, oblivious to the horrors in the curator's office. Coming to a halt, they were met by Aednat, who was standing in their way.

Ian grabbed Rebecca and stopped.

"Why the hurry?" Aednat asked, not really caring for an answer.

Staring at this young woman in a panic he tried to keep his composure and not scream – which was all he wanted to do. "That man..." He pointed back to where they ran from. "He just fucking killed himself."

"What?" Aednat replied, for once showing some emotion other than disdain.

"He cut off his *own* fucking head!" Ian yelled at her. People in the foyer were starting to pay attention; whispers of '*What did he say?*', '*Don't listen*', '*He's mad*', '*someone died?*' could be heard.

Rebecca was crying without realizing. When she did she wiped the tears away and regained her composure, as best as she could. "We have to call the police, right now!"

Before Aednat could answer her or Ian's pleas for help, her phone beeped loudly. A shrill tone repeating. Not like a phone ring, but akin to an alarm. One that pierced through the foyer.

This was soon followed by dozens of other people's phones within that foyer following suit and emitting the same repeated alarm. Until most of the people were looking at their phone – answering that exact same alarm.

One family all looked at their phones, which all made the same noise. Amongst another family, only the mother looked at her phone's alarm. Her husband looking at her curiously, asking, "What the hell is that?"

Those who did not have a beeping phone looked at the people that did, confused. Then the ones that did, slowly turned their attentions to Rebecca.

On the beeping phones was not a long message, but a symbol and a single word. On a red background, the symbol was a circle with two vertical lines going through its lower half. Underneath that symbol, a word was written. A simple word: '*Reset*'.

Rebecca turned as she started to realize that all the people were now looking back at her, blank yet intent. Those without phones continued to look around in confusion, asking what was going on to anyone who may answer. But no one did.

Ian, still emotional from his outburst to Aednat, looked around at the people staring at Rebecca. "What the fuck is this…" he asked.

A man barged past them in a panic, someone chasing him. But before he could escape, a long heavy blade – swung by the woman chasing him – came down and split his skull in two, the blade cut down to his throat, his head now divided down the middle.

Seeing this, Rebecca's terrified scream pierced through the room as Ian dragged her backward.

By now, all the people with phones who'd received the alarm, had also brought out knives, machetes, blades of all kinds. Hidden in handbags, up sleeves, in inside pockets.

Heather was a loving mother.

She had raised her two children, Agnes and James, all on her own. She was a bastion of single motherhood. A victor in the struggle so familiar to many other single parents. The children's father had absconded years ago with most of her money and possessions, leaving her almost destitute. She had gone to the police, but they did not care to even follow up with her. She tried to get the help of a lawyer who just gave her bad advice and a large bill to pay for the privilege. It was only with the help of her loving family and friends, that she'd managed to pull herself up off the ground that she had been emotionally thrown down on to – and only recently that she'd been able to re-focus all of her energy and attention on raising these two magnificent children the best way she could, making ends meet by taking any freelance work she found.

This was all made so much easier by the intelligence of her children. Mature beyond their years, the epitome of good, well-rounded kids. Agnes was now 7, James now 5 and both could already be seen as future leaders.

Agnes had asked to come to the museum so she could look at the medieval sculpture exhibition which had just opened. James, though not caring for sculptures, loved being with his family, so was more than happy to go. And Heather could not love them anymore, or be happier in her life.

As Heather dug her blade deep across the throat of her daughter, then turned to her terrified son and stabbed him through his eye, piercing his brain – she felt nothing. Her phone had beeped. She had her command. The mission was greater than the distraction of her life in this place. Greater than the lives that, at the end of the day, were not real to her.

Around her, those who did not have an alarm were panicked, trying to escape the museum. But they were being set upon by those who did have the alarm. Attacked with knives. Killed quickly and brutally. As those with the alarms knew of those that didn't instinctively.

Rebecca was in a daze. She stared at the multitude of murders occurring as Ian dragged her to the exit. The victim's bodies fell and gushed all of their blood supply over the marble floor.

"You have to come with us!" Aednat shouted as she blocked off the escape route where Rebecca and Ian were running to.

Almost as a reflex from her years of self-defense classes, Rebecca quickly lifted her leg and kicked Aednat squarely in the groin. Her boots were heavy and her kick had an incredible force behind it. Aednat fell to the floor in an instant. The pain of the kick was intense and debilitating. If she was to live much longer, Aednat would have had to have been hospitalized for this.

Through this almost insurmountable amount of pain, Aednat grabbed the blade in her hand and tried to take a swing at Rebecca's legs, attacking in fury. Rebecca had no time to try to counter this attack – but before anything else could happen, another blade came down and sliced through Aednat's wrist, sending her severed hand – still grabbing the blade – to the floor. She screamed as a man stood above her angrily. "She is not yours to kill!" he spat venomously at her, as he plunged his now bloodied blade into the top of Aednat's skull.

The man then turned to Rebecca. "It is *your* time now. You have to meet your Goddess." He spoke emotionlessly, as Ian watched on in a panic.

Rebecca and Ian then backed away, looking around them in a daze. Most of the people with alarms had successfully dispatched those who did not. Lovers turning on lovers. Children turning on parents. Parents turning on children. And now they all turned to her.

"Praise her name!" one voice shouted from the advancing mob. Soon they all chanted the same...

"Praise her name!"

"Praise her name!"

"Praise her name!"

..as Rebecca and Ian stumbled towards the last two people blocking their exit.

They were not violent people. But to escape this insanity, they were about to unleash an instinctive fury they had not ever thought themselves capable of. And it started with an uppercut when the first person tried to grab Rebecca's wrist shouting, "You're coming with us!" Rebecca's clenched fist connected upwards with Heather's nose, breaking it on impact, unleashing a torrent of blood in that second. The bones from the nose splintered upwards and into her brain – extinguishing her life in an instant. An end to a life too quick for a woman who meted out such tragedy to her two murdered children. Ian meanwhile had grabbed Aednat's fallen blade – with her severed hand still attached – and was swinging it at any aggressor he could.

Rebecca did not know she had ended Heather's life, as she and Ian were now running to the exit, punching and slashing at anyone who came in their way. No one had been trying to use their weapons on her, nor even attempting to stop her with violence. Ian was safe as well, but only due to his proximity to Rebecca.

Outside the museum, in the many streets which sprawled out from its large stone steps, much of the same was happening as what had happened inside. There was a massacre erupting, swiftly followed by a mass panic. Screams of people being hacked up by strangers and loved ones. Tourists, businessmen, taxi drivers, homeless people. There was no separation between killer and victim. No apparent methodology or obvious intent.

Nothing except they all wanted Rebecca. When they noticed her exiting the museum, they turned their attentions solely on her, and away from their own victims. The lucky few who were not killed straight away by these murderers scrambled away as fast as they could. The even fewer lucky ones, who were not already injured and about to bleed out, made it at least a street or two away before they collapsed. But no one would survive. Those who got away did not get far and were hacked to pieces by those turning against them – or worse, taken by the oncoming dark.

PART 2
The Descent

"The path to paradise begins in hell."

Dante Alighieri

Stowe Haven

Nestled on the edge of a seemingly never-ending stretch of moorland lay the small fishing village of Stowe Haven. With no neighbors within a day's ride, it was isolated as far as any place was within these isles. This small village was reliant solely on its own fishing and farming to provide its food, and also sustained itself by being the trade post for those smugglers who wished to avoid more "legal" docks which lay around the shores of the country. Wishing more anonymity due to the nature of whatever illegal or immoral item their cargo was - From human trafficking to weapons dealing, Stowe Haven allowed anything to pass through their waters. Refusing to abide by any rules of government or royal decree, Stowe Haven was the last lawless town in this land; a veritable Wild West in one community of less than 200 people.

On this wintry night, snow was falling in a silent dance. The continual torrent of thick snowflakes fell in all directions, crossing each other and never colliding, as if following a predetermined pattern. The rhythm of this blizzard was evident if one were to take the time to witness its display of order within chaos.

Out to sea, each of these flakes were obliterated in an instant as they hit the water. The thick falling blanket becoming nothingness as each flake's journey was extinguished as it collided with the ocean.

For the men on the two small rowboats, it was a different matter. The snow fell and built up on them as well as their boats, before the pulsing gales blew the flakes off into an airborne powder, off to their next stop within oblivion.

The boats, each carrying three men, moved slowly through the waters toward the docks of Stowe Haven. Through the surrounding howling wind, their oars could not be heard and with no lights to guide them, the blanket of falling white shrouded their approach. Not that anyone would see them at this time. Past midnight, the village would be asleep; slumbering until the dawn awoke them to another day's labor – even in the harshest blizzards, the farmers and fishermen of the village never stopped when daylight was present. But as soon as darkness came, it was a different story.

Stowe Haven's docks were made up of three moorings: one for large ships, which ran the length of the cliff-face along the right side of the harbor; one for mid-sized boats which ran along the opposite cliff and the last, the mooring for the smallest boats, whose small wooden jetty lay in the middle of the harbor –the one that these two small boats headed toward. The other two moorings were better for a surprise attack, but worse for distance –

and as it was the middle of the night, stealth was not the highest priority, especially as they were not planning to be quiet in the battle they were about to commence.

At the front of the lead boat, Gobolt's grin was wide. Covered in a heavy cloak, which protected him from the blizzard, he wore his leather battle armor underneath. In his hands, he held two small runic carved scimitars; one side sharp, the other side jagged with razor teeth. He was ready for what was to come, but he was also tired. Tired of the constant struggle. The never-ending fights. When one evil died at his hand, another came into view. It was an eternal parade of evil being thrown at them. For years now, he and Ferenc had fought and beaten everything pitted against them. Ferenc, though, did not know of Gobolt's wish for the fighting to end. To the outside world, he was a powerful and determined warrior and his true face was never seen, the face of the man wishing to live in peace, away from the nightmares, somewhere by the sea, farming his own land. He would even leave his quest for vengeance against the Black Witch, if it meant a quiet life. But Gobolt knew dreams were only that. He found his fuel to fight through his friend's determination and endless supply of rage against those who sought to harm. So, it came to be that as long as Ferenc fought, he would fight too. And when he would fight, he would be nothing less than the Gobolt talked of in whispers. The man so formidable in battle that even his inner wolf hid from him. Not the truth of his condition, but one he was happy with being perpetrated by those who speak of him.

The small jetty came into view through the thick blanket of falling ice – their blinding protection from being sighted by people on land.

Turning back, Gobolt looked at the king's soldier beside him. "Chin up, lad," he said, his grin still stuck to his face.

"Yes sir," the soldier replied. This soldier's name was Avershaw.

Though all these soldiers had seen battles galore, fought demons aplenty, they were now to face something worse – witches. And they were not feeling the warm embrace of bravery. The kind that Ferenc felt. They just felt the chill of potential demise at the hands of unforgiving evil.

"If we die today we die. Nothing can be done. But if we win? Ah… now there'll be a story to outlive us all. And when we win, we're that one step closer to having a peaceful nights rest."

Avershaw nodded. He was used to duty, used to laying his life on the line for King and Country. Used to battling evil. He had seen a lot over the past seven years of fighting for the crown. But now was different. He had seen what a witch was capable of once before – and that was more than enough for him. If he lived a thousand more years, he would have been happy to never face the wrath of such a foulness in person ever again.

In the midst of a blistering heatwave, a younger Avershaw stood on guard outside the Royal prison. Having only been a King's soldier for a year, he was green when it came to battle. He had been taught to fight and beaten all other soldiers in practice combat – but he had never killed anyone. Never had to. And in this position, it was very unlikely to happen soon. He was charged with entrance protection to the sub-levels of the king's prison. A place where real evil was kept.

Brought into the fold by the king himself, Avershaw was the newest member to join the battle between light and dark, something he did not at first believe. But since his induction, he had been shown not only the darkness that lurks in the periphery of humanity's gaze, but also the hidden innocence that deserved protection from that evil. Guarding a prison would normally be a demeaning position, but what was below was not something that should be guarded lightly. He had seen many of the prisoners being brought in. From hulking beasts to incorporeal phantoms – the curtain of reality had been well and truly pulled back. So, he was glad to remain here until the king decided that he was ready to progress to a higher rank. A promotion which was due at the start of spring – after 18 months of learning, he would then be due to train for the first battalion and would join the actual fight, finally putting his sword to the king's work.

As the sun beat down on him, Avershaw remained focused. He would not let discomfort deter him from his position. He looked ahead, to where the main prison lay. The prison made for humans. Through the windows, he could see the guards milling around the corridors of this virtually safe environment. He could see some of the prisoners being escorted around. All oblivious to what was below his feet. The real prisoners here. None having the slightest inkling as to what he protected them from. They would not understand that his job was to not stop anything going out – there were plenty of guards down there to serve that role – but to stop anyone coming in. To protect *them* from the truth.

The large wooden door beside him opened with a loud and forceful creak. Turning, he saw Gobolt stare out at him, wide-eyed and covered in blood. "Boy, your services are required downstairs. NOW!" he yelled.

"What about the post?" Avershaw asked, knowing full well that this could be a test to see if he would abandon his post for any reason. Gobolt never played fair when it came to teaching his new recruits.

"Fuck the post. Now come on before I drag you unconscious down here," Gobolt uttered as he disappeared back inside.

Though he knew better, he could not say "no" to a direct command. And besides, that man scared him. He had heard the other soldiers telling stories of the wolf man, so knew better than to second guess.

Locking the prison door behind him, Avershaw saw the darkness settle down the steps of the staircase that led below, his descent only being lit by occasional torches on its narrow stone-clad walls. Gobolt walked in front as the spiral stairs went deeper. He did not turn as he spoke the words Avershaw did not want to hear: "It's the witch."

As he reached the bottom of the staircase, Avershaw saw why he was needed. One of the regular guards was sat on the floor, his blood staining the dirt around him to a deep almost black color – he was dying slowly. The skin on his face had mostly been peeled off. His hands were weak and grabbing at any remaining skin it could, his subconscious aching to peel off the rest. All that he had left was the chin, part of his scalp and his eyelids. His nose was already torn off, as were his cheeks – all exposing his skeletal interior. Strangely he did not scream – he just moaned under his breath as he gently clawed at one of his eyelids. In his mind's eye he was being attacked by flesh-eating ravens., the witch's illusions taking full effect.

"Jesus, save me," Avershaw uttered in terror as he saw this poor soul under a witch's spell.

"Nothing he, or you can do to stop it," came the reply from Gobolt, who was looking down the hallway in front of him.

Turning, Avershaw pleaded, "We have to get a doctor."

"He's gone, boy," came the reply. "No medicine can stop him doing what that devil is making him do. Now come on… We have work to complete."

Looking around, Avershaw noticed the lack of other guards. Normally there would be half a dozen men here. Standing guard. Down the hallway he could see something, but was unsure exactly what it was. Some movement in the shadows.

Gobolt walked forward, towards the man tearing himself apart and looked apologetic to the new recruit. "What I need you for, is a mission of mercy."

Avershaw looked confused.

"This," Gobolt pointed to the man on the floor, "is no way to go. We have to show kindness."

Taking out his hand-held scimitar from its sheath, he held it up.

There was nothing Avershaw could do to stop him plunging his blade through the skull of this dying man. Nor would he. He was showing mercy to a man in the torment of a witch's curse.

Slowly, as Gobolt removed his blade from the man's head, Avershaw asked in a hushed tone: "Where is it?"

"That cunt's locked up now," the large man said as he wiped the blood from his blade onto his tunic. As he stood back, the corpse fell to the dirt, the soft and gelatinous pulp of what used to be its face, hit with a squelchy thud.

"I need you to help me down there." Gobolt pointed with his blade down the hallway.

"Where are the other guards?" Avershaw enquired.

"That's what I need help with. She took them," he spoke as he took a last glance at the dead guard on the floor. "And we have to help them like this one."

Avershaw, despite his lack of battle experience, would not hesitate to put a dying man out of his misery, especially one under a witch's spell. He remembered King James' texts about witches. He'd memorized a passage because it scared him to his core:

The fate of our world is governed by two certainties. 1) Good and Evil are a balance which cannot fall in favour of the latter. 2) There is no evil living in God's lands greater than a witch. For they seek to not to only destroy mankind, but to watch us tear each other apart whilst they gratify themselves carnally.

He presumed Gobolt would show him the guards in a similar horrific state and was just along to be another blade as the weight of responsibility for such a dark task was too much for just one man. But he presumed wrong. He was needed to fight.

Walking down the long narrow hallway, Gobolt and Avershaw walked with their swords drawn. "Don't worry" Gobolt said quietly. "I locked them in, so no one's jumping out at us… I hope." His words instilled fear, even though that was the opposite of his intent.

Each door they passed had a wide, thin slit in it, enough to see whatever inhabited the cells. As he walked, Avershaw saw glimpses of the imprisoned menagerie. Most were quiet. Waiting. Some were wailing in joy at what was happening with the guards. Some feral and in a ravenous fury were hurling themselves at the metal doors, trying in vain to escape. There were beings made of light, of faeces, beings resembling reptiles, beings with multiple heads. All here for a good reason. And if released, they would leave a trail of mutilation in their wake.

At the end of this hall, a door leading to the higher security area was closed with a lock. This door led to the cells reserved for the worst of the worst. And it was in here where they housed their most dangerous: the witch known only as Saskia. Hailing from the dark forests of Germania, her capture had been years in the making – and one Gobolt took great pride in.

Stopping by the door, Gobolt turned to Avershaw. "What lays beyond here, is nothing pure. None of them are redeemable. None can be saved from her grasp – even though she's back in her cage."

"I understand," Avershaw replied.

"Do you?" Gobolt hated having to ask someone so untrained to take part in this, but believed he could not do it alone – at least he thought he could not. In reality he could easily defeat many men at once. He just had no confidence of certainty – and would rather someone beside him in battle. "I'm asking you to kill the men you know. Your compatriots. I'm asking you to forget their humanity and slaughter them. As they will slaughter *you* if you don't. Then they will do worse. Much worse."

"Aren't they like this one..." Avershaw spoke, whilst motioning with his head back down the hallway to the dead man.

"Like him?" Gobolt said finishing the sentence. "No. They are up and ready to kill us. About six of them in all... I think."

"And the others?" Avershaw didn't know why he asked this. He knew the answer. He knew the rest were dead. A chill fell over him. But he felt assured that he had the hand of his God on his shoulder. "May God be with us," he said as he readied his sword.

"Your God can eat my shit. And whatever you do, don't look in the fucking cell. Ever," Gobolt said flippantly as he unlocked the lock, turned and opened it with a sudden forceful jolt.

Inside the room was a sight no mind should ever process. The room was soaked in blood and shit, and had no humanity left here. The bodies of the slain lay in pieces over the floor and all the men under the witch's control – now in a state of undress – were each devoid of their old selves.

Two of them feasted on the body of one of the slain, gnawing on the rancid bowels they had just removed, with each bite arousing them. Another guard was thrusting himself deep into the skull of another victim's decapitated head – rutting as if his life depended on it, growling as his engorged member was rammed in and out of the corpse's eye socket, which only grew tighter around him, the bigger he got. One other was furiously ripping another dead victim to shreds, even though his victim's life had long left – he still clawed in fury into the dead man's chest. Ripping chunks off at a time, as if wishing to tunnel through. Another of them was defecating on the floor then rolling in it like a wild animal. The sixth stood against the glass at the other end of the room, the window to the cell of the witch. He pressed his whole body against the floor-to-ceiling stained glass – a holy barrier which evil could not cross. Sobbing toward what sat in the shadowed corner of the cell, prostrating himself to his new master.

When the door flung open, all the men stopped what they were doing and for an instant, a silence fell over the room. They then turned toward the two interlopers – the men that were here to end their lives.

Scrambling towards them, they roared in animalistic fury. Gobolt looked to Avershaw "Be strong!" he shouted, as he raised his blade and advanced on the men. In a cold sweat, Avershaw did the same.

The battle was short-lived. Their blades found their targets with ease. Gobolt was more skilled than any of them and managed to dispatch four in quick succession, his blade cutting through their hearts and throats with devastating accuracy.

Avershaw was faced with the furious man with the severed head stuck on his still erect member. He roared like a lion at Avershaw, his eyes as blank as death. Even though Avershaw only saw this man's eyes for a moment – and before managing to swing his sword through the temples of this advancing animal – he noticed the lack of life in them. As if they were made of clay, they looked unreal yet somehow alive.

The last man against the glass was also Avershaw's to take care of. And so he thrust his sword into the back of the man's neck, severing his spinal cord in an instant – and making a loud crack as his sword hit the glass on the other side. Pulling it back, the man fell to the floor, dispatched in an instant.

Though he had never killed before, he had been trained for years of how to do it – But now, in less than one minute, he had killed two men, and without a scratch on him. He thought he would feel bad after killing. He thought that the guilt of murder, even for a good cause, would leave him cold. But it did not. He felt justified and prideful. He felt more in the grace of his higher power.

A light giggle sailed through the air, from deep within the other side of the stained glass in the cell. Looking at Avershaw from hearing this, Gobolt was wide-eyed and shouted "Don't look at it!", as he pulled his blade out of the groin of the last of his attackers.

But it was too late.

Avershaw saw the witch. He had looked up into the eyes of Saskia. And unlike the monster he had expected, he instead saw a young girl. Barely ten years old, grinning an evil grin, directly *at* him. Naked, yet clothed in dirt. In an instant, her grin started to fall as her mind advanced towards his, ready to devour it and turn it to her favor.

Before anything more could happen, the hilt of Gobolt's blade smashed into the back of Avershaw's skull, knocking him out cold in an instant.

"Stupid bastard," he said as he looked down at the unconscious man he had just saved. "One rule," he muttered. "You only had one fucking rule."

"Oh, my dear Gobolt." The sweet and innocent sounding voice of Saskia spoke from her cell. "Do you not want to gaze upon my ripe body? Do you not want to fuck this little cunny with your hard cock?"

Gobolt smirked, not looking once at the monster. "That actually works on men?"

"Sometimes. But I guess it will not work for the likes of you. Pity," came the small girl's reply. "But you cannot blame a young girl for trying."

As he picked up Avershaw with ease, he flung him over his broad shoulder and turned to the open door, saying one last thing to the beast. "You? Young? Right… Well next time we meet, I'll be putting something hard in you. But it won't be my cock and you'll *not* like it at all."

"Promises, promises," Saskia laughed to herself.

But she did not laugh when Gobolt executed her the following day, decapitating her, then burning her body to nothing but ash. She had screamed at him for clemency. Pleaded for mercy. Pretended to have been cured and that she was a real girl again, the demon inside her having left her. All futile attempts – ones every witch tried before execution.

Avershaw had witnessed this execution. From the naïve man he had been a mere 24 hours before, he had suddenly aged and grown more determined in the holy fight ahead of him. But from this encounter in the prison, he did not escape unharmed. For the second the witch was in his mind, she had left her mark. Her indelible mark.

Her terrifying mark. A mark he would never speak about, nor ever escape. In the corner of his eye, for as long as he would live and even when his eyes were closed – Saskia was there. Standing. Grinning at him. Even beyond her death he would still see her. Up until the day he himself would die, she would always be in his periphery.

Alive.

Tormenting.

Ferenc was first to put his foot upon the creaky wooden jetty of Stowe Haven, his boat mooring there before Gobolt's – he and the two other soldiers now stood in complete darkness facing the slumbering town, the lack of illumination necessary to aid their mission. No one could know they were coming, the element of surprise was their greatest weapon when battling those other than human. The howl of the wind and the thick curtain of snow blocked their view of the town itself, so in preparation they withdrew their weapons from their sheathes and readied themselves, as Gobolt's boat moored alongside theirs.

The King's Guard all carried the same weapons; a single curved scimitar which broke apart into two lighter weapons. Though usable as one, it was equally ferocious and deadly as two – and each blade was etched with runic symbols and forged with holy water. The king was adamant that any battle must be fought with sacred weaponry and enlisted the assistance of the church to aid in their creation. The king, though very secretive, had to tell some people of his mission as even though a king, he needed other resources on occasion. And for this he hated that he had to ask the church. Not because of any differing ideology, but because he knew they were corrupt as an organization and were not all they said they were. They were, though, a necessary evil. They were too concerned with maintaining their subterfuge of being God's church, so chose to assist in the king's requests.

"You think we'll die today?" Gobolt asked Ferenc, as the snow fell with a howl around them.

Ferenc had now been battling with Gobolt at his side for several years. He had been fighting the king's battle ever since he'd been made the offer in the Nevermore Chambers and had not regretted it for a moment. Together, he and Gobolt had vanquished many a demon, freeing innocence from the dark grasps of corrupt souls. And though it had been a good fight, they had seen many a hardship. No matter how hard they trained their men, there were always casualties. The king's men were not as accomplished as fighters as both of them were and no amount of teaching could prepare a recruit for the reality of war. Avershaw, though, was the exception. He was alive through some miracle, no matter the wounds he had previously endured. No matter the situation he had found himself in. He had always – against the odds –survived to fight another day alongside them.

"My friend. We may die. We may live. But we will take some of them with us," Ferenc said with a grin. He knew full well of Gobolt's exhaustion with the good fight. And he too felt the pangs of missing normality. But to him, some things were more important than any personal desire.

The noise of the wind silenced his words from the other men's ears. But they knew their mission; Stowe Haven was where their battles had led them. There was a coven here, the size of which was unknown. Their prominence in the town was unknown. But everything led here – to the alpha witch, the one whom all the others they dispatched followed – Elizabeth.

The six men walked down the jetty, blades in hand, leather armor clad. They all wore metal helmets, emblazoned with the first battalion of the King's Guard symbol. A double-headed lion holding a scimitar in each maw.

The village was still out of sight due the white blanket constantly falling around them, the light from the moon being the only illumination offered and that was minimal and ineffectual.

They stepped off from the wooden jetty and onto the beach. Ferenc presumed it to be made of pebbles and driftwood, as each step cracked underneath his boots.

Then, stopping everyone with an outstretched hand, he motioned for his men to gather round – To get close to listen to him above the storm.

Soon they huddled around him as he spoke as loud as he could without the sound being able to travel outside of their group. "Men. We are here to do what we do. Now the coven may be one house. Maybe two. But we will need to start from the outside in a circular pattern, looking for their symbols. Just remember, protect the innocent. Protect—"

"Sire…" Avershaw interrupted. He was looking down at his feet as he spoke. "I think there may be no innocence left here anymore."

Ferenc and the other men looked at him curiously, then they all followed his gaze to the beach. In between the pebbles and driftwood under their feet were bones. Many, many thousands of bones.

Trying to focus as much as they could within the moon's illumination, they could see that the bones stretched over the entire beach, not only mixing with the driftwood and pebbles, but greatly outnumbering them. This was made up of more bones than the entire population of this town had within them.

In the corner of Avershaw's eyes, Saskia laughed. "I will enjoy this..." she said to him quietly. Determined, and as he usually did, he ignored this possession and fed his anger into gripping his blade handle harder.

Gobolt could tell that the bones they stood on came from humans of all ages, but belonged mainly to children – he could feel in his gut that witches were the things who had done this, and he could not wait to exact his vengeance upon their monstrous brows.

"I guess the mission has changed then," Gobolt said to the men. Some of the newer soldiers were visibly upset by what they stood on. Ferenc, though seasoned, was not so strong as to be impervious to this horror. Seeing a smashed baby skull amongst the bones chilled him to his core, but they all had to get used to suppressing any emotions that crept upon them – at least until they were safe and alone. Only then could they let their feelings of torment and fear flood out.

"Men," Ferenc said as he raised his scimitars out to the middle of the group. Signaling them all to follow suit, by all holding their blades up together – which they quickly did. They stood swallowing their trepidation and uniting for the cause.

"For the good," Ferenc said in a firm voice.

"For the righteous," Gobolt continued.

"For the innocent," all the men all said in unison, as they turned to the village.

As they walked further up the beach of bones, the village itself came into view. Soon the horror that awaited them became clearer.

Most of the village had been destroyed. Many houses now were burned to the ground. The remains of the people who had previously occupied the now-charred shells lay dead, piled on top of each other on what would have been the entrances to their homes. Their bones removed then thrown onto the beach, joining the hundreds of other crushed skeletons the soldiers now walked on.

At the precipice of the village, where the bones ended and the winter-frozen dirt and grass began, the six soldiers of the king stood ready to fight. The snow was quickly letting up around them, as if Mother Nature wanted to show them the extent of the witches' massacre and to make their approach easier – or alternatively work against them by alerting any witches there to the soldiers' arrival.

The falling flakes got lighter and their descent started to slow. The moon was now given a chance to shine fully through the thick clouds onto the once-peaceful village of Stowe Haven.

Ferenc glanced at the destruction that lay ahead of him. He looked over his shoulder at his men and nodded for them to advance – and to be at the ready.

The blizzard had now ceased its howling and was becoming a silent night with a light snowy drizzles. The once visually impassible white curtain was now just the sporadic and quite beautiful decorative framing for a winter scene. But not this scene, here the snowfall only led to giving the grotesque remnants of what was a village, a more ethereal and otherworldly appearance.

Each footstep the men took cracked as the ice and snow beneath them gave way and compressed to support their weight. Now with the winds having miraculously ceased, the sounds they made were more audible than they had been. Loud enough to be heard by anyone nearby.

Gobolt looked at the men and with a whispered breath said, "Light footsteps. Don't let the unholy cunts hear ya."

Ferenc, at the head of the posse walking up to the village, smirked at Gobolt's words. English was his fourth language, behind Hungarian, Romanian and Germanic – not that he had spoken any of those tongues in years – and Gobolt was in large part his teacher for what he did not know before, mainly curse words and 'cunt' was the one he heard the most from his friends uneducated mouth. Followed up by 'cunny', 'twat' and 'cock'. Learning the English words often shocked Ferenc, not through their vulgar usage, but as they were all about genitals. In his native language insults were more based on status and lack of parentage. So, learning this language's more colorful output was often very entertaining, though baffling. He himself rarely cursed. Not through any sense of decency, but only because he preferred the comfort of silence to the scream of abuse.

Avershaw was at the rear of the group as they passed the first burnt-out shell of a house. The skins of three children and their mother were thrown on top of each other callously, their backs having been ripped open in order to extract their skeletons, leaving their head skin intact without any damage. Terrifyingly, these flat and hollow faces stared out in an eternal scream of pain. He swallowed hard as he saw this.

Ahead of him, the other solders all fought back any negative feelings at seeing this violence – anger, revulsion, shock – all of them needed to concentrate on their silent passage through the ruined village.

In the corner of his eye, just out of focus, Saskia sat giggling to herself. Having been with him for years, Avershaw was used to ignoring her presence. But he could never not hear her. No matter how much he ignored her, he could not escape every word she uttered into his mind.

"They are beautiful, aren't they, my sweet?" she whispered as he glanced at the remains of the children. "But I ask you… what is missing?"

Hearing this – and going against all he had tried to teach himself – he reacted. Slowing for a second and looking harder at the remains.

"Oh, my darling, you hear me!" she whispered again with delight. As he looked at these hollow remnants, he started to understand the answer to her question.

Turning, he walked up faster, as quietly as he could, to catch up to Gobolt.

Hearing him approach, Gobolt turned, questioningly looking back. As he got nearer, Avershaw tried his best to lessen the cracks sounding from underneath his boots. But there was only so much he could silence. "The bodies," he whispered to Gobolt,

"What about them?"

Ferenc had stopped, as did the other men, then stepped back to hear what was being said by Avershaw. Breaking the advance meant it was something of note. The other soldiers also stepped in.

"What is the problem?" Ferenc interrupted.

"Speak," Gobolt said in hushed tones to Avershaw.

"The skins are there. The bones on the beach…. Where's the rest? There's only a tiny bit of flesh back there. And where's the blood? I cannot see a single drop on the ground. Or on the skins."

Ferenc hadn't thought of this.

Gobolt looked to him. “Killed elsewhere, you think?” he whispered.

Ferenc nodded with a look of concern upon his face. None of these men knew the purpose of what they saw, or the details of what had happened here – but now was not the time to discuss it. He motioned with his head to carry on in the direction up the hill.

Gobolt turned to the rest of the men. “All of you. Be fucking vigilant,” he said as he nodded in appreciation to Avershaw, then turned to follow Ferenc up the hill, to the crest where the village continued down into a valley.

“Do you want to know why they took their insides?” Saskia asked in her childlike voice.

Avershaw ignored her. He *had* to. He could not give her a bigger place in his life than she already had.

“You just have to say ’yes’ and I will tell you all,” she said as he continued to pretend that she did not exist – that the voice in his mind was only that.

But she was not in his mind.

She was a parasite and had infected his very soul.

The Evolution Will Not Be Televised

The city was burning.

Buildings aflame.

Massacres happening wherever people stood. There were two factions – not just good vs evil, but inhuman vs human.

Rebecca had seen a glimpse of the truth as she escaped the hordes of murderers chasing her. They had turned and killed anyone unlike them, but not all of them were victorious in their missions. As Rebecca darted through Leicester Square, barging her way past anyone in her way, she saw something she still could not fully understand.

She was now in a Chinatown alleyway, where she tried to process everything as she fought to regain her breath.

She had lost Ian. As they had run past Madame Tussauds, their grip on each other's hands had been separated as a blade sliced through the air, cascading down and severed his grip at the wrist. Turning, she saw her friend – now in unbelievable pain – screaming 'RUN' at her.

And with that, her fear pushed her to abandon him, sobbing as she ran away. She did not know what became of him, but could only presume these monsters had dispatched him the same way they seemed to have dispatched others. She heard him scream for her to run and she did. But she felt like she might have been able to save him nonetheless. If it wasn't for her cowardice.

Almost hyperventilating, the tears streamed down her face silently. She did not know why they did not try to kill her, as they did so many others. She had no idea why they tried to grab her, to take her to 'her destiny' as they all seemed to believe. She knew nothing except one thing; they were not as they seemed. What she saw that she could not understand, was as she had crossed the square, she passed a man who had not been killed by one of the murderers and was now besting his attacker by punching them repeatedly in a vicious rage. As she passed, this now victorious victim spilled backward after seeing something on his attacker – the face he was punching had now broken apart. Showing something beneath the skin... A blackened, scaly and monstrous face.

As Rebecca saw he was not one of the murderers, she screamed at him '*Come on!*'. But all he could do was stare wide-eyed at this beast. This monster being the woman he had spent the last two decades with. Now, she was laying on the floor – her true features splitting through the skin, staring back at the man she had loved and now tried to kill.

"What are you?!" he screamed as he now lunged forward, tearing at his wife's face. Exposing more of her real form; She was terrifying, with gnarled features and sharp teeth hiding underneath the fake flaps of skin which made up her pretty human mask.

Rebecca saw this for a fleeting moment, just before the man was set upon by a group of people – presumably other monsters – then hacked to pieces. She turned and ran towards Chinatown as one looked at her and screamed "*You will sacrifice the young on your altar of blood*!"

Being physically imposing had always been the bane of Rebecca's life. From getting called all the colorful names under the sun at school, to being maligned by most producers as to not being '*feminine*' enough, her size and look had always been a burden; one which made her turn to learning how to defend herself. After all, she might as well make her size count for something – and in this instance, it was the best decision she had ever made. Escaping these murderers was made easier as they had no chance against her physically. She knew the punches she had to land in order to send them crashing to the asphalt. She knew where to kick to make sure they didn't stand up again

quickly. And as long as they all seemed intent on capturing her and not using their weapons, she could continue to evade them. Of course, she knew this could only last so long. She was exhausted, yet knew the area so well that she knew where to hide. She knew the alleys and corners of this city. She had used them enough in her youth. stealing forbidden moments with so-called beautiful girls after a night out. Those wishing to experiment, but not enough to be seen. These alleys and backstreets had seen more of her than any other place she had been.

Grabbing her phone from out of her pocket, she quickly loaded up her news app. The prime minister gave a speech about Scottish fisheries. A has-been filmmaker and author in Hollywood arrested on pedophilia and bestiality charges. Blah blah… but nothing on what was happening now.

Trying another news app – nothing. CNN. Nothing. BBC. Nothing. Sky. Nothing. Even the tabloids. Nothing.

She quickly decided to do the only thing left that she could think of. She had to call her mother.

Leanne was sitting in the front pew of the Nevermore Chambers, looking up at the painting behind the altar. On the floor in front of her lay Phyllis' corpse. But now her body was decimated, the very flesh ripped off her bones. As if vultures had picked her dry.

"Ma'am?" Helen said softly from the back of the room. Clipboard in hand. Her expression full of worry. "She's evaded them."

Leanne, not addressing this just smiled. "My little bird," she said to herself, with her gaze not breaking from the painting on the wall. "You always knew how to fly away."

"Excuse me?" Helen asked, unable to hear her words.

Turning in the pew, Leanne looked back over her shoulder to Helen. "My dear," she said, and smiled. "Did you expect anything else of her? She has always managed to surprise us."

"Should I tell them anything?" Helen asked.

"No, they know enough," she said in thought, before taking a pause to turn back and look at the painting again. "Tell me, is it all set up at Parliament Square?"

"Yes ma'am."

Leanne looked at her watch. "And the incubus is ready?"

"It is..." Helen smiled. "She looks healthy."

"A few years early… but, she's been waiting decades. She can assume the mantle as many have before." A phone signal rang out from Leanne's handbag, cutting off her train of thought. "I thought we turned all of these off?" she said as she pulled the phone out. It had on the display the words *Little Bird calling*. "Well this is a first, she obviously doesn't know yet."

Picking up the call, Leanne's expression suddenly turned to fear and panic. A powerhouse performance, which eschewed believability. But this performance was only in her face. Her body language remained as it did before; calm and steady.

"My baby…" she said, terrified. "Thank Jesus…." She sounded as if she was sobbing, breathing fearfully. But her body language proving it was an act. "Where are you? Please help…"

Rebecca spoke quietly into the phone. "Mum… I don't know. I'm in Chinatown. Where are you? I'll come get you."

"Helen tried to kill me…" Leanne continued. Behind her Helen's eyes widened at hearing this. “But I managed to stop her. Then they took me… Please… I’m so scared.”

“Who are *they*? Where are you?” Rebecca whispered. Her expression grew more determined as she heard her mother’s reply. “Parliament Square?”

“They grabbed me. Put me in a van. They said they’ll kill me if you don’t show up. But I can see out of the window. I see Big Ben.”

“Fuck… I don’t know what I should do. Are there many people there?” Rebecca answered.

“I…. I… Please… Save me.” Leanne then hung up the phone. “Shut them down… NOW!” she said aloud and firmly to Helen. Helen then quickly exited the room.

Back in the alley Rebecca looked at her phone display. She brought up the contacts and tried to redial Leanne. But instead of connecting she was met with the dead line tone. She tried again. And again. But nothing. She looked at her signal. It had gone from full strength to zero. Nothing.

She had to get to Parliament Square.

Leanne stood up from the pew and picked up her handbag. Turning, she walked to the exit of the chamber, glancing back one last time into the room.

“It is done, ma’am.” Helen said from down the hall. Leanne could see her at the base of the spiral stairs leading up to God Begot House. She nodded understanding, looking uncharacteristically emotional.

"Is everything okay ma'am? You seem… sad."

Leanne forced a smile. "44 times… It's quite a feat, isn't it?"

"Yes ma'am."

"Of all the many times. This was by far my favorite. Just a shame, that's all."

"Maybe the next will be better?"

"I am afraid I do not know if that will be the case. She has said she will be witnessing this end," Leanne said softly.

Helen's expression was now a mixture of joy, sorrow and confusion. "Is it over?"

"I hope not. But we work at her word. Maybe there will be another path for us to follow…"

Upon hearing this, Helen glanced down sadly.

Leanne continued, "We may as well shut off the rest. Just keep the center in motion. Close off all unnecessary areas."

"Yes, ma'am…" Helen then said carefully, "Can I ask…. Do *you* think it will end now? Not be a restart?"

Leanne did not reply. What she kept unsaid and what she tried to block out of her own mind, was that she could feel that Rebecca would never complete the destiny. And that the Goddess knew this, so was deciding to end it all. Having informed her of the events at the Wentworth Museum, the Goddess had smiled and spoken about events coming together nicely – which made Leanne believe that *everything* would end. This world would just cease to be. just as it was always intended to do. No restarts. No do-overs. All the 43 times before, never once had it ended as it should have done, so each needed to be restarted instead of extinguished. All from the beginning. Getting it right – this was the intent from the very conception. At first the plan was simpler, but with access to infinite resources, complete power over the reality of the realm and an infinity of time to get it done right, Leanne was free to try increasingly outlandish scenarios to enable the end game to come to be. All with a singular purpose: to corrupt Rebecca's soul. But her soul did not tarnish, no matter the scenario.

This kind of corruption was no easy task, as the purity of innocence was not an easy item to break – especially one as pure as her. And this was not the real-world that Rebecca thought it was, so nothing was as simple in this place. Through the symbolic nature of this purgatory, Rebecca had to corrupt herself with a supreme action. And had not done once before. Each time the plan had ended early for whatever reason and needed to be restarted. But *this* version of the world. Version 44 – they had never come *this* close to fulfilling the destiny of *Mater Tenebris*. But now she knew it was about to end one way or another. Even if by some miracle, it was just a restart, this reality had to end before it could begin again. But she knew in her corrupt heart it was over. The prophecy would come to be somehow.

The bright glow from the 57-foot-high curved advertising screen cast an eerie glow over Piccadilly Circus, the changing images on the screen throwing the only light in the area. An ever-changing kaleidoscope of colors swamping the darkness of the place. All other light sources were now non-existent, probably for the first time in many decades, since this area had become a tourist trap. The illuminations of the area were usually on 24/7, as it was a hive of city life at whatever the hour may have been. But this wasn't the case anymore. All of the surroundings were devoid of power. No light was cast from anything -- even the sky had turned black. No moon or stars could be seen on this black ceiling. This eerie night which seemed to have arrived in an instant, was a night that carried with it the stench of death.

From the streets which sprawled out in front of the Circus's advertising screens, to Leicester Square which was located nearby, to the walkways of the Southbank and all across the city of London and out across the country – this story was the exactly same. Whether a bustling metropolis, or an isolated farm, or a small seaside resort town – it was only about 30 minutes ago that they had all been warzones filled with people turning on others and slaughtering them, and now these places were merely a wasteland of death. Those who did not get the message had been summarily wiped out. And if not already, it was only a matter of time. On the breeze, you could hear the screams of the last remaining ones being dispatched. The ones who got away and hid, the ones who thought they lived in safety. The ones who thought they knew their loved ones, their friends, their family – whomever it was who had the call and now turned on them with extreme and violent prejudice. Cleaning up the world before the end. Not allowing anything birthed into this reality to survive.

The ones that escaped and bested their attacker's advances thought that they would get away, thought they had survived – but the escape they thought they managed to achieve was short-lived; the darkness was now closing in on this entire world. An eternal darkness which ate at the very fabric of reality.

Standing above the corpses of w his twin baby boys, Davis looked down without any emotion, bloodied knife in his hand. He turned and looked around him. So many dead lay here, and their murderers walked through these fields of corpses, ensuring the lives were indeed extinguished.

The advertising screens nearby suddenly went dark, the electricity no longer feeding them. M, making a loud clank as the power was shut off.

Davis was now standing in pitch darkness, his eyes emitted a muted glow., an eerie spilling of light where humans should have none. But he and his comrades were not human. Turning, he dropped his knife and began to walk away, through the darkness, over the bodies and in the direction of Parliament Square. The rest of these murderers did the same. The darkness they were all trapped in now dictated the path to their destination. Each and every one of these people with the same light which shone deep in their eyes.

As Davis walked he glanced down, looking at the fallen dead as he went. He saw a few of his kind lying still amongst those who had been murdered. Seeing his brethren sprawled out dead made him feel a pang of sadness and upset, but seeing the bodies of those who they turned on, he had felt nothing at all.. He stopped and stood over a female creature like him, one who had been bested by one of those humans. He saw her human mask ripped across her face, most of the skin now missing. Her eyes were open, but without any light within them. Lowering himself on his haunches, he reached down and closed her eyelids – her monstrous demonic face now looked asleep.

Gritting his teeth in anger as he looked at the dead monster, he grabbed the blade from her hand and carved into his own throat in a quick and decisive action. Then with his other hand, he dug his fingers deep into the bleeding wound and with a vicious yell ripped the skin upwards, over his chin and clean off the back of his head. L, letting the whole head of skin now droop off the back of his neck like a hood. Empty and bleeding it squelched downwards. His exposed demon face was now on full show. H, his true form released, glistening with the blood from his human mask. Almost reptilian, his purple-black skin was tough and armor-like, his eyes glowing brighter now without any human pretense.

With his tongue, he loosened the top and bottom dental veneers and spat them out to the ground. These fake prostheses had covered his real teeth -- his small, pointed and vicious teeth, for many, many years.

He let out a furious yell, his emotion boiling over. Finally, he was able to escape his human mask. He stood up with purpose, looking around at the others of his kind. Many of them looked at him with a smile, happy with his shedding. Taking his cue, they started to follow suit as they still walked in the direction of the square. Cutting their masks off to reveal their true monstrous selves. Their blades slicing through what had been a prison for them for decades.

Before joining his kind in their procession, he looked down and saw his veneers lying on the asphalt where he had spat them out. The light from his eyes reflected off the spittle which remained on them. With no more than a moment's hesitation, he stamped his large boot on top of the fake teeth, cracking them into pieces with one stomp. He was done with this charade. He knew there would be no restart. This felt unlike any other time. And if it came to be that he was wrong, he would re-pledge his fealty to the cause and get a new pair of veneers and a new face.

He was happy to be given the gift of ending the lives of the false ones. The ones he had to live amongst. When it started, it was just his kind who were there to enable Rebecca's destiny. To carry out the will of the Goddess. To blacken the innocence of the chosen one. But as the restarts got more elaborate and more complex, as their attempts bore no rotten fruit, more people were needed. And these drones were created – beings who could only exist in the realm they were created in. Beings who were temporary. Made of flesh and blood and as human as Rebecca, but not born in reality. Only born into a fake world and this fake world they would need to die in.

Despite being nothing without the illusion of this world, they were still creatures and able to work against the plan. They had their own morality. Their own beliefs. So, like actual humans, needed to be corralled, kept in the dark from the reality of the world in fear they would act against it. And when the time arose, when an end was in sight – whether a restart or the end itself – the faithful were rewarded with the bloodletting of their drones. And each faithful had their own drones. Some even bred themselves, through coupling with their drones. But the faithful were the Goddess's only chosen. The drones were simply meat used to make this reality more than just a purgatory of corruption. And the bloodletting was not only a reward but a sign that they knew their purpose.

If there was ever an occasion where one of the faithful believed the illusion and chose not to end the drones they were with – their lives would be determined to be extinguished as well.

No drone could ever understand the truth. They could never fully realize the condition they found themselves in – not that they ever were given the chance.

Ian could feel his own heartbeat banging loudly through his head. The pain he had from the wound where his hand was severed pulsed with each beat of his heart and cut through his nerves like a red-hot blade. The wound was tied off with his belt, stopping the bleeding as best it could. But he was pale from the blood loss which he could not stop, the light from his phone providing the only illumination as it lay screen-up on his lap.

Lying inside a smashed-out storefront, he was propped up against a wall next to a metal carousel of banal tourist greeting cards. Hidden from the view of the street outside – the street that carried a throng of monsters walking in procession – he stared out, hidden from view. Controlling the noise of his breathing as best he could.

With a large bloodied blade in his hand, he was propped up next to a female member of the faithful. With a large hole stabbed through her heart from the blade in Ian's hand, she was dying. Bleeding out, with her face mask half-ripped away.

After he was separated from Rebecca (as well as his own arm), Ian thought his life was about to end. The blur of terror was spinning around him, in a furor of panic he saw the inevitable. But now he was sat next to a carousel of cards saying 'I Love London' and other such phrases, wondering how he was still breathing, how he'd bested this thing dying next to him.

Since he was a boy, Ian had never been the kind of person to keep himself to himself, or stay out of other people's business. He was the inquisitive one. Someone who would have made a superb investigative journalist, if it wasn't for his terrible grasp of the written language. And now, his mind raced with possible explanations. Terrorists? Aliens? He had no idea. But he glanced down at the dying thing beside him. The thing, whose monster face hid beneath its female human face.

"What are you?" he asked in a whispered tone. "What the fuck *are* you?" He was terrified at whatever these creatures were, but this one was not a threat to him anymore. She had no energy to call for help and was quickly bleeding to death.

This monster next to , the one who chose the name Samantha, laughed painfully as a cough rose up and spluttered a smattering of blood from her half-skin-covered mouth, showing the lower veneers to be missing.

"You think this is funny?" Ian asked, repulsed at her callous laugh in the face of her being bested in their battle.

"You think you're lucky, don't you?" Samantha asked with a pained smile. "You think you can survive this?"

"You're the one who's dying, not me," he retorted.

"Maybe. But when the darkness comes. You will die anyway. Your kind cannot survive the reset… Me killing you…" She coughed between her words. "Me killing you…You dying… Would have been a kindness. Now you will be one of those who get eaten by nothing."

Ian had no reply to this. He just looked down at her, feeling sick. But he felt compassion.

Compassion even for *this* thing. Her coughs and pained whimpers were heartbreaking, no matter what she was or what she wanted. She was still in pain.

"Do you want me to finish this for you?"

She looked at him with sick glee. "You ask before you kill?"

"You're in pain. I... Thought I would offer." He shook his head. *Why did I bother asking?* he thought. He didn't know how to act. He didn't know how to properly navigate this insane situation.

"You offer me compassion? I would not offer you the same.," she spluttered under her breath.

"So, what are you? An alien?"

This question caused her to laugh again. "No… You are the alien one. You were created for this reality." She took a breath in, a wheezing breath, a breath that would be one of her last. "We exist despite it. You exist because of it. And… N-n-now…" Her words started to stutter as her life was ebbed away. "Now…"

Ian looked at her grappling with trying to grip onto her life, but failing in every way. He felt evil being the one who did this to her. No matter his attempts to justify his actions. He was a murderer. Whether she had tried to kill him or not. Whether she was human or not… Nothing stopped his creeping guilt.

"Then the world will go dark and you shall be eaten alive …" His eyes widened as she spoke. "Eaten… by the shadows …" She grinned as her life was almost gone. "And the one you know as Rebecca shall lead the damned."

As her last breath escaped her body, the blood in her slowed, but continued to pulse out of her chest wound.

The last of the monsters had passed by the open store front. The sound of their procession had now disappeared into the distance. Though it was too dark outside to see properly, he presumed they had all left and he had successfully evaded their culling. The sounds of the innocent screams had now dissipated, and the monsters were gone – they'd taken their massacre out of his hearing range. The screams he had heard earlier still played on repeat in his head, as clear as if they were still happening. The confused screams of loved ones being betrayed in the most grotesque way echoed throughout his memory.

Staggering out onto what was the pedestrianized zone outside of the now- destroyed souvenir shop, Ian glanced back, the glow from his phone's torch now being the only illumination in these streets. The advertising screen which cast its solitary glow had turned dark only minutes before. L, leaving all the streets in a deep bleak shadow.

He had left the now-deceased female monster lying in the shop where she had fallen. His light swashed over the smashed door and windowpane, now in bloody pieces on the ground. The body of the old man whose weight smashed through the glass in the first place was now in two pieces across the threshold of the shop. His eyes removed, with his sockets staring blankly in Ian's direction.

Winching in pain and cradling his wounded arm, he had done his best to not break down. Whatever this was, would now serve no purpose with any negative debilitating emotions. He had to remain calm and strong.

Turning around, his light moved across the many dead bodies which were strewn over the ground– of all ages and sizes, they were massacred in every way imaginable. Some gutted, some beheaded, some ground to a pulp, some stabbed, some shot, some hanged. But no matter the dispatch method, all of them – bar none – had their eyes cut out. Removed and nowhere to be found. Even the newborn laying in front of Ian had suffered the same fate.

Looking away and swallowing his revulsion and upset, Ian staggered on slowly. His light wasn't strong enough to provide a very clear path, but was good enough to show him his immediate surroundings.

Up in the distance, he could see the sky had a flickering orange glow. Whatever was there was burning, large and furious, and the monsters were all heading towards it.

His mind was racing from hearing Rebecca's name, spoken by a vile creature who tried to kill him. *Lead the damned? Rebecca?* If this *was* about her, she would logically be where the flames were. He should try to save her. Even with one less arm and suffering severe blood loss, he should try. He was her friend, after all. She would do the same for him, *but* he remembered that she did not. She'd left him as he lost his hand. But he *should* try to save her.

No matter how much he told himself this, he could not bring himself to comply. He knew she was in danger. He knew these *things* wanted her for some insane destiny. They even probably wanted to sacrifice her to whatever stupid God they praised. They probably wanted to torture her. Drink her blood.

Wait…

The painting…

His mind clicked. Correlating the events around him and what they were at the gallery for. The speed at which this horror erupted had totally thrown him and he hadn't noticed the links that presented themselves.

But even with these thoughts, even knowing he had to try to save her, he found himself moving in the opposite direction, his light leading his way. Clambering over the hundreds of dead eyeless bodies in his path, navigating himself through the carnage. He felt lucky that his home was in Camden Town – the opposite direction to where the monsters were heading. He could just hide out in the safety of his own surroundings. He had food. Water. WIFI. He would be fine.

Racing as fast as he could down the middle of the streets, around the discarded cars and vans, over the murdered bodies, Ian struggled to keep a clear view. Waves of dizziness hit him over and over. The hand holding the phone was also holding his arm stump – the stump which ached as it was bleeding despite the belt tourniquet. His running had sent blood flowing around his body at a higher rate and forced its liquid way through his makeshift solution.

As he approached the Tottenham Court Road and Oxford Street intersection, he had slowed down to a stagger. Breathing heavily, he tried to see anything around him, but only had a limited view from his torch – which stretched to about ten or so feet.

He closed his eyes tightly, trying to blink away the nausea and dizziness. His only thoughts were that he had to get home and that Rebecca *would* forgive him. And *he* would forgive her.

Taking a step nearer he was suddenly plunged into darkness, as his torch shut off.

"Fuck!" he spluttered in a panic.

Turning the torch to his face, it suddenly shone bright into his eyes, blinding him for an instant.

Slowly opening them again, he turned the phone back to in front of him. Its torch cut out yet again. He shook the phone in his hand, but nothing happened. Turning it back to him, it burst back to life as before.

"What the—?" he said, pained and hushed.

Turning the phone away from him once more, it – as expected – shut off. Moving his hand to the left, it slowly burst back to life. Back to the center – Shut off. To the right – Back to life.

Looking up in front of him, to where the torch would not shine, he felt a coldness. A sudden icy grip caressed his whole being.

In front of him, the darkness was total.

There were no shadows.

There was nothing.

It was as if the world just ended there.

As he turned the torch to the left, he could almost see a line where the total darkness started and the night without illumination began.

A low crunching noise alerted Ian to something on his right. On the asphalt, next to where he was standing, the remains of a teenage boy lay. Ian looked down, expecting to see a rat, or something scuttling around. The boy was dressed in a white shirt and black tie and his badge read “Elder White’. In this boy’s hand, he still gripped his copy of the *Book of Mormon* -- and this holy text was his last determined thought. He refused to let it go, even as his throat was being torn away from him and his eyes removed before he expired. His last thoughts were of meeting the Lord and being welcomed by Jesus’ embrace.

Another crunching sound. It was coming from the total darkness in front, where the lower half of the young Mormon’s body lay.

Backing away, Ian sensed the danger. But before he could move, a long black tentacle burst forth from the darkness and attached itself to the corpse of Elder White and dragged his body back into the blackness. The sound of the boy being pulverized and consumed echoed throughout the silence of the intersection.

Scrambling to turn and run away, Ian hoped his luck would hold out.

His frantic motions sent the torch beam in every direction as he moved back from where he came, past an abandoned van navigated at speed by a fallen cyclist. Trying anything to keep his focus. T, to quell the effects from his blood loss and stop the vomit that threatened to escape from his guts. But his body was reaching its maximum tolerance to the trauma and damage. His mind was also close to its breaking point.

Behind him more tentacles burst through the eternal darkness, grabbing the bodies of the dead that lay on the street, each one dragged back into the dark and consumed with a grotesque crunch. With each body that was dragged back, the darkness pulled itself further into the waiting night, its impenetrable blackness consuming all that lay within its path.

As he was about to turn and glance back, to see how far he was from what was advancing on him, he was thrown to the ground with an almighty force. A tentacle had smashed into his back, forcing him to the ground like a rag doll. The breath from his body was forced out as his ribs cracked upon hitting the asphalt. He would have screamed in pain, but there was no opportunity.

The tentacle crushed down upon him like a ton of bricks, knocking the wind out of him. The tentacle's suckers pushed him hard and unleashed sharp bony spines from their fleshy centers. These spines pierced through Ian's back, ripping through his insides, making their way through all of his internal organs and gripping them tightly.

Raising him into the air, the tentacle swung backwards. Unable to breathe or move or even make a sound, the blood poured from Ian's mouth as tears started to flow down his cheeks. Before retreating into the darkness, the bony spines from his insides pierced through his eyes and spread out like budding flowers, spraying blood as they blossomed.

Ian wanted to scream. Wanted to run. Wanted to hide. Wanted to be safe. But instead, he fell to the exact fate the dying monster in the shop prophesized for him. He was indeed eaten by the shadows. The shadows which now advanced bit by bit. Grabbing the slain bodies and dragging them into the nothingness in which it dwelled.

Rebecca looked out from the alleyway she hid in and could see what was happening in Parliament Square.

In the shadow of Big Ben and the Houses of Westminster a huge pyre burned furiously. I, its flames reaching high above the surrounding buildings. In front of it lay a 20-foot-high pile of dead bodies, a fleshy hillock where on top sat a large sacrificial altar made of bone – the same one which previously rested within the Nevermore Chambers.

Walking up the mound of corpses, stepping on the flesh and bone of some grotesquely fashioned steps, Helen carried in her arms what appeared to be a large fleshy organism. A large cocoon-like thing which slowly pulsated, as she walked past flaming torches, each casting its glow onto the fleshy pulsating membrane.

Rebecca watched as she saw this woman, her mother's assistant, place what was in her arms down onto the bone altar. The questions drowning her mind were insurmountable, but she was only focused on one thing – to find and save her mother.

Yet, between her and this scene, stood thousands upon thousands of 'people'. The ones that slaughtered the innocent. All facing the altar, in wait. All in various monstrous stages of skin undress. Some had shed their flesh suits completely and now stood with their demonic glory on full display. No clothes. No coverage. Just showing their purple-black mottled and ridged osteoderm – that similar to an alligator skin, which covered each of their emaciated bodies. Some stood still dressed in their human disguise. And the rest stood somewhere in-between.

With a scream, Rebecca's attention was refocused to the front of the crowd where she saw her Mother, Leanne, being tied to a spike which was dug into the ground and raised up twice the height of anyone here.

"Help me!" she screamed.

Rebecca knew she could not make it past this army. She couldn't just run through and grab her mother.

She had to find another way.

The Spiral to The World

"That thing clawed itself out of his fucking skull!" Gobolt exclaimed as he gazed out of the window of the king's tower. His leather armor was now beaten, worn and blood-soaked, his face a mass of bruises and swelling. If his eyes were not already swollen and constantly leaking he would have probably broken down in tears. Not one for public emotional displays, he knew no one was impenetrable to the toll of witnessing the pure horror that he had witnessed in the previous two days.

Stowe Haven seemed like years ago. Despite his inability to sleep since witnessing the events surrounding the Blood Queen's descent, it was almost a distant memory, his mind protecting him from reliving the horrors in too vivid a detail.

"And this was Avershaw?" the king asked as he sat on a high-backed wooden chair at one end of the room. This tower housed the Royal audience chamber for the king's men of the First Battalion, a place where the king could speak freely within his own palace to his secret brigade. Flanked either side of his modest wooden throne stood two stoic and red gowned guards, complete with their red metallic helmets.

The king was finding it difficult to follow the whole story. With Gobolt not being the most verbose of his subjects, he had to try to take the story piece by piece, filter out his pauper's language and garner its real meaning.

"Yes, it was fucking Avershaw! I just said that." Gobolt turned, looking back at the king. He was never one to hold his tongue to anyone, even a king. And the king was well aware of that and forgave him this, as he knew there was no offence intended. For if there was, a king would be in his rights to execute a subject for such an insult – but Gobolt would not be held to the same standards as normal men. He had saved the King many years before, wrenched him from the mouth of evil before his soul could be corrupted. He was the one who'd showed him the realities of this world.

"Please, my friend. Take it slowly… You were all walking through Stowe Haven. It was snowing. And the villagers were all dead. Correct?"

"Massacred. Skinned. Disemboweled." He spoke quietly and with venomous remembrance within his words. "Men, women and children having their lives cut from them, so their guts could make that fucking devil's temple." He took a breath in. He didn't want to remember. He never wanted to see that place again, even in his own memories.

"Men… this is an evil we have yet to best… stay alert, Ferenc said as they stood in the center of the village. With burned-out houses and skins of the dead surrounding them, the men of the First Battalion gazed in horror at what lay in front of them; a large structure made entirely of the insides of the villagers, their guts and flesh making the walls and roof to this unholy creation. A 20-foot-high building with a single opening at the front. A doorway framed with the flesh of babies. Still in the shape of their bodies without the skin or bone, all embedded into the rotting flesh walls, each facing out and holding hands, positioned around the entire circumference of this large entrance.

Glancing around cautiously, the men looked for any sign of the evil that had created this, any movement at all. But there was nothing. Just the falling snow around them. Gobolt presumed that the moisture from the corpse-made building avoided any snow from settling on it. But Ferenc realized the snow fell everywhere *except* that house. There was a perfect circle in the storm of falling flakes, a circle which formed around the building, as if the blizzard itself refused to grace that grotesque structure with its renewing winter fall.

The men looked steely but nervous. They knew their role. They accepted that they might die for the , and it was still something that they would do gladly. But even the most dedicated servant of the King felt fear, and this was the worst they had ever felt.

Avershaw, meanwhile, was trying to concentrate. In the corner of his eye, Saskia looked out, her face a picture of twisted glee. She could see the house.

"The queen! You brought me to the queen!" she screamed in his mind. He gritted his teeth trying to shut her out, but she was too loud, too deafening in her cackling joy. He tried his best to keep hold of his sanity and position himself back into the reality which they had found themselves in.

"Hey!" Gobolt hissed at Avershaw. *Had he not heard the first time I called him?* Gobolt thought. Lifting up his scimitar, he waved it in front of Avershaw's face, trying to get his attention.

In an instant, Avershaw snapped back to reality and looked at him, looking drained and shocked. "Who the fuck *are* you talking to?" Gobolt whispered harshly.

Oh no, Avershaw thought. *What did I say? Did he hear me speaking to her? But I didn't say anything. Did I? God in Heaven, please let me weather this storm.* "Shhh... my pretty," Saskia's voice said to him. "Let us go inside."

"Get your head in the moment and out of your arse!" Gobolt said as he turned to the other men "Now, let us go inside. End this fucking evil."

Ferenc nodded in agreement.

"Is this witches? Without doubt?" one of the soldiers quietly asked.

"We do not know for sure." Ferenc answered as he motioned for Gobolt to move into the building. "But most likely. And we must be prepared to fight the Devil himself."

"Or herself..." Gobolt quipped, readying himself. His blades were held up defensively as he took cautious steps to the building's entrance.

"Yes... or herself," Ferenc replied. Following the men in, but before turning forward, He glanced at Avershaw behind him before turning to move forward. "Take the rear."

Avershaw nodded nervously as he took the last in line position of the men. He gritted his teeth almost to breaking point, getting the focus he needed. Ignoring the songs that Saskia now sang in his mind;

"Bring me their lives, Bring me their death. Bring me their young. Bring me their heads. Bring me their hearts. Bring me their souls. The queen will devour all the unborn."

Over and over again, she sang it on repeat.

He should have warned his men. He should have told them about Saskia. But at the end of the day, it would have done nothing. The events would have come to pass no matter what he had done. Even if he'd ended his own life years ago, these events would have still happened exactly as they were fated to do.

Stepping over the decaying flesh of the threshold and into the room where the men now stood, he looked around. The whole of the inside of the house was also constructed from the insides of the villager's bodies. On the floor, walls and ceiling, you could identify parts of victims. A heart here, a liver there. A spleen. An intestine. All was familiar in design, but putrid and terrifying in execution. The stench was steadfast in its determination to never decrease in its ability to sicken the men to their cores. Though the freezing temperatures helped stave off the decay, the guts and flesh nevertheless still decomposed at a slower rate. The intestines still leaked out the contents of their attached bowels. The rotting meat and excreta caused a haze of purification, which few people could weather.

Ferenc lifted a jar from his pocket and opened it. Sticking a finger in, he then withdrew it, revealing it covered in a thick spiced paste. Smearing it on his top lip, it masked the invading odor of decay and filth. Holding the jar out, the other soldiers, one by one, followed suit. Each smearing the strong mixture of spices close to their nostrils.

As Avershaw did, Saskia complained. "I want to smell the dead!" she screamed. But Avershaw blocked her out as best he could, his attention now drawn to where the men in front now headed; down a large spiral staircase in the middle of the room. Following them downwards, he took each step carefully. Glancing back occasionally to ensure no one was attacking from behind. Each step he took cracked slightly, as human bones made up each and every step. Bones small and large. The only bones not part of the beach. And each step leading down into the unknown.

The men descended. Ferenc and Gobolt led them at a slow deliberate pace. This caused the impatience to grow – not in the men – But in the witch in Avershaw's mind. She was in a fervor.

Screaming at him to hurry. Hurling the most despicable insults at him. Pleading with him. Anything to get his attention. To get him to answer. But nothing worked.

She then gave up.

After about 10 steps further, she chuckled to herself, her fury switching off in an instant.

"I don't know what I find funnier… that you are determined to think you can ignore me, or that you actually believe that I am trapped here."

Avershaw stopped in his tracks as he looked at her. For the first time in years, he actually focused on her in the corner of his vision. Sat in his periphery, smiling whilst looking downward.

"What did you say?" Avershaw asked her, out loud. The soldier in front of him turning as he heard this. "Huh?" he asked.

"Oh… Are you ready for the big reveal?" Saskia asked as she stood up and grinned whilst emitting a hideous cackle. "Get ready…"

"No…" Avershaw said quietly, as he realized what was about to happen. He then glanced to the soldier in front of him, taking his focus off Saskia. "Run…" he pleaded to the soldier, as tears started to fall down his cheeks.

Saskia screamed loudly as she ran towards Avershaw, arms outstretched, hands forward clawing at him.

"RUUUN!" he screamed as the rest of the men in front all stopped and turned.

Before they could prepare themselves, or determine what was happening, both of Saskia's hands burst out from Avershaw's eyes, her forearms breaking the sockets of his skull open, then splitting the surrounding skin. The men in front who saw this recoiled in horror. Not knowing what they could do to help. Ferenc and Gobolt could not see what was occurring, as they were around the corner of the staircase.

They could only hear the screams.

Saskia's arms wrenched their way out of Avershaw's skull, splitting it in two. His screams cutting short as she pulled herself through his brain and out of his skull.

A grotesque rebirth.

Ripping his whole body in half, this young witch emerged naked, clawing herself out of him, blood-soaked in the crimson torrent that spewed out of her host – all whilst screaming her battle cry and clamoring towards her next victims; the soldiers on the stairs.

"What's happening?" Gobolt screamed whilst trying to see over the men behind him. But before he could get any reply, he saw the attacker. The young witch, clawing her way over the soldiers. Ripping the throat out of one, then clambering towards the next, just as that man she had just killed fell to the ground. By the time Gobolt and Ferenc could see her, all but one of the men were ripped to pieces by this beast, her nails and teeth eviscerating all those in her path. And with the staircase being so cramped and small, there was little escape.

Gobolt's eyes opened wide as he saw Saskia biting through the skull of the soldier in front of him. Her jaw opened to an inhuman degree, her teeth small and serrated. Her eyes wide and bloodshot.

"Don't look at her!" Ferenc screamed to him, as he grabbed Gobolt's arm and pulled him down the steps. "Hurry!"

They ran further down the human staircase. Faster and faster, further and further downwards. Panicked and keeping their attention forward. Behind they could hear the wails of Saskia, as she ran after them. Gripping to the ceiling for the whole of her descent – clawing each step downwards like a spider.

Avershaw's body lay splayed apart on the stairs, in a fleshy heap next to the bodies of the three other soldiers – but unlike them, Avershaw was not actually dead. Not completely dead as only his body was without life. For her remained with Saskia. In the periphery of her vision, as she clawed her way on the ceiling, faster and faster down the staircase, pursuing Gobolt and Ferenc, Avershaw sat – having swapped places with the witch, he was now within *her* mind. *Still* alive. And *still* in torment.

The staircase came to an end, as Ferenc and Gobolt spilled out into a large room. This room was also made from the insides of the villagers, just as the rest of the building at the ground level above had been. These walls, ceiling and floor were all a pulp of guts and flesh, lined with gargantuan inhuman bones to hold the whole structure up.

The stairs had spiraled downwards for what seemed like an age before breaking out into this room, so that they must have been a hundred feet under the ground level at least.

Before they could register the detail of the surroundings, they could only check to ensure that there was no imminent danger before they split apart and stood either side of the entrance to the foot of the staircase. Their blades held up. Hiding in wait for the witch to follow. Motionless as they planned for her to be met with the full force of their fury. Both were tirelessly trained and worked in perfect sync as a team. They didn't have to tell each other what to do, or what they were about to do. They knew instinctively what the plan was. And it had been this way for the past few years. They had confronted and beaten evil after evil. But in all their years extinguishing the dangers in the darkness, they had never seen a parade of death quite like this. They had followed the clues left by a trail of dead bodies – but had never before seen a whole village wiped out. They had never witnessed evil manifest in such a way as was displayed by this building's very existence.

The feeling of Stowe Haven was no longer like a town, but felt like an oppression. As soon as they stepped their first foot onto the bone-laden beach, their hearts sank and the dread felt all-consuming, as if all goodness that had ever existed there was now replaced by the air of torment. When they walked up past the first row of burned-out houses and saw the skins of a man and his pet dog, Ferenc had said to Gobolt, "This is what it feels like to have nothing left to live for." Gobolt found that a strange phrase, but now as they waited for the witch, he totally understood it. The feeling crept into his very being and quite literally was consuming his will to fight. But both he and Ferenc were stronger than this force. It may have been eating away at their subconscious, but their desire to fight, their desire to vanquish the evils in the land, far outweighed any negativity here.

"And you are sure it was the same witch? Saskia?" the king asked Gobolt, who now sat down on the chair in front of him.

Nodding, Gobolt smirked. "I only saw that devil for a split-second. But I knew it was her. No doubt in my mind."

"And how did she get there?" the king asked. "Was her execution not fulfilled?"

"Oh, she *was* there. And she *was* executed before." He looked into the King's eyes assuredly. "I burned her body myself." Taking a moment to pause, he wiped the moisture away from his swollen eye. "She even told me as much, as she did this to me…"

No one came from the staircase, Ferenc and Gobolt looked at each other. Ferenc shrugged, then motioned with his blade to walk further into the room. Gobolt looked around, then nodded back to him.

Taking steps into this room away from the staircase, Ferenc sidled up beside his compatriot. "Call me crazy, but that *was* her, wasn't it?" he whispered to Gobolt, whilst keeping a keen eye on all corners of this empty room.

"I have no idea how... But yes. Seems the cunt lives on," Gobolt responded in hushed tones.

He took a step forward, as Ferenc was looking the other way checking the stairway entrance. His foot then slipped through the flesh, deeper into the guts and filth.

With a grunt of surprise, he turned to Ferenc for help, but before he could reach out, two arms burst from the floor and Saskia clawed out at him, ripping him downwards. Her hair covered her face as she screamed a blood-curdling cry, grabbing wildly. Suddenly the surrounding body parts turned swamp-like and lost all of their solidity – even the floor where Ferenc once stood was now falling inwards.

Crawling up to his face level, Saskia pushed Gobolt down and he fell up to his shoulders into the rotten muck of the carrion. She battered him repeatedly in the face with her head and fists. He tried his best to grip onto anything solid, but it was futile. He was at her mercy.

"And that was a doorway, I presume?" the king interrupted. "Through the floor, itself?"

Gobolt nodded. He could still hear in his mind the voice of Saskia as she dragged him through the gore. Whispering in his ear. *"You will praise me. Praise my name. Worship me. Saskia is your God now..."*

Swallowing hard, Gobolt breathed in. His wounds were aching. His face swollen from being beaten. The exhaustion from his battle almost insurmountable. But he continued. He had to. This was just the first shot. There was much more of the war left.

"The problem, my king..." Gobolt continued, "is that I cannot tell you much of what happened next."

"How so?" the king enquired – more surprised as Gobolt did not call him *Jimmy* or *James,* which he seemed to have a wont to do when they were speaking in private.

"The little bitch's fault... I don't remember how... Don't know how long.... Don't remember much... But I came to looking down on Ferenc... I was half-stuck in the fucking ceiling." He closed his eyes for a moment before continuing. "Saskia was down next to... That thing... We must have fallen through to another room. But I..." he swallowed hard. "I didn't make it much further. I think that little whore's cunt did it on purpose. Just so I could watch her take him down."

In an expansive rotten chamber, deep below the surface of Stowe Haven, lay Ferenc. He was beaten and bloodied laying on the fleshy floor. Trying to catch his breath. He attempted not to let his gaze focus on anything around him – on any of the monstrous walls, which unlike the walls in the chambers and stairwells above were patterned over its entirety with skinned human faces. Thousands of them. Circular and covering every inch of these walls. Indiscriminate in age, color or sex This pattern stretched from floor to the top of the high ceilings, to all corners of this room. The paste of spices he had wiped on his upper lip had now been smeared away by the battering he was just gifted. He tried his best to keep the repulsion from ejecting his last meal. He tried his best to not be the victim *they* wanted.

Standing above him, Saskia looked down with a grin. Her small fists bloodied and clenched.

"He looks like he wants more," Saskia said whilst looking back.

"We have an eternity…" came the familiar voice from atop the large throne at one end of the room – a throne made entirely of human bodies. And in this, this demonic chamber, this chamber fit for a queen, she sat.

Elizabeth.

In her full glory.

As Ferenc saw her, he had accepted he would not see the light of day again. And that *she* had won.

"Do you really want to die?" Elizabeth, looking the same as the last time he saw her, smiled. She did not show a single minute of age on her face from the years that she had been gone – the years that he had known her to be dead. "Okay then. I can accommodate your desire, dear husband."

"It's not her!" came the familiar voice of his friend. Looking up, Ferenc saw Gobolt half-stuck in the flesh of the ceiling. Not dragged all the way down to floor level like he was, but left up there to watch, to witness what was to come. Gobolt was not tormented by this situation as some would be, but more determined. Determined to save his friend. And then… Determined to leave this life of battle as he had always dreamed. This *had* to be his last battle. He knew that much. When Ferenc was safe, he would leave the sword behind. But until then, woe betide any evil which might cross his path.

Saskia, skipping over, looked up at Gobolt. "Shhh! You are my puppy and you will obey me!"

Laughing at this, Elizabeth stood up from her throne of death. "Now, now young one. You full well know he is not yours to own. Our mother marked him, not you."

Gobolt heard that and looked down at Saskia. *Their mother? The Black Queen?*

"What the fuck did you say?" he bellowed from the ceiling to Saskia. "Your *mother*?"

Saskia merely looked up and smiled. "Didn't I tell you?" She spoke slowly and with conviction belying her youthful appearance. "All those years you held me captive? Did I not mention that I knew of you? That she told me of you? Of what you tasted like? Of what she told me about the wolf she marked with a bite of her own?" She giggled as she saw his reaction of silent shock.

Elizabeth walked slowly to where Ferenc lay. "When you both came to the castle. When you came home with your *dog*. When you ripped apart my grave and looked at my corpse." She glanced up to Gobolt. "You both thought I could not hear you?"

"*Fuck you!"* was all that Gobolt could think to spit in hate at her.

Ignoring this, she continued. "I got what I deserved? May I rot in the fires of hell? Isn't that what you said as you presumed me dead?"

Gobolt screamed in anger as he tried to get himself free, unsuccessfully.

"And you…" She looked down at Ferenc, who was still trying to get his breath and stop himself vomiting. "…you said I was the devil? Well, not quite… But I *did* get what I deserved. And *so* much more." She looked to Saskia and held her hand out. "Now come… we must go." Saskia ran to hold it.

As Elizabeth looked down at this little witch, she smiled as she saw something. Something deep in her big blue eyes. "Is that a guest I see?" she asked.

Saskia nodded with a sick smile. "Can he be mine? If I cannot have my mother's pet?" she said joyfully.

"*I AM NOT ANYONE'S PET*!" Gobolt screamed, at the top of his lungs.

Elizabeth did not listen to the fury coming from above her, as she answered Saskia. "Of course, you can, little one."

She then waved her hand toward her throne, a wave which caused the bodies that formed it to start to twitch and move. As they moved, the crude stitching holding them together ripped great tears into their skin. They each then, raised up to their feet (and those without feet, to their stumps.) and made their way over to where Elizabeth stood. All thirteen of these battered corpses then encircled her, Saskia and Ferenc. Some had no heads. Some had no arms. Some were just legs on a torso. All dead. All under a witch's spell.

"Are you ready?" she asked Ferenc, as Saskia crawled up into her arms. Elizabeth cradling her like a baby, as Saskia began to suckle on her exposed teat.

The bodies standing around them walked closer. And as they did, all the faces which pattered the walls of the room, closed their empty mouths and eyes. As the bodies got closer, they started to meld together, into one another. Their skin and flesh becoming gelatinous and combining with the torso next to them. Until they became a dome of rot which covered the three. The ground beneath them, then started to give way and they sank downwards. Elizabeth smiled down at her beaten husband. Saskia was in bliss suckling the rancid milk of the Blood Queen. Ferenc wept. All whilst Gobolt was left above – staring in shock.

"I think it is time I introduced you to our daughter," were Elizabeth's last words before the ground swallowed the three whole and the chamber started to collapse in on itself.

"How on earth did you escape?" the king enquired, leaning forward, captivated by Gobolt's words.

"I climbed up. Through the muck and shit," he mumbled to himself. "Felt like it took days."

"And what was up there? Did you see any more witches? It could not have just been two of them, surely? That could do all of that?" the king asked, surprised by almost all of this story. Never in his life had he heard of an evil deed of such a scale. For evil to wage such a bold move upon hundreds, if not thousands of lives – was almost unheard of. Especially in this realm.

"I have seen a lot in my life. Gods who can change the world on a human whim… Demons wishing to be angels… But this was… I don't know how to fathom any of it… She was there. And she dragged him down to fuck knows…" Gobolt stood up painfully. "And to answer your question. No, they were not alone."

Through the flesh-soaked ground of the building in Stowe Haven, Gobolt forced his hand outwards. Breaking through to the village. Having crawled up through the rot and flesh, he had finally broken free to his world. As he lifted himself up he breathed in painfully and deep, having not had much oxygen on his ascent. He clambered to regain his composure. The air up here, though still heavy with the rot from the villager's dead bodies, was pure in comparison to the chamber he was previously in.

But before he could rest, the building around him started to collapse in on itself like the horror did below.

Though hurt and beaten, he scrambled to his feet and ran out of the door before he got caught in his wake. But, instead of meeting the abandoned village. Instead of seeing the burned down town, he was met with hundreds upon hundreds of pairs of eyes staring at him. All witches. All wearing the skin suits of the villagers which had been piled outside the gutted houses. The witches' eyes staring out toward him as they started to advance.

Glancing down, Gobolt only just realized that his blades were no longer with him. Both having been lost deep beneath in the flesh he escaped from. Gritting his teeth, he clenched his fists hard. *If this is the end*, he thought, *I will take some of these unholy bastards with me.*

The witches standing around the circumference of the area where the building was now being consumed, slowly walked toward him. Step by step. The building itself had now sunk deep down and the ground was becoming a sinkhole next to him.

"Come on then…" he raged at the oncoming figures. The villagers' skins that they ill-fittingly wore, sagged off from their naked bodies. As they approached, they didn't utter a word, not look to be attacking.

Glancing around frantically, Gobolt estimated there must have been at least five hundred of them.

"And how do you know they were witches?" the king asked.

Gobolt just shot a blank look back at his king. He knew what they were. He didn't have a single doubt. He could smell their kind. He could smell the demons within them.

As they got closer, he got ready to fight, but instead of going after him, the one nearest motioned for him to move out of their way.

But he did not. He couldn't fathom what was happening. So, they walked around him. This procession started to crawl into the sinkhole of human remains. Crawling downwards to their Queen.

"They didn't harm you?" the king enquired before continuing, "Do you know why?"

Gobolt did not answer.

"*Fight me*!" Gobolt screamed as he punched one of the witches who passed him. Their villager skin ripping downwards with the force of his punch, away from their face, exposing their demonic expression to him. One of… Nothing. No expression. Blank. No pain. No anger. No hurt. Just an emotionless glare, before moving again and continued their path to where they could crawl into the rot.

As he stood aghast, he saw hundreds disappear from where he had escaped from. "*Why won't you fight*?!" he screamed again, squaring up to the passing abominations.

One witch, an old woman, stopped in her tracks as she looked at him intently. He just stared back at her. Every fiber of his being wanting to strangle the life out of her. She stopped then peeled her face downwards, so she could look at Gobolt face to her own face.

"You think you look better without it?" he snarled at her.

He lifted his fists ready to hit. But was stopped by her cackle.

"My little Lycan... We won't lower ourselves to fight your kind. Not today... Not when our queen calls us."

"What?" he asked, confused. "How do you know what I am?"

Laughing the witch peeled the old woman's skin back over her own face and continued her journey, but not before calling back. "We can smell the wolf on you, just as you can smell us."

Watching the last of them disappear downward, Gobolt felt castrated by their avoidance of him. He just wanted to fight. He just wanted to find his friend and save him from the evils below. He wanted to avenge the deaths of his comrades. But all he could do was watch a legion of evil pass him by without a care. Considering him too low a being to interrupt their unholy pilgrimage. Without a weapon, he would not get far. And sacrificing himself from rage would do Ferenc no good.

Never before had he wished for the moon to be full. Never before had he wished for his curse to have reared its monstrous head and enacted his fury upon them. The wolf would have had a chance.

Gobolt could not tell the king about the Black Witch. About that evil being mentioned at all, and that they considered him *her* pet. He needed to block out his revenge. He needed to focus and find a way to save Ferenc. The Black Witch would wait until another day.

"I can guess your next request, Gobolt," the king spoke as he stood up. Walking slowly over to him, he raised his hand and placed it on his shoulder. "My dear man, you do know that where you want to go, is in all likelihood a one-way journey?"

Gobolt nodded.

"And you think I will just allow you to go alone? When we have an army at our disposal? You know I cannot afford to lose you as well as Ferenc..."

"He is not lost. He was kidnapped," Gobolt uttered sternly, under his breath.

"Of course," the king replied apologetically for his callous phrasing. He knew that Ferenc was invaluable and with Gobolt by his side, were the heart and force of his holy crusade. But he also knew that if he lost Gobolt as well, he would only have an army without their generals. Despite wishing to deny Gobolt his request to follow, to accept the wounds of battle and carry on – he knew he could not make him comply. He would be hunting for Ferenc no matter what his royal orders were.

So, he conceded, "I will only allow you to go with the full force of our might behind you. We lost the first battalion already. We need to address this injustice. And hopefully, find Ferenc. You cannot go in as outnumbered as you were."

Gobolt knew that leaving the realm of reality was an almost suicidal task. One he had done only once before. But was not the same place he had to go to now. The world he went to was the world between worlds. A place of void called The Balance. A holding space for Gods to dwell. But where he wanted to go was below that. A place where even the Gods had not ventured. Far below. It was the place where the darkness itself was born. A place he had only heard about in cries and whispers. A place humans would define as Hell. A place he probably deserved to go. To be amongst the murderers and monsters, and with each fiber of his being calling for him to just leave, run away, live his life far from this – he knew he had no choice. He would *have* to save Ferenc or give up his life trying.

"I'll get him back," Gobolt said as he looked up at the king.

"Are you willing to pay the price for finding the path?" the king asked calmly.

"I don't have much of a choice, do I?" he replied. "I cannot leave him there… I cannot leave him *damned*."

The king nodded. "I know I cannot stop you. So, please. Be careful. You cannot trust the gatekeeper. Tread *carefully* through the woods. One misstep from that path…"

Gobolt smiled. "Don't worry. I won't let them get me. I've seen it before, Besides, I will have your army, right…"

No matter his words, the king sensed there was something Gobolt did not tell him. "Come back alive… Please….” he said sincerely before continuing. “I only have one other request for you.”

Gobolt nodded, knowing what was to come. “I know what you want…”

“You need to take the priest,” the king confirmed.

“Even as dumb as I am, I see his worth in going there...” Gobolt spoke with a tinge of melancholy. “But he ain’t walking by my side as an equal... I don’t trust him...”

“…So, what do you propose?” the king asked, knowing he would have no choice but to accept whatever Gobolt demanded.

“No matter what you think of him, the Priest can’t be trusted on his own two feet in his own reality,” Gobolt said as he mentally prepared himself for what was to come. “And he won’t like it one bit.”

Deep in the bowels of the earth, Ferenc’s thoughts were now only on his daughter. The daughter Elizabeth had spoken of. The daughter she said he would meet … And that was the only thing he ever wanted to do. Meet the child that death stole from him, before he could look into her eyes. His only comforting thought in this nightmare. His child – His Hanna – might still be alive.

The Grotesque Path to Hell

In the wetlands to the east of the city lay a thick wooded region known locally as The Bowels. A place which got its name from the grotesque smell of rot and shit that seeped out from throughout its trees. A smell that originated from the heart of the woods, deep in a large swamp. Deep down through its filthy water, to where a creature lived. A creature of immense power.

Villagers from the surrounding towns knew to steer clear of The Bowels, for many had disappeared when they ventured too far beyond its thick and almost impenetrable tree-line. For that creature within the swamp was not the only thing there. His acolytes were in vast numbers, spread over the whole of the forest. These other beings roamed the area searching for lives to take back to their master. These creatures were half-formed and humanoid. Only standing a couple of feet tall, they had blank features, hairless and formless bodies, with only a rough estimation of any human detail. Their hands with no fingers, faces with only eyes and mouths. Their skin gelatinous and translucent through their mostly organ-less body. Only through their head, behind their eyes, could a small brain be seen. One no bigger than an apple. Without a thought of their own to carry, these pale spectral beings slithered on their hands and feet along the dirt, leaving a trail of slime behind them. Hiding from sight, until they happened upon prey. Only when in arms' reach would they reveal themselves, with an expression of innocence on their face, they would seem harmless and otherworldly to their intended victims, who would see no threat coming from them. But when they could get close, they would open their mouths, emit a high-pitched scream and launch themselves, mouths agape, at their chosen victim. Not drawing blood when they bit down (as they had no teeth to pierce the skin) their body would start to consume their victim, their gelatinous skin breaking apart and covering as much of the victim's body as possible. Never alone, they would soon be joined by other nearby acolytes who would follow suit, scream and launch themselves at the victim. Their bodies fusing together to form one thick layer of skin over the entirety of their victims. And if there were multiple victims on horseback, they would do the same to each of them. No matter the species. No matter the number they appeared in. For the acolytes would always outnumber whatever army would dare venture inside.

When these creatures had formed themselves into the thick skin around whatever victim they wished to attack, they would work in unison, walking these victims to their fate. To the hands of their master in the swamp. Their movement giving the illusion of the victim walking of their own free will, but *they* controlled the journey. No matter how hard this victim tried to struggle to escape, they could not break free. They would only be able to breathe and emit a small muffled scream from a gap the acolytes left under their nostrils – Otherwise they were trapped.

The forest itself was far reaching and had a circumference which would add a couple of days onto a traveler's journey circumventing it. And because of this, many travelers who happened upon the thick tree-line decided to cut through the forest, hoping for a shortcut towards their eventual destination on the other side. The locals near the forest had tried their best to dissuade any travelers, but these warnings were always met by deaf ears. If they had a chance to happen upon these travelers and warn them of the monsters within, they would be met with scorn and derision. Dismissed as local folklore which was meant to scare strangers away. Little did they know that these villagers would be the last humans that they would see. Only when the villagers tried to block the path to the woods, cutting off the supply of victims to the monster in the swamp, would these acolytes come past the tree-line and take villagers instead. So, for the past few decades, an unspoken truce was understood by all. They would not stop any travelers. They would not block the path. In return for their non-involvement, they would be left alive – an uneasy bargain with an unseen devil.

Sometimes though, despite knowing the dangers, some foolish people went into the forest. Fully willing to battle monsters, all in search of an imaginary treasure they thought must exist. Some also heard the tales and discarded them anyway, determined to get through fast enough. None of these people though, no matter their plan, were ever seen again.

The only people who could leave this place alive were those who came to bargain with the monster in the swamp. For this monster was a gateway to every other realm. It held the key to the path to any reality, any possibility that any person needed to venture on, this monster could open that gateway – provided they agreed to the price.

The king had chosen many years ago to leave this monster alone, allowing it to commit its atrocities for the greater good. He saw the value that this monster had. He knew that without its ability to hand, his men could fail in their future missions. Of course, he could always find other passages to other realms in other places – but *that* way you would not know where you would end up in the infinity of eventualities, or when in time these other passages may lead you to. The monster could pinpoint not only a particular time and place but could also find out where it is you *needed* to go.

The Bowels were not strictly part of human reality. It was an overlap of realms where the monster was the sole gatekeeper and this was the only one of its kind, anyone knew of in this world.

At the entrance to the woods, Gobolt got off his horse and took a few steps toward the imposing and thick tree-line, which stretched far either side of him. Ahead of him, a large pair of gnarled trees, entwined their leafless branches together and formed a kind of archway – an entrance inside – beckoning any stranger into its dominion.

Turning, he glanced at the men behind him. The trail of a thousand strong king's men. His own army sent to follow him below – the army he was never going to use. The ones who had come this far to complete the illusion of compliance to the king. These were fighting men, but innocent men. Men who didn't deserve the corruption of hell. Standing in five-man rows, they stretched back as far as the eye could see. On their journey from London, they had all set out on horseback and traveled the four days' ride to what would become their encampment in an adjacent valley. Having left their horses behind and each dressed in full armor, each one of them carried scimitar blades with runic carvings etched onto them. They stood, motionless, waiting. Awaiting the command to walk into the battle below. Awaiting their general's command. But Gobolt would *never* give that command. He had brought them as far as he was willing to take them.

The night before, Gobolt slept a restless sleep. Waking up in a cold sweat. Seeing in his dreams, the deaths of all these men. He knew where he was going was a fool's errand. He knew that even with a million men, he would probably not survive. But he was indebted to his friend and would willingly give his own life to try to save him, but could not damn these innocent soldiers alongside him. Not to mention his other half. His Lycan half – which was a week away from appearing – and was an unknown quantity in any other realm. Who knew what would happen to the man if the beast was loosed? He had a recurring nightmare that he would turn on his own men and that was something he could not abide and was most afraid of. Killing the innocent. Becoming what he vowed to destroy. There was an exception to his determination to not damn another soul – apart from his own life, he was also willing to sacrifice the life of the Priest to the possible death that might be waiting in the realm below. Though fighting on the same side, he never trusted or liked that demon. Once a harbinger of death from one of the other realities, this demon had changed allegiances and found the same God as the King. An allegiance which secured his freedom. And a faith which he followed to the priesthood. Not that the church knew of his demonic reality, for he kept that hidden deep inside. A being with two bodies who dwelled in the same shell; on the outside was seemingly normal male human skin, but on the inside – on the reverse of this skin – was his demonic side. A side that resembled a diminutive scaly-skinned slug. Without legs this demon was merely a torso with two long arms, on which he stood up and moved around with – arms twice as long as his small body which hung off his multiple-eyed face. This twisted creature, when needing to show his human side, would fold itself inwards –

through its own dark green chest – and turn his demonic shell inside out, producing a normal-sized human male form, with all limbs intact.

This demon had a name. A name which Gobolt refused to call him. He would be called Priest and that was that. No matter what the King commanded. Despite the royal pleas to accept this demon as one of their own, he had seen what this Priest had once been responsible for. For he'd caught this demon in the first place. He had seen the destructive influence it had wrought. It was a demon who offered the innocent a devil's bargain, in order to corrupt their souls. Within his human skin, he used his wiles and magic to twist the minds of the impressionable, to appear to them, masquerading as an angel. Offering them anything they wished for in payment to carry out a holy mission. They could have anything in the world in payment for carrying out God's work; Riches. Power. Revenge. Sex. *Anything.* All for the simple and non-negotiable price of extinguishing one 'evil' life. A life they didn't know. One chosen by this disguised demon. And no matter how steadfast they may be to not take another life any cost, the Priest would trick them, infecting their mind, whilst in his angelic guise. Before they completed this task – and they *always* completed it after his work to corrupt them, he would go to the next person and offer them a name to kill. This offered name would be the name of the person who took the deal before them and the evidence he would show them, was of them killing their assigned person – who was the person before that. A never-ending cycle of violence and sadism.

Gobolt could have seen a possible redemption had it not been for this demon having committed his evil thousands of times over. Had he not appeared to people world-wide. Offering the same deal. Tricking with the same tricks. Damning the poor into a promise of a better life. Corrupting their soul and forcing the next person in line to kill them.

Despite this glee that he garnered from the violence, the Priest supposedly found his faith and then asked for forgiveness for his actions. A request accepted and then given absolution by the king. All of this against Gobolt's advice. He did not believe this Priest. He thought it all a ruse to keep him from losing his life – a desperate attempt to cater to a king's religious foolishness.

Gobolt accepted the king believed in his Christian God. He knew there were beings who claimed to be Gods. And beings who had created worlds. But none were the childish invention that his beliefs followed. And the idea that a demon, a being from another realm which had seen many Gods rise and fall throughout existence had suddenly believed this primitive human invention, was laughable. Like a renowned scientist suddenly abandoning all they knew, to changing their whole belief system to tout the healing power of crystals. He knew the Priest had to be hiding his real intent. And though he could not trust him, he had to hope that at least a part of the Priest would value his own life. For if he tried to turn on Gobolt, he would ensure a deathly fate upon him. Yet, this Priest, despite Gobolt's misgivings and mistrust towards him, *was* needed. As Gobolt had never been to any of the realms deep below, whereas the Priest was born into them. And having a demon by your side in a demon land made the most sense, even without the basis of trust. Besides, Gobolt doubted it would be a successful journey and would prefer to take that possible corruptive influence away from the King, and damn it back to the realm it came from.

It was how the Priest would join Gobolt on this journey that was the one condition asked of the King. A condition that the Priest naturally protested, but it had fallen on deaf ears. With a Royal agreement, the Priest would have to be in his demonic form for the entire journey downwards. All whilst strapped to Gobolt's back. He would need to stay in his diminutive real form, unable to fold himself inside out, into his preferred human look. Stuck with Gobolt until he allowed otherwise.

Unknown to Gobolt, the Priest was not pretending in his beliefs. He *had* seen the light in the king's teachings. As he served time for his crimes, in the depths of the Royal Prison, where the king had taken to speaking to the inmates. All in order to learn more about them, about their kind. Most of the prisoners, though, he got nothing from. Most spoke in hatred to their captor, who sat wishing to listen. Offering them kindness in return. The Priest was different, though. He actually read the book which the king had offered him. And through the words of these fantastical pages, he saw some light in the darkness. A better path. A path he wished to be true, whether a human invention or not. And through the years of captivity, he became a willing pupil. From his cell, he was taught the theology and meaning of the scriptures of this faith by the king and when he believed that this prisoner was honest in his convictions, he arranged for him to attend a seminary school, whist under constant guard and only in his human form. And throughout it all, the monster that Gobolt called the Priest renounced his evil ways and wanted to atone for the deaths of those he had taken. Though he knew Gobolt had not believed in his faith conversion, he would never stop in his attempts to convince him of his remorse and wish for atonement. And though he would have preferred to stay, he saw this mission to save Ferenc as a final way to prove that he no longer had any allegiance to anything below. Even having to stay in his demonic form – which he hated and saw as a reminder of his ungodly past actions. He would do whatever it took. And it was a mission to save Ferenc, a man whom – like Gobolt – did not trust him, but did not treat him with the same verbal scorn. If he was to be invaluable in this rescue. If they made it out alive – maybe he could earn his acceptance from the man who had once captured him.

This Priest in his demonic form was now held with leather straps to Gobolt's back as he walked along the dirt track into the thick woodland. A full leather satchel strapped to one side. They walked, leaving this army waiting at the entrance.

This army had been given the strict order to wait until they were signaled to follow. If the signal did not come within two days, they had to return to the king. They had to presume Gobolt and the Priest had been unsuccessful in securing their passage, and did not survive the meeting. They could not afford a war with this monstrous gatekeeper. They all knew the dangers of this forest. They knew they could not afford a battle here. The cost of life being too high.

As far as they knew, Gobolt had to speak to the creature in the swamp first. To pay for passageway to the realms below. To be shown the path through the limitless eventualities and realities which splintered off from this world, the path to where Ferenc was taken. And without the help of the creature in the swamp, they would never be able to find the single needle in the haystack of limitless sized realms. But in truth they would never enter this forest. Gobolt and the Priest were in this alone by choice. By Gobolt's choice, and the Priest believed the subterfuge as much as the army did.

Gobolt had been here once before and, until Ferenc was taken, had vowed to never go back. He had met this monster. He had paid the price – and to Gobolt, the price was too grotesque to agree to again. But for now, at least… he had no other choice. To some degree, he was glad that this monster had not been destroyed and was given the king's grace to exist.

As the gnarled tree's arched entrance disappeared into the distance behind them, Gobolt walked with trepidation upon the dirt path. A single curved rune-etched blade in his hand and the demon Priest belted on his back, he carried on.

The Priest looked around silently, fearfully. For even evil was scared of what lay here, as they were as much in danger as any human. If the acolyte creatures saw anything that entered their lands and deemed them a worthy gift for their master, they would be taken and their master took every gift with glee and death.

With each slow and purposeful step, Gobolt kept his attention to his periphery, keeping watch for any approaching acolytes. The Priest looking more fearful the closer into the forest they went.

"If you see one, you'd better say..." Gobolt gnarled to the beast on his back. "They won't help you escape, so don't think of doing any double-crossing."

The Priest accepted long ago that he should not talk back to this man, but let the barbs aimed at him be left unchallenged.

"I shall let you know," was all he replied in his guttural voice.

Gobolt wanted to provoke the Priest, to get him to react negatively. To prove the king wrong. But the priest would never allow himself to falter in his redemption path. And even if he knew that, Gobolt would still never stop trying.

Hearing a rustling of fallen dead leaves, Gobolt stopped in his tracks.

Silently he waited. Listening. Hearing some more rustling.

"It may just be a rabbit," the priest whispered.

"Ain't no life here, demon..." he retorted viciously. "*Show yourselves*!" he then shouted out.

Nothing.

No sound.

The rustling now stopped.

But Gobolt knew better. "*Show yourselves*!" he shouted again.

After a few more moments' silence, they saw a movement from the bushes. A small featureless creature. An acolyte. Looking out at them with an innocent expression. Its mouth open and a sexless, almost terrifying voice came out. "Come closer..."

"Maybe it's just the one?"

Knowing better, Gobolt lifted his blade to this creature, who was about 20 feet away. "*All of you. Show yourselves you motherless fucks*!" he screamed.

Not altering its expression. This creature opened its mouth again. "We can help you..." it said.

"We can help you both!" it repeated. But this time in union of thousands of other acolytes. All now raising their heads from their hiding places. All around Gobolt and the Priest. From every bush and tree, as far as they could see. Their question trying to lull their intended victim into believing their benevolence.

"Just one of them, eh?" Gobolt smirked quietly to the priest.

"What can we do?" they said. "Tell us…What can we do?" They started to slowly advance on Gobolt's position. Their tiny alien-like bodies slow and awkward as they slithered on all fours. Their voices, seemingly innocent, were laced with menace and tinged with malevolence.

"Stay the fuck back! *We are here to see your master*!" he shouted at their advance.

"Can we get you anything?" They all spoke in their bassy voices, the nearest now almost reaching Gobolt and the Priest's position on the path. "Let us help you," they continued.

"*We want passage*!" Gobolt screamed again, the priest now convinced that they were about to meet their demise. But instead of attacking, upon hearing his exclamation, the creatures all stopped in their tracks, moved backwards and disappeared out of sight. Back to where they were hiding before. Leaving the Priest and Gobolt alone on the path once more. These acolytes hiding only visually. For they were always there. Always watching.

Silently and knowing that his exclamation of intent would soon make its way to the creature in the swamp, he continued down the path deeper into the forest, safe in the knowledge, that for now at least, he would be allowed an audience.

From where his army waited to where the swamp lay, was about a day's walk – a day that Gobolt and the Priest spent enduring the extremist elements that did not exist outside of this forest. Trapped in its own realm, the forest crossed every eventuality, and was home to many ecosystems which collided with each other. The deeper in you went in, the more the weather changed on a dime, and the more alien the life that grew around you became. The closer to the swamp you got, the more fantastic the flowers, plants and trees turned. As well as the flora and fauna, the smaller insects, arachnids and reptiles also grew stranger to look at – and these small beings were the only living things that that the monster and acolytes allowed to exist alongside them. Anything mammalian or with any real sentience would be offered to the monster to do unspeakable acts to.

A small spider living in the undergrowth by the outer tree-line, would appear to be of a normal variety, but deeper within the forest, where the realms bled into one, there would not exist such a normal arachnid like that, but instead would be something almost nightmarish in appearance. Much larger, more legs, more eyes, living in the undergrowth of some strange colored leave and branches – ready to attack and kill any passerby.

The changing weather system could never be prepared for. Mild and temperate one moment would soon give way to a blustery wind, then to light rain which slowly grew more torrential by the step, until the rainfall began to freeze as the temperature dropped to subzero degrees, then the blizzards, the tornados and heavy snowfall would follow - until finally, around the area of the center of the woods, around the swamp itself, there was a debilitating heat which always stayed the same. A thick and sadistic temperature akin to the Sahara in a heatwave.

The swamp itself was the focal bridge between all realms and caused this overspill of life and death into this reality. Parts of every realm it touched, had some influence here. Even if it was only one solitary plant, there would be some trace of every reality within this forest.

Gobolt had crossed all the variant weather systems within the forest at a brisk and determined pace - silently and purposefully he strode through the harshest of weather conditions and through the most fantastic of wildlife. The rain from the monsoon had now frozen as he continued to trek through the arctic level freeze and into the area where it was now melting off him, as he walked through into an oppressive 120-degree heat. He struggled to get his breath under control as he walked closer to the swamp's edge, finally at their destination.

The heat in this swamp baked the putrid stench that bubbled up through the thick brown water. Worse than the most rancid sewer, worse than the most pungent rot, this swamp was the boiling pot of all things rancid and hung in the air with a thick greenish brown mist.

When entering this heat, the stench hit Gobolt's throat – he tried to hold back his vomit, but failed, just as he had failed the first time he had to endure it. Strapped on his back, the Priest was unaffected. He just stayed silent. He could smell exactly what Gobolt could, but the smell of waste and death was not something that could make someone like him sick or repulsed. But what it did do was remind him of the realm where he came from. A place he wanted desperately to forget. He now considered London his home. He considered humanity his people. He considered the one God his savior and King James his leader.

Now with a huge smear of strong spiced paste under his nose, Gobolt took a step into the thick oozing swamp. The strength of the stench around him was only dulled slightly by the spices smeared into his mustache. And that was just enough to stop the uncontrollable vomiting, but not enough to quell the nausea which raised in him like a repeating tidal wave.

"You know what we have to do here, don't you?" Gobolt asked the Priest as he took another step in up to his knees. The thick sludge of waste that made up the swamp tugged at his clothes, beckoning him downwards.

"The King told me," the Priest confirmed.

"Well, the King has never been here. And we only tell him the things he needs to know. He doesn't know the price each requester has to pay."

The Priest looked confused as he asked, "You have to give him blood, correct?"

"No blood, no," Gobolt replied coldly.

"No?"

"Just hold your tongue down there," Gobolt requested. "And whatever you see, it is not for the king's ears. As far as he knows it's a passage payable in blood. And that is how it will stay"

“Why not tell him?” the Priest asked, fearing he may have spoken too much. But Gobolt did not censure him this time.

“This is a place of evil. He knows as much as he needs to.” He stopped as the water got to his waist. He took a breath in and gathered his bravery before continuing. “He has not seen the face of real evil, nor should he know of the nightmare things we have to endure for *his* fight.”

The Priest was silent in reply, understanding what Gobolt asked. He wanted to protect the king from the truth for his own sake. But he had no idea what the truth was… Yet.

The next step Gobolt took was into a large patch of quicksand-like filth and he fell in, as the muck started to pull him under with unbeatable force. “Hold your breath,” was the last thing he managed to shout before he was dragged under by the foulness. Pulled into the darkness of the excrement of the swamp.

The Darkness of the Dark

Ferenc remembered little after he was dragged down by Elizabeth. In his memory, he only saw flashes of images; Gobolt surrounded by rancid flesh. The young witch, Saskia, beating him with a sickly smile, then Elizabeth's wide grin as she held a blade toward him. He remembered her words, *"I told you what I would do..."*

And now, he could not see and could not move. He could only hear and feel the wind on his skin. He presumed he was paralyzed by some witch's spell and was forced into stillness. His mind was a fog, and he had trouble holding any thought for long, before that thought was lost and he had to start over again. He felt almost drunk without the dizziness. He didn't feel bad. He just didn't feel much, expect the mental fog and the noises he could hear.

"Your grace?" He heard a woman's voice. As far as he could tell, a voice unknown to him. "We have her," she continued.

A cackle he had recognized now filled the air within the room – it was the laugh of Elizabeth – unmistakably. His dead wife. From the acoustics, he could safely presume that they were in a room of considerable size. "Wonderful!" she exclaimed with glee.

"Can I ask my Goddess a question?" came the unknown woman's voice again. Ferenc could hear the fear that laced the edges of her voice. The quiver in her words as she spoke to Elizabeth.

"My dear, you have given everything to me. The least I can do is answer you. Please… What is your question?"

"Is… is it over now?" came the question from the woman.

A pause.

Ferenc did not know what any of this meant, but he was intrigued to know what was happening here. He could feel his mental grip on the subject and his memory of the last few seconds fading.

"Only in as far as this idea can be. It was very inventive of you… Using the world yet to come… And I loved your use of humanity," Elizabeth said kindly. Kindlier than he had ever heard her voice sound before. "My Hanna will feed well from the desperation of torment."

"I shall prepare the rebirth."

Ferenc's mind stuttered in its fog. Hanna. How could he forget her? He was here listening to this conversation from his mental prison without a care in the world. Even forgetting the evil that Elizabeth had become. Like he was half-watching a play, he was just blankly hearing events unfold. But now, he remembered his daughter. *What did she mean? What would she feed? Is she indeed alive? Is she here?* He tried to scream aloud. He tried to yell to the Gods to allow him his moment. But nothing. He was still just trapped within the darkness. Listening. All he could do.

"This Rebecca, that is her name at this moment, correct?" Elizabeth asked. Ferenc could only presume the woman nodded, as he heard no vocal affirmation in reply. "No point holding this charade up any longer. I see those out front have already begun to shed their skins. So, I think we are at about that time, yes."

A small child's cackle could be heard. A cackle he knew well. Saskia. "Finally," this young witch uttered to herself.

"Do you wish to see her now?" the woman asked.

"Why not? May as well stoke the fires and see what burns. See if we can amplify her anguish," Elizabeth replied.

Ferenc heard a single set of footsteps on the concrete slowly walk away – he presumed that this unknown woman was the one to exit.

It had been nine years since Hanna had died. She would be a small adult by now. *Elizabeth must have stolen her away and…* He dreaded to think more as to what she had gone through. He could only assume this Rebecca *was* Hanna. His mind was still a fog of confusion, but he thought he'd pieced that together correctly.

"Oh, my dear, sweet, beautiful Ferenc..." he heard Elizabeth say. Her voice getting closer to him, as he heard her stand on something wooden to get nearer to him. "How I wish you had seen the beauty of my world and joined me willingly. You could have sat by my side, whilst we bathed the innocent in their own mother's blood." He could feel her breath on his cheek.

"But I shall tell you a secret," she whispered into his ear. "I prefer you like this." He then felt her kiss him on his forehead, before she retreated away from him. "So does young Saskia."

Saskia cackled again. "He is beautiful!" she said.

"Ah!" Elizabeth interrupted. "You must be Rebecca!" she exclaimed.

Hanna! His daughter! She was here!

"Who are you?" came this stranger's voice. An adult voice. Not the voice of a child. His heart sank as he realized he was wrong. This was *not* his Hanna. His mind had taken the words spoken and fitted them to his own narrative. Rebecca was an adult and someone else's child.

"Me? I am just here to take you from this world. To feed your lineage..." Elizabeth spoke with delight. "Are you not happy to see your mother?"

There was silence at first. This stranger, Rebecca, did not reply to this instantly, but after a few moments said, "You are not my mother..." she spoke hatefully.

"Leanne…?" Elizabeth called out.

"What?" Rebecca exclaimed, surprised, as Leanne walked in. "Mum! What's happening? Are you ok?"

"What's happening?" Leanne, this other woman's voice, mocked back. "What's happening? Mum? Mum?" she cruelly said. "Come to save your sweet old mother, did you? Dumb fucking bitch."

"Mum?" Rebecca said, her emotions in turmoil at this. "Please…"

"May I?" Leanne asked Elizabeth.

Ferenc did not know these people but could hear the hear the hurt in Rebecca's voice and the stone coldness from this other woman, Leanne.

"Of course," Elizabeth replied. "Show her your face."

"What are you….? NO, MUM!!"

A fleshy ripping sound could be heard, hidden amongst the terrified, panicked exclamations from Rebecca – soon followed by her scream of terror.

"Ta daaaaa!" Leanne said with a cackle "Don't you love your mother's real face?".

"Get the fuck away from me!" Rebecca screamed, her love now turning to fear and hate at this *thing* who spoke to her. Ferenc could hear scuffling and presumed this Rebecca was being held down by some people, or some things.

"Now, now… calm down." Elizabeth said as her voice got more distant, presumably walking away from where Ferenc was.

In this room, this stone lined chamber within the Houses of Parliament – a room now under Elizabeth's command – Leanne stood, her human face torn off to reveal her demon face. She watched with glee as Elizabeth walked confidently up to Rebecca, her long red dress flowing behind her like some Hollywood starlet at a film premiere. She looked confident and cruel as she stood in front of the two guards holding Rebecca firmly in place by her arms.

"Get the fuck away from me!" She spat her words at Elizabeth.

"Now, now, little bird, language!" Leanne spoke with a serrated-toothed smile. Rebecca glanced at her in shock. She did not know how to process anything that was going on. She could only look in terror at the woman she called her mother. This grotesque monster wearing her skin.

Behind Elizabeth stood a dozen figures in long white robes, with white veils covering their faces. Their heads bald, their figures feminine. They all carried long golden spears. There were her guards. Not that she needed any. But in this realm, Leanne had prepared for most eventualities.

In the middle of these guards, sat a large wooden throne where Elizabeth had sat. In front of it, sitting cross-legged, was Saskia. Smiling in glee at the proceedings. Like an obedient dog, she stayed silently in place as her Goddess addressed Rebecca.

Above the throne, on a large black metal frame, hung the complete skin of a flayed man. Displayed like an army's banner - this man's skin had been stretched out with wires attached to its frame, pulled as taut as it could be. Displayed spread-eagled in full nakedness. This man's empty eyes and empty mouth overlooked the whole scene with a terrifying look of surprise.

Ferenc did not have any idea that he could be this man. He did not remember his death. He did not remember Elizabeth slicing his skin from off his body. He did not remember laying on the ground in agony, as his skinless corpse was feasted on by her and Saskia.

He did not remember the moment of death.

He just could hear his wife. His evil wife. The wife whose corpse he had buried – now here in this impossible place. He could hear her words corrupting this woman called Rebecca. And he could hear the truth about where he was and what was intended. And he could do nothing at all to stop any of it.

Three Keys and an Offering

In a candle-lit cavern deep underground, Gobolt lay in a puddle of swamp filth. The Priest was no longer attached to his back, but still lay on the dirt in his demonic form only a few feet away. Both were unconscious. The small gelatinous creatures from the forest had brought them there from the land above. Now retreating, they walked up to the walls of the cavern and disappeared within them. Their bodies breaking apart and dissipating into the very dirt, only to reappear from the depths of the swamp water, far, far above. The visitors delivered to their master.

The cavern was made of mud and filth, the ceiling vaulted with bones. Gobolt and the Priest were lying on the floor of a long narrow hallway. A hallway which led to a large, dark room at one end.

Down each wall of the cavern hall, skulls of many kinds of animals were embedded in into the dirt at eye height. Within these skulls rested wax candles – alight and illuminating the hall with their flames. Human skulls, horse skulls, as well as many other skulls of more fantastical creatures. Skulls from beings not of this world, the ones that had bled through from other realms and been captured and killed. Ones which suffered the wraith of this monster.

From the dark room, a movement of water could be heard. But nothing could be seen. The blackness in that room shrouded everything and not one candle could be seen inside to bring illumination to it.

Gobolt didn't feel unconsciousness take him as he was dragged downwards into the swamp, trapped in the powerful muck and dragged by the hidden acolytes. The Priest, though, did. He felt the excrement-filled water break into his lungs, filling his whole being up to the brim. He could feel death upon him. A death he thought would never come for a long, long time. Not claiming immortality, he had just hoped to live his full demonic lifespan. He felt the hands of the acolytes grab and claw at him, yanking him further into the depths.

Coughing up the wealth of the muck he had drowned in, the Priest's eyes burst open as life flooded back into his body and the filth from within his lungs expelled itself from his mouth and onto the solid mud floor. He drew in a huge breath of oxygen as his lungs expelled all of the foreign matter. Coughing the last of it, he slithered to his elbows. The lower tail-like half of his body dragging behind him. He looked around as he gained his composure. His many red eyes darting around, until his multiple gaze landed on the dark room at the end of the hall. His breathing became erratic from his rising panic at the realization of what lay inside. They were here. At the precipice to the monster *itself*.

Crawling over to Gobolt, the Priest shook his unconscious body. "Gobolt! Wake up!" As he did, the large man moaned. Alive but not awake as yet.

The Priest lightly slapped Gobolt's face a few times. "We are here! Please… Awaken," he continued.

As his eyes burst open with a jolt, Gobolt drew in a large breath of air and sat bolt upright, his lungs contracted and expelled the same swamp water which the priest had ingested – spraying it out in front of him and over his feet.

Struggling to regain his breath, he saw the Priest was now off his back and next to him. Then his gaze went to the room which lay ahead. Scrambling backward he grabbed his scimitar from his belt and crawled to his feet, his head pounding from pain. The near-drowning they'd both endured had a much more debilitating effect on Gobolt, but you couldn't tell from the strength he exerted now. He quickly patted down the satchel, making sure the contents inside were still secure. He wiped the muck still present from his only working eye and spat some dirt from his mouth onto the floor

"Welcome…" came a cracked and grotesque voice from the darkness of the room ahead of them. Which caused both of these men to divert all of their attention towards that monstrous noise. They both stared blankly and fearfully toward the dark room which lay ahead of them. There was no time for Gobolt to think clearly of what he needed to do – he just had to get on with what he dreaded was about to happen.

"Do not be shy…" the voice slicked out from the room. Every word with an infected and rotten tinge to it. The sound of filth itself. "Come forth… What do you two shamans wish for? What led your journey path to me?"

Gobolt glanced down at the Priest who was propped up on his hands, dragging his demon form behind him. "Are you ready?" he asked. To which the Priest glanced back up in terror. His many eyes displaying his trepidation. The fact a demon was afraid of what lay in this room was very telling of the level of danger they now faced – as this monster was not affiliated with anything except his own nature and would as easily kill a demon as it would any other kind of being. The power it held greatly outshone the mere parlor tricks that the Priest had up his metaphorical sleeves and most magic other similar beings had mastered.

"I'll never be ready…" the Priest answered quietly. "Should I get on your back?"

Gobolt looked forward to the room. He could hear a low laughter. A guttural terrifying and quiet chuckle from the being who sloshed around in the very liquid it resided in.

"We got no time…" he replied. Then – and against all better judgements – reattached his scimitar back onto his belt. He then, slowly, walked forward toward the dark room ahead of them. His previous plan to keep the demon Priest strapped to him had already failed. Failed even before they got to the realms below. There was no point continuing with that charade now. He was there with him. There was no escape yet.

As they approached the doorway, the vomitus voice continued. "Please come in… I shall be with you shortly…"

As they took a step from the dry mud of the hallway floor, they walked into a pool of liquid. A liquid which made the swamp water from above seem comparatively clean and healthy. In here was a lifetime of liquid waste, interwoven with decayed and rotten body parts which floated haphazardly within it. In this darkness, they could not yet see the full extent of the horror within this room.

The Priest slithered in, landing shoulder-deep in the sewerage which coated the floor. He moved through the waste on his arms, next to where Gobolt stood, looking forlorn as the liquid lapped against his shoulder and all over his submerged body. The stench of the room was a secondary grotesquery to the knowledge that Gobolt had of what was to happen.

In the depths of the dark shroud that the room enjoyed hiding in, a deep monstrous snorting echoed from what they presumed was an adjacent room.

The guttural rumbling inhalation was soon followed by a hacked cough. A deep and rattling sound, which sounded like a large beast regurgitating its fresh kill.

Gobolt looked down as the light from the hallway behind him, reflected onto a tongue which floated by in the filth, knocking into his knee. A tongue which had been bitten off. The severed end having large gouges made by many teeth across it. He would normally wish to take in a deep cleansing breath, in order to regain his composure, but a deep breath in this room could be a fate worse than not breathing in at all.

"That is better..." came the monster's rancid tones as he came closer through the darkness into the room. This monster crawled its way through the shadows, the splashing and sloshing of shit and rot announcing its arrival. But neither men could, as yet, see any part of this creature which greeted them.

"So, man-wolf.... You crave an audience with me, again? I like doggies." The voice dripped with bile, with a mock childlike verbiage. "Will you pay the price a second time? I remember greatly enjoying the first."

Steadying himself, Gobolt nodded. "Yes, sir." He spoke quietly.

"Sir? SIR?" it spat from within the shadows with a cacophonous anger. "How dare you. How DARE you!" it suddenly erupted with rage, the liquid beneath it crashing out in a wave as it slammed its furious arm downwards. "You will address me as your GOD!"

Closing his eyes for a second and not showing his inner smile, Gobolt felt a pang of happiness. Part of him enjoyed seeing the rage of a lunatic. The sheer madness of the petty most evil beings possessed.

"Apologies. My God," he said in reply.

With a sudden air of reversal, the monster spoke happily. “Oh please… No need for that.” It then clamored forward at surprising speed, stopping only a few feet in front of them. The light from the hallway behind them cast a glow onto this thing, exposing it from the shadows it had previously hidden in. This thing – like the Priest – slithered on two clawed arms, dragging its gnarled back end behind it. Significantly larger than the both of them, it looked down with a gleeful and revolting smile. Despite its hulking arms and back, the rest of this monster’s body was twisted and gaunt and only a huge bloated belly showed any signs of flesh. Vile skin covered this demon. It was pale and blotched with sores, both open and healed. The open sores seeped with blood and pus down its mottled body into the liquid below. Though in a cold, wet environment, this monster was dripping with perpetual sweat, that caused his body to glisten repulsively. Its bloodshot demonic eyes sat in a permanent state of venturing in opposing directions. They were welled with moisture, which one could presume may be tears, but this monster had never had an emotion besides sadistic glee or anger in its long and despicable life. As it smiled down at them, its yellowing rotten teeth were on full display for them to see. And as it spoke its smile never seemed to fade. “That King James… He is looking very ill, nowadays isn’t he? Is he dying? Tell me all about it.”

As he spoke, the skin from his face started to sag down, revealing his hidden demon face below. It was a human made skin-suit he wore. And due to his size, was made-up of more than a dozen bodies. Crudely stitched together to make what should be a form-fitting look, but instead was ill-fitting and terrifying to behold. But this monster did not see the horror on display. As far as it was aware, it had put on its favorite human suit to meet these visitors. To greet them as it saw itself – as a being exuding beauty, intelligence and wit. Which was what made this monster more terrifying. Its mind had turned rotten over the centuries. It had cannibalized itself to the point, where it was not able to follow logic or a continuing conversation.

"You have seen the king?" Gobolt asked.

"Of course. I visit the palace often. Only last year, in fact…" the monster lied, having never left The Bowels in its entire existence, which Gobolt knew and knew better than to correct – so he just stood there silently. The Priest, meanwhile, looked up in terror at this insanity on display. Unable to say a word.

From its collapsed human skin nose, a smattering of blood seeped down over its lip and with a single motion it lifted its hand from the shit and rot water, and rubbed away the blood from its mouth, then drew that stained hand back over its blackened tongue, lapping up the crimson with glee.

"Please… Sit… Tell me of your pain…" It motioned to the room. A room where no chairs could be seen in the very limited light. Only the rotten water that soaked their ankles and this grotesque being in front of them.

With that, the monster slithered off into the darkness. The surrounding water sloshed as it disappeared into the shroud of the shadows.

With a spark from its hand, the monster – now at the other end of the room – ignited a flame from within its boney hands and passed this fire into a small trench that was dug into the dirt walls, igniting a liquid deep within them. This flame grew and followed the thin trench upwards and all around the room. Illuminating in its fire the full horror of the monster's lair.

Along both side of the room were wooden cages, each housing emaciated and naked creatures of all descriptions. Looking weak and forlorn, they groaned as the light hurt their eyes. Some were heavily injured and had been left dying in their own filth.

Hiding his shock, Gobolt's attention was drawn to the table in front of one of the cages. A table he was very familiar with. A table from his last visit. A table with four wooden bowls resting on them. Three black and one white.

The Priest could not contain his horror. Since his conversion and his renouncing of his demonic side, he had become more than accustomed to humanity and the way they lived. Choosing that as the way he wanted to be. He craved humanity and this… this display of cruelty, in a setting filled with rotten flesh water, was something that sickened him to his core. Though from the same realm and with similar traits to this monster, he was nothing like it. Even at his cruelest, he had not sunk to this level.

“I sense disdain in your pet…” The monster looked over to the Priest. Slithering over with glee, it moved in the water nearer to them. The monster peered down on the Priest's diminutive size, and smiled at the sight of him barely keeping himself out of the rancid water. Seeing his arms and body mostly sunk in the filth, with his many eyes darting around in fear. Turning to Gobolt the monster spoke with sickening glee. “I never thought I would see the day…” before turning back to the Priest. “A demon of a Christian God.”

Gobolt knew not to interrupt or question anything from such a malevolent evil. So, he stood silently. Obediently. His gaze drifted upward and noticed the ceiling of this cavern was littered with, what at first glance, looked like sleeping bats hanging upside down, as if they were in wait for the night to come, but there would have been no escape for them if they had any breath in their lungs. As Gobolt's eyes adjusted he noticed that though they were indeed bats, they were far from alive. Each had been mummified, bound with twine and cover the ceiling like grotesque decorations.

The priest shifted uncomfortably, distracting Gobolt's attention away from the death above him, and he was quickly met with the Priest's eyes full of fear. He wanted to speak, but Gobolt shook his head silently, signaling for his unwanted companion to keep silent – which he understood. He trusted Gobolt, despite the hatred he showed in return. He was trusted by the king, so was trusted by association.

The monster bent over the Priest and took a guttural sniff inward. The skin of its nose, barely holding itself together, with no bones to keep its form, flapped as its wearer inhaled deeply. Closing its eyes for a second, it then exhaled a putrid sigh. "Ah… I adore the smell of misguided faith…" Looking back down at the Priest, the monster's smile dropped to a snarl. "You think you can come into my dominion with your impotent God in your rotting heart?" it growled.

Gobolt looked on, trying to hide his shock at what the monster said. It could smell the Priest's belief? Demonic abilities should no longer surprise him, but this one did. He was sure the Priest was a liar and a wolf in sheep's clothing; waiting for the king to expose his weakness, before this demon would strike, and repay the kindness given with slaughter. *And now it seems he was not lying? He was wrong about this Priest?*

"Please... My one true God." Gobolt spoke aloud to the monster, stealing its attention away from his demon companion.

The monster turned with a sudden switch of emotion, from rage to glee. Hearing this adulation arousing every part of his putrid existence.

"I come before you with a request. A request that's beneath your limitless power," Gobolt continued stoking the flame of the monster's ego. "A request you would be benevolent to accept."

"Yesssss…" the monster hissed with excited pleasure, turning its body toward Gobolt. Allowing the Priest to breathe easier, if only for a few moments. "I am, as you say... powerful… Aren't I? Eeeeeeeeee!" Its own words fanning its delusions.

"I come before you to offer all I am to you, in exchange for your grace and safe passage." He spoke his rehearsed lines.

The monster now in front of Gobolt, with a smile much larger than before said, "You talk so well, for an animal so primitive." With a motion of its hand, it waved towards the table carrying the wooden bowls. "Then show me your offering," it said excitedly.

As Gobolt turned and walked toward the table, his legs heavy as they moved through the excremental corpse water. His thoughts still resided on the Priest and the fact he was not lying about his conversion.

"And where do you wish to go, hey?" the monster asked as he clambered besides Gobolt on his way to the table.

"Down to the lower realm… If my offerings please you enough and if my keys guide you," Gobolt said as he got to the table, opened his satchel and removed its contents; three wooden gourds and a leather-wrapped package. He placed them on the table.

As he took them out, the monster sniffed in again. Smelling the contents of these items, even though sealed. His cloudy eyes alight with exhilaration. "Oh, you spoil me. I can smell the life and death they carry…"

As Gobolt opened the first gourd, he glanced downwards at the prisoner of the cage in front of him. A thin, humanoid creature. Starved and beaten. Its face displaying two lines separating the skin – one horizontal and one vertical – with both crossing paths over the tip of its nose. Separating its features into 4 equal sections. The hair on its head had been torn out, leaving its scalp a mess of open wounds. It looked up at Gobolt wearily and pained. Mouthing the words "*help me*" as much as it could, without being seen.

The monster, noticing Gobolt looking at the prisoners, placed one of its grotesque and gnarled hands on the small of his back, sending a wave of nausea throughout his body. Something he hid the best he could. "These are my friends," it said as it stared at the caged prisoners, who now looked more afraid, with its attention turned to them. "They are my friends, for milking," it continued.

Changing the subject, it motioned to the crudely painted white wooden bowl on the table. "Please… Show me what you offer your , as you say, God."

Discarding the first gourd he opened, he then opened the second on the table, the one he wanted most. The one with the important offering. Picking it up, he poured its contents into the white bowl. The contents being Gobolt's seminal fluid. The only currency this monster ever accepted. The "milk" of which he spoke. And the amount poured out had taken many days to produce – for the larger the offering the happier the monster, the safer their journey. The gourd had been full and now the bowl was nearly overflowing. The monster was beyond ecstatic as it sniffed the air at the bowl. Each inhalation giving him a hit of pleasure.

His expression then turned to fury, but not at Gobolt or the Priest but at the prisoners around the room. "And you, you pitiful examples of life," it began to shout at them. "You give me soured dripping, when this beloved follower brings me *AMBROSIA*!!" Its hand punched the wall over the table, sending a rumble down the cells beneath. The prisoners that were conscious cowered.

From the middle of the room, the Priest saw something he would never have predicted. Out of sight of the monster – who was now closer to the bowl of semen and sniffing it boisterously – Gobolt had removed a dagger from the front of his tunic and thrown it under the table to the prisoner who previously asked for his help. That prisoner quickly grabbed the gifted blade and hid it under its leg. Trying to conceal its happiness, its eyes said thank you more than it could ever say in words. With a sense that something more was afoot, the Priest looked around the room and saw that at one end – next to a large pile of bones, which jutted a few feet out of the water – was a large stone counterbalance on a rope. This large weighted rope held the cells doors shut.

At the table, the monster steadied his orgasmic senses and looked toward Gobolt. His now favorite follower. "So… give me the keys and you shall get your payment. As you *more* than deserve my grace…"

On the table, Gobolt poured the next full gourd into a bowl, a gourd full of his urine. The next filled with his spittle. Both of these being full in their containers and now poured out, nearly spilling over the rim of each bowl. Next, he opened the leather wrapping and exposed a few days' worth of his own collected feces - the stench from it, almost making him gag for the past few days of travel. He was glad that the Priest, nor any of the army questioned the odor from the satchel, as it sickened him to think about what was about to happen. And how these "keys" were used by the monster.

Ushering Gobolt to the side, the monster looked at the table. "You will need to leave soon. As I am getting tired." It spoke low with a mock pained tone, its eyes staring at the bowl of semen. It was all it thought about. It wanted these guests gone so it could enjoy this white offering.

Grabbing the bowl of spittle, it lifted it to its mouth and lasciviously spoke. "The spit…" it uttered as it drank the entirety of the liquid in one. Thick ropes of mucus spilled out of the sides of its mouth and dripped down its face. Without a moment of hesitation, it continued. "The piss," it hissed with glee as it picked up the second bowl and drank it down while. With this second offering swallowed, it turned its attention to the third bowl. "…And the shit. The key I triumph over…" it rasped. As it did, it scooped up the contents of the bowl with his hand and forced it into its open and excited mouth.

Swallowing the excrement, the monster's eyes started to light up – not metaphorically, but literally. A low glow turning into a bright shine, illuminating more of the horrors of the room.

Turning its head, the monster spoke with a perverse relish. "I have consumed your past and can see your journey path clearly."

It turned its bright gaze to Gobolt, who winced at the brightness. "The path you seek is to the Blood Queen?" it asked.

"Yes," Gobolt replied.

Raising its hand, a bright light broke through the skin on its palm as it pointed towards the far empty wall of the room. As the light hit that wall, the mud and dirt which made up its structure started to break apart. Slowly at first, then in chunks. Until a large man-sized passageway appeared. What lay inside was shrouded within the darkness from where it led.

"You chase your own death with your quest..." the monster said as the light within it started to fade back. "You know this, correct?" it asked not wanting an answer, as it glanced back intently toward the remaining bowl of semen. Wishing to be alone with it. The dark passageway to another realm remained open at the far end of the lair. The Priest looking toward it.

"Now leave me..." the monster said as it motioned to the passageway. "I need to rest." Not turning to either of the men whilst it spoke.

Gobolt nodded to the priest, and they both started to walk through the horrific muck they waded in toward the entrance to the realm below.

The Priest scampered in a panic toward the entrance. From inside, a cool breeze traveled through and hit him in the face, the unfamiliar scent of this new place strong in the air. He looked to Gobolt who just motioned him inside. Nodding weakly, the Priest crawled gladly from the muck and into the entrance to the realm below. He pulled himself inside and onto the stone ground on the other side.

Gobolt turned before he stepped inside the passageway. The monster glanced towards him. "This bridge shall remain open until you return," it said as it turned back to the full bowl. "...but it shall be open for no longer than a day."

"We won't need it," Gobolt said as he smirked. The Priest looking at him from the other realm, wide-eyed and confused. The monster *also* turning to him. No one had ever wanted a one-way trip before. It looked to Gobolt as it noticed his cocky grin. A dawning realization of trickery flooded over the monster – but before any more could be said, Gobolt picked up his scimitar from his belt and swung to his right, slicing through the rope holding the cage doors shut.

"NOOOOO!" the monster shouted in anger, its eyes bursting with rageful light.

The creature that Gobolt gave the dagger to was now launching itself from its cell, toward this monster. The four sections of its face were now open – the human face folded back and unseen. A large circular leech's mouth that had hidden beneath these folds was now fully exposed and open, ready to attack.

As the monster screamed toward the passageway, this leech landed on its back and bit into its head with his circular mouth. With the dagger in its hand, it stabbed wildly at any flesh it could reach. The rest of the conscious prisoners hurried out of their now open cages and joined in battling the monster. Getting their revenge as they all attacked it en masse.

As Gobolt retreated into the passageway, he glanced back at this vicious scene and saw the leech deliver wound after wound to the monster's face, the blade piercing both its eyes and tearing its human mask clean off. The other escaped prisoners clamored over its body and ripped the skin and flesh from any part they could claw at. Thick black blood oozed out through its wounds and into the water below.

One of the final things that this monster ever saw was the table being knocked over, spilling the full bowl of semen into the water below, its gloopy contents disappearing beneath the muck. Very telling was that the monster was more distraught at losing the contents of that bowl, than the clear and present prospect of losing its own life at the hands of those he tortured.

Screaming a final and terrified yelp, the monster's body jerked back as this leech creature ripped out its throat with his circular mouth, forcing this monster's grotesque body to sink in to the cold darkness of its own death.

A fitting end for such a vile thing.

And with its death, the acolytes above ground started to fall apart. Their vague forms losing all of their cohesion as their gelatinous bodies fell into themselves. Piece by piece, turning into a thin liquid whilst letting out a small howl of despair. Then each sank into the dirt of the forest ground, their deaths as intrinsically linked to the monster as their lives were.

As their existences were expunged, the many thousands of deathly howls that rose from this forest echoed throughout the trees and carried out into the reality of the world. A howl that no one heard. Their deaths forever unknown.

Within this new realm that the gateway led to, the Priest stared upwards – all of his many eyes were wide and filled with a mix of deep terror and awe. Gobolt had not as yet looked at their surroundings whilst the gateway closed in on itself – he was feeling content about the monster's demise, looking at the wall where they had walked through. He didn't care that the passageway was now closed, essentially trapping them here. And for that moment he didn't care that he might never see his world again.

Turning to the Priest, he noticed the shocked expression on his face and for the first time smelled this realm. The stench of rot disappeared and had been replaced with the odors of this 20th century city; motor fumes, oil and pollution hit his senses like a freight train.

Following the Priest's scared gaze, Gobolt looked upwards, taking in the overwhelming sight of these towering monstrosities that stretched up around them. A wave of nausea and dizziness seeped over him as the skyscrapers loomed above.

They were stood in the middle of a street in this desolate city. Cars abandoned on the streets around them, no people in sight – just these two men and the city. Now in a place and time they were unfamiliar with – this hellish and oppressive place – the buildings of glass and stone which surrounded their vista raised like leviathans around them, stretching up to unfathomable heights and bearing down onto them on the street below. These man-made colossi were so unbelievable in size to them that the priest could not stare up anymore and quickly succumbed to his nausea, vomiting the contents of his stomach on the asphalt below. Unable to take in the sheer scope of where they were. Though a demon hailed from these below realms, he had never seen anything like this. His realm was a place of pure darkness – a wasteland of complete absence. A void filled with monsters – not this place of glass, stone and steel.

Neither of them could find the words. The Priest then looked to Gobolt as he wiped the vomitus from his mouth, hoping for a calming word. A plan. Anything to assure him that they were not stuck. That there was a greater design at play. But instead he noticed Gobolt's expression of encroaching dread as he looked up at something high between the buildings.

Something this Lycan did not think he would ever see again.

"Oh fuck, no..." Gobolt said, as his body ran cold with fear.

Despite the feeling of sickness washing over him in pulsating waves, the Priest looked up again, so he could see what filled Gobolt with so much terror. His many eyes widened as he realized what it was…

…Between the buildings…

…Higher up than anything else…

…The full moon hung proudly against the starry sky.

PART 3

Asphalt & Blood

"We are each our own devil,
and we make this world our hell

Oscar Wilde

A Break from Reality

"You, my sweet pretty one, are not real." These words rang through Rebecca's mind like a freight train. Ever since the woman in red spoke those words, Rebecca had felt her grip on reality starting to slip through her fingers. In less than 24 hours, she had seen her whole world, as well as the worlds of others fall to rot and ruin. She had witnessed her own life be systematically dissolved from her heights of fame and fortune, to abject nothingness. Her whole past had been made null and void, with her having no other choice than to be a passive observer on this downward spiral of a journey.

Her family was gone; the one she knew as her mother now stood in front of her, laughing at her daughter's mental anguish. Taunting her screams as she tore off her human face to reveal a monstrous face below.

Her only real friend was gone. As they tried to escape the madness, hand in hand, they were separated by a falling blade. Instead of turning to grab him, she ran as Ian was set upon by monsters.

She had abandoned the only person who truly loved her.

Her whole life was gone; She had seen this city turn on itself with extreme prejudice. She had seen the innocent slaughtered en masse by beings from the darkest passages of biblical verse.

And somehow, she was part of it all. Whether in the painting, or in their words, she had been a focal point of these beings and their attacks on the innocent. Maybe, she hoped, maybe *none* of it was real? Maybe she was – at that very moment in time – locked within the safety of a hospital, suffering paranoiac delusions of grandeur. Maybe she was trapped within her own demented imagination. Maybe her mother was waiting for her to wake up, sat lovingly at her bedside, stroking her daughter's hand, as she suffered these nightmares. But it all felt very real. Very present. Despite the extremity of madness this world seemed to be suffering. Despite it all seeming unbelievable and impossible – she knew and it destroyed her inside. She *knew* it was all happening.

The monster from underneath the skin of her mother now stood beside the woman in red, talking with a demonic dark smile. Hearing her mother's voice come out of this creature was stuff of nightmares enough – but seeing the skin that once coated her mother's face, now torn off and lying on the stone floor in front of her – the same face she kissed the forehead of nightly – was what finally broke her will. *This cannot be happening,* she repeatedly thought in her mind. Even though she knew it *was* happening.

Forced into a kneeling position on the floor, Rebecca's hands had been tied behind her back. She was flanked by two large demon guards, dressed in long red robes. Each held a spear in their claws, which they pressed against either side of her throat – stopping the possibility of any movement from her. Not unless she wanted to have her neck ventilated.

No matter her hopes and denials. She was a prisoner, trapped in this insanity.

Her eyes darting around in a daze, trying to make sense out of anything, she noticed Helen – still wearing her human skin – looking back at her with a seemingly apologetic smile.

In another version of the world, Helen had grown up with Rebecca from a very early age. Of course, Helen had never been a *real* child, only merely pretended to be one within adolescent skin. A hard job to act as an equal to someone else so young, being many decades older. In this previous version, it was also Helen that Rebecca had lost her virginity to – a step in the plan of that failed attempt, deemed at the time necessary by Leanne. Sanctioned by the Blood Queen herself. And something that Helen could never shake from her memory, even though different versions of the world had since come and gone. A silent longing that that this version of Rebecca could never remember. Helen fell in love in that version. As much as a demon could. Her being in love with something not entirely real, and merely an abstract avatar, would never change her actions. Because she placed her faith way above any of these strange emotions, so would never even consider deviating from the plan. Yet, that did not change the pangs of nostalgic emotion that she seemed to feel. Seeing Rebecca captured and on her knees made her – at least for a moment – wonder if she could ask to be her lover again upon the next reset. To be her first love once more. It had never happened in any other version of reality, but that one, many cycles ago – and it was the first time she felt any genuine joy in being here. So if it *could* happen again – she wanted that.

Rebecca meanwhile looked at her with sorrow, knowing that she was not human, that no one here was one was. Closing her eyes for a brief moment, she wished this scene away. She wished that she was back on the stage, flirting with her co-stars, thinking her life was *finally* back on an even keel.

As Elizabeth spoke to Leanne, Rebecca could not concentrate on the words. She was too trapped in her confused fog of torment.

"That was a brave attempt. You should not count it as any sort of failure." Elizabeth spoke kindly. "You created a rich and varied existence. One we could improve on."

Elizabeth walked over to where Rebecca was being held, watched her as she danced on the precipice of tears. Fighting them back, but they kept pushing nearer and nearer.

"Your anguish looks delicious." She said maliciously, in an accented and melodic tone.

"Why are you doing this?" Rebecca asked weakly, her voice breaking with emotion as she tried to keep her composure.

Elizabeth smiled at her prisoner as she crouched down directly in front of her. With one hand, she stroked Rebecca's face in a caring manner.

"Why?" she asked. "Why is an explanation too large for you to fathom, my sweet? You were not created to understand. Just to die to feed the one who is to come. To offer your corruption."

"Why me?" came her reply. She was surprised she had kept her tears back so far. They were hiding on the edge of her current emotions, but she still managed to push them far away.

"Another why? Well…" Elizabeth said as she pointed outside, "did you see the altar as you came in?"

Rebecca did not answer. She didn't know what she remembered at the moment. Everything was a haze. She thought she saw her mother's assistant carry something to somewhere. But couldn't say what it really was, or where it really was.

"Well, on that is the real you. The you that came from me – my daughter." Her voice was now almost sincere in its tone. "And you… as I said. You are not real. So, your sadness is nothing more than simply forged upset for a life that never existed."

She watched as Rebecca tried to make sense of the words, but it was futile to even try. It was just more information on top of a wealth of other incoherent information. Without the knowledge theses demons possessed of this world, it was almost impossible for her to grasp anything in the state she was in.

"Please don't kill me..." were the only words she could muster up – and it really was the *only* thing she honestly cared about at that moment. All that she had left was her own life. The life she *felt* was real, even if this woman in front of her, deemed it otherwise.

Elizabeth glanced back to Leanne with a smirk, then to Rebecca. "Kill what? I have said, you are not real. Outside, *that* is my real daughter. You... you are just an avatar in this failing reality. One made to blacken her soul. You are ingredients we have conjured in this world."

Rebecca stared blankly at her captor. It was no use her trying to understand this anymore. There was not going to be any explanation good enough for her. Something outside was the real her? This was the mother of it? She is her mother too? But she is not real. And what about Leanne? What about the monsters? What about the painting and the old lady? What about her whole life? The questions were insurmountable. But what else could she do? What else could she believe? Her mind flicked between resigning herself to her inevitable death, all within this insanity, to trying to convince herself that it was not *her* that was not real, but none of *this* was. That idea that she couldn't be in her right mind was the only rational explanation.

Elizabeth smiled at her prisoner and spoke quietly. "Both you and my real daughter are beautiful. Though, you both take after your father too much."

Rebecca looked into her eyes. *My father*? she thought? *What father?*

"You have his eyes…" she said, before biting her lip, as she seductively remembered before continuing, "the eyes I only just ate a few hours ago."

Rebecca could not answer. There was nothing she could say.

Elizabeth turned and motioned to the flayed man, whose skin stretched in the frame, high above the throne. Her father. Ferenc. "…And there he is," she exclaimed proudly. "Your mighty father. The great Count Ferenc. Scourge of the Ottoman empire and now flag to the Blood Queen!"

Still unknowing of his own condition, Ferenc had heard all that was said in this room, but by now his memories had all but faded. He could no longer place the voices to people he knew. He could no longer remember one person from his life. The one whom he had known as his wife was now just a stranger's voice. If he could talk, if someone was able to ask him for his full name, he would not be able to give it in reply. He was no longer Ferenc in his mind. He was just there and without a memory of the horror and torment.

He was happy being there.

His memory was no longer a part of his world.

He just... was existing.

Looking toward the guards, Elizabeth nodded a silent command.

Obeying her order, they removed their spears from Rebecca's throat in one synchronized action.

Turning her head to look around, without fear of skewering her jugular, Rebecca then stared at Elizabeth in a panic. "What's happening?" she asked.

Elizabeth's happy expression had now dropped at hearing this. She looked toward her prisoner with annoyance. Shaking her head as she walked back to where Leanne was stood. "Questions, questions…. Is that all this puppet is good for?" she sighed.

"Please? Please can someone… please tell me what's going in… It's all a joke isn't it?"

The flood gates eventually broke and for the first time in decades, tears began to stream down Rebecca's face. "Mum… please…" she continued, as the guards then took her arms and yanked her to her feet with force.

Elizabeth looked to Leanne. "I *think* she means you?"

As Helen watched, the guards led Rebecca out of the room, kicking and screaming to no avail, being taken to where she was to die. Here, at seeing Rebecca crying whilst being dragged away, Helen felt something *more* than nostalgia. Something deep inside. Was it guilt? No. It couldn't have been.

"Her confusion is wonderful despite being annoying," Elizabeth said as she walked up the small steps to her throne, then sat down.

"What do you command?" Leanne asked.

"Perform the ceremony," came the order. "Let us end this once and for all."

Leanne motioned for Helen to join her. As they walked together, she quickly noticed Helen's expression, which showed some confusion.

"Are you okay?" Leanne asked.

Helen smiled politely. "Yes ma'am. Just wishing to be part of the next one, that's all."

"Aren't we all... Now take that off." She motioned to her assistant's face. "You don't need it anymore... I've almost forgotten what you really look like."

Helen nodded. "I will do as soon as I get a moment, ma'am." She would, of course, follow this order to the letter, but she would still miss her skin. She would prefer to wear it forever. She had grown quite accustomed to it. If she was to be honest with herself, she would say she preferred to be human than a demon.

Outside the building, next to the altar atop the pile of bodies, a few feet from the last step of the bone staircase leading downward, Rebecca was now tied to a large stake.

Looking back on her rescue attempt, if she could have seen through the panic and fear she was now consumed by, she would have noticed how easy it was to "save" her mother. Through the throng of thousands of beasts which flooded the square, she managed to make her way past them all – all of them turning away at the right moment so as not to see her. None of them having any suspicions. Of course, it was all a trap. But a trap she could not fathom a reason for. What they had told her had been vague at best and confusing at worst. It was what she would expect from the mad running the madhouse.

At the top of the steps, behind where Rebecca was held, Helen now stood with Leanne.

"May I just have a minute with her?" Helen asked hopefully.

Reluctantly Leanne replied, "I will give you a few moments as a reward, but only a few."

Smiling in thanks, Helen turned and walked toward Rebecca – though she did not notice her approaching from behind. She was too terrified as she stared out to the now larger, more raucous crowd which lay ahead of her. All these monsters staring back at her in awe. Thousands of them filled the square – each of them wore some or no human skin and their glowing eyes stared at her with intent adoration.

"Hello you," Helen said kindly as she walked in front of Rebecca, whose attention now quickly switched toward her. Her terrified expression remaining on her face, knowing that a demon resided behind the human mask.

"Please… Help me…" Rebecca said weakly.

"Oh, I can't do that. I just wanted to say hello. I really loved our times together. Not that you would remember. It was many realities ago. Now you just remember me as your mom's assistant."

Rebecca looked upward for a moment, the tears filling her eyes again.

"You shouldn't be sad." Helen said. "You are going to help make our God."

Rebecca then blinked as the droplets dripped from her eyes, and she looked back down. She was exhausted by this madness. "Just tell me... please..."

"Tell you what?" Helen asked happily. She may have felt emotions for Rebecca, but she *was* a demon at the end of the day, and didn't care about the torment this captor was now evidently experiencing.

"What am I?" Rebecca sobbed. "Am I real?

"Oh Right. Yes... No. I mean you're not. The queen is... well, not the most verbose of people. I can break it down very simply for you, okay?" Helen beamed. "After all... You did make a demon cum. Which... No-one here would believe if I told them..."

Cum? thought Rebecca. *What is this thing talking about?*

"So..." Helen pointed to the altar on the other side of them. Directly at the large fleshy, pulsating cocoon on top of it. "That is Hanna. That is the real you. Got that so far?" Rebecca didn't answer. She just looked at the grotesque mount of flesh laying on the altar – beating with a dull heartbeat. "And you..." She pointed to Rebecca. "You are like an empty plate... And this..." she motioned all around her. "This is the oven making the food."

Rebecca was keeping up with her, but it was still making no sense.

"And this oven... Each situation. Each event within it... which we engineer for you. It created an emotion. A psychological marker... All geared for you to experience and ingest mentally. So you... the plate... would soon take what you experience and distill the ingested... stuff and it would be essentially food." The joy she had whilst explaining this was evident. "And the real you over there – she needs to feed. She needs to be prepared for what is to come. She needs to have her soul blackened. To do that, we make plates like you. Mirrors of her, but not her. And prepare them with the right food on top. Then she eats them. Ingesting the experiences. So, when the time is ready... she can rise to lead us all... You get that? At least the metaphoric intent?"

Rebecca tried to wrap her mind around this insane moment. Until all that could flash within her mind was the old lady. The one who spoke to her at the theater with the painting, in what seemed like a lifetime ago. "She wasn't talking about me..." she muttered.

Helen asked, "Who wasn't?"

Rebecca looked into her eyes. She had no idea if she would understand it, but she continued. More to herself than to Helen. "The painting... It was her... Not me..." She looked at the cocoon on the altar.

Helen smiled more. "Yes! Phyllis! Exactly!"

Rebecca's exhaustion was now insurmountable, her mind only barely keeping a grip on consciousness, and her body only held upright due to the ropes which now secured her to the stake.

"She was speaking to Hanna through YOU! So when Hanna feeds on you… she will see that moment…"

Leanne coughed from behind. Motioning for Helen to hurry up, to which Helen smiled and nodded back.

"Well, just wanted to say goodbye. I have to go now. It's about to start. I hope we get to be close again one day," Helen said, her smile not fading once during their conversation.

"Please…" The emotions rose up in Rebecca like a returning tidal wave, brimming over again the edge once more as she repeated yet again. "Please help…"

Helen then leaned into Rebecca before she walked away, back to Leanne. "You should be happy. You're part of a beautiful plan. A *beautiful* plan. And if there is a next time with a new you. A new plate... Whatever name they give you… I shall be there too." She grinned lasciviously. "And you can make me cum like you did before."

Leanne watched as her assistant walked back to her side. "That was quite an explanation. Plates? Is that the best you could come up with?"

Helen shrugged with her smile still in place, not caring what Leanne had overheard.

Saskia sat at the base of the throne staring up at Ferenc's skin, still displayed for all to see. Her small thin legs crossed, her elbows resting on her knees and her hands propping up her chin. She had a smile plastered wide upon her face. A smile so pure and genuine, that on anyone else, you would presume them to be incapable of evil. But on her, made her much more terrifying and sinister.

From the corner of her eye, Avershaw looked on and wept uncontrollably.

"Do you like what we did to him?" Saskia asked her prisoner with glee. "He looks much happier now, doesn't he?"

She laughed as he wept harder.

"Are you enjoying your pet?" Elizabeth, still sat on the throne above her, asked.

Saskia, looking at Ferenc and not at her Queen, answered. "Yes… He keeps crying. It's wonderful."

Elizabeth smiled. If her real daughter could be birthed half the person Saskia was, she would be happy. In a perfect world, she would give Saskia the mantle of savior – the mantle now held by her flesh and blood daughter. But no matter how much magic she knew, no matter the power that her and her kind had, they could not change what was to be. She knew though, that no matter what Hanna became, she would always prefer Saskia. Her little beautiful and cruel sister. Cut from the same cloth and made by the same evil.

In the crowd, Davis stood in his full demonic form. He had waited a long time for this moment. Unlike Leanne, he had hated this version of reality from its very inception. In its previous incarnations, he had been given a much larger role in the *great plan,* but he was now relegated to a mere bit part; Once he stood tall and proud as an infernal guard to the Queen, but now he stood in the square amongst the myriad of other lower beings.

It was in this position he found the pure torment that was living in the banality of humanity. The sheer drudgery of the working class, the class he was ordered to become part of. To live the hellish boredom, ready to be in action when requested. A perpetual feeling of being ostracized by being made to sit in the wings, only fulfilling any purpose when the chosen one life's decisions dictated.

Playing out nearly four decades of the savior's life – even over a compacted timeline – felt like an eternity to him. Having to live alongside the drones was his biggest misery, and one he could only cope with by using any spare time he could find to live another life parallel to his own. A life he created in secret where he would hunt and take his frustration and anger out upon the kind that caused him agony – the drones that existed to fill the gaps. Without purpose and there only as decoration, existing on their own and out of the realm's purpose – ones who would never need to interact with the chosen. This was his target for their fury. The drones who resembled the ones that he had no other choice but to interact with, or worse still, rut with – the ones he had to hide in the guise of a being a father or husband to – he tortured and killed. Hunting the humans he hated *so* much.

Of course, these crimes caused the perpetrator to be hunted by the police – this was a fully functioning world after all, not a playground. This murderer was classed as a serial killer, together with a profile of being a tall black man in his 30s and someone who was highly educated, most probably wealthy. So, being in the skin of a short white man in his 60s, with no education who lived on the breadline, meant his crimes were never going to catch up with him. Not that it mattered as this was a fake world.

In his mind, this was all necessary. If he did *not* do this, he would not be able to fulfill his role. He and his family would, on occasion, have to be in the same area as the chosen. Eat near her in a restaurant. Be at a certain place when she walked by. Anything that was commanded. Naturally, as he was a faithful follower, he would do what was asked – as every player on this stage would. But he had to have his outlet, his way to survive the banal existence he saw himself in, until it was all over. Until this world was done and he could petition for a better role to play next time – and a better skin suit – if there were to be a next time.

Now in his true demonic form, he looked up to where Rebecca was tied. He felt a wash of relief come over him. Finally, he was free of the shackles he imagined himself in. As he stood amongst his brothers and sisters, he smiled as this world was finally at its end. She was captured. It was almost feeding time... He could feel this world breathing its last, and in the distance, he could hear the darkness closing in, as a deep, booming and echoing roar was heard. A roar which filled the crowd with glee. They all erupted into an uncontrolled cheer.

The end *was* indeed nigh. There was no turning back the clock now. This reality was over.

As another roar boomed through the world, Elizabeth looked out of one of the windows from her seat on the throne. Saskia broke her staring at Ferenc to look to Elizabeth with glee, excited at the sound of the final beast getting nearer

"And so it ends," Elizabeth said with a smile. "You may return now. I release you, Sister."

Saskia asked as she stood up, "Are you sure?"

"You are not required to stay for that arrival, but more importantly, you have not been home since she, our mother, awoke." Elizabeth paused for a moment. "And I know you have been waiting for me for me to release you"

Letting out a childish giggle, not saying another word to the Blood Queen, Saskia turned and skipped out of the room. Happily on her way home.

"Forever a child," Elizabeth mused happily to herself as she watched Saskia leave. Her bare feet padded on the stone floor, echoing into the air as she went.

Ferenc heard all that was said, but had trouble placing any of it in a context that he could understand. He was too concerned with trying to recollect his own name. He swore he had one. He must have had one.

And once he did.

He just wanted to remember that.

Just that *one* thing.

But it was lost to him.

In the crowd, Davis felt the wave of celebration that spread throughout his brethren. They all raised their arms toward Rebecca. They all shouted in unison '*Mater Tenebris.. Mater Tenebris. Mater Tenebris.*' All stood, impatiently awaiting the feeding to come.

At the stake, Rebecca had succumbed to the realm of unconsciousness. Unable to carry on trying to fathom her predicament, her mind gave way and gifted her with a kind respite. It then gave her the memory of better times, far away from where she was now. Dreams of love, life and happiness. The last dreams she would have in this world.

In a small dark room, Saskia pointed to a large metal cage.

"Get me one," Saskia commanded the guards. They were in a room not in the world she had just been in. But one in a place of infinite darkness, the place where the roars came from. The place where the tentacles came from, which took Ian away from this life. The demon's realm. The *real* demon's realm behind the curtain of this fake world.

Inside this cage were a dozen varying fantastical beasts. Scaly, furry, bald, small, big. The only thing they shared was the fear they felt, that consumed them. They knew they would never escape with their lives, but had not quite accepted their fates – they feared the end as much as any other being would. They were not, though, prisoners of a crime. They were not serving out a sentence. They were instead, tools that the witches used.

"I need…" Saskia said, as she looked at all of the prisoners cowering in their confinement. Pointing to a fish-looking creature at the back of the cage, she spoke with glee. "That aquatic one."

One of the guards grabbed a chain then opened the large metal door to the cage. The prisoners backed away as he lumbered toward them with a terrified expression. The fish creature tried its best to hide behind some of the others, but fearing for their own lives – even if they were to never escape – they pushed this poor creature out toward the guard, keeping their eventual fate as far from them as possible.

As the guard wrapped the chain around the fish creature's neck, he yanked it, choking the poor thing with the chain acting like a leash, keeping it in place.

Dragging it out of the cage, its webbed feet clambered for purchase but got no traction on the hard, cold floor. It wrenched and grasped wildly at the guard, trying everything its weak small body could do to escape from this goliath and more importantly, the fate this witch had for him.

"Hold him still," the young witch commanded, as the guard grabbed the fish creature by both arms and held it in front of him, off the floor, its front facing her.

Without a second's pause, she launched toward the creature. With her hands outward, she landed on the prisoner's chest, clawing at it ferociously, ripping into his moist and scaly skin with ease. Digging deeper into him at a terrifying rate. The creature screamed as much as he could, struggling with all the strength he could muster, but it was all for naught – the young witch had now clawed deep into its chest, killing it within seconds, then started to crawl her way inside the large open gash she had made. Instead of ripping her way out from the back of this now-deceased body and onto the guard – she was going elsewhere.

From inside her eyes, Avershaw sat in hell, having witnessed Saskia climb into this poor doomed animal, then pull her way inside it. Deep into the carrion, where a shadow formed; a shadow which she crawled toward with glee.

The guard dropped the fish creature's carcass to the floor, its body now devoid of the life it once had. Then he dragged it with the chain to the corner of the room, and placed its corpse on top of a pile of a dozen other dead rotting creatures. All with their chests burrowed into. All having suffered the same violent end.

The remaining imprisoned creatures howled in fear, screamed and cried at what they knew their demise was set to be.

Avershaw watched as his captor swam through the depths of the shadows. The surrounding water was impenetrable like blindness. He could feel them swimming upward, but could not sense a depth of the water.

After a few moments, they broke through the surface of this thick dark liquid. Saskia gasped for air as her lungs filled with oxygen. In this black-watered lake, a lake of incredible size, one that would seem like a sea to those not knowing that there was indeed land either size, or that it existed way below the natural sea level for this realm. This realm where the creature she travelled through had originated from and lived in this very lake amongst others of its kind.

Looking around the distance, through the failing sunlight, her eyes met with a small island in the middle of the dark water. An island which measured only a hundred or so feet in diameter. Sitting on top of this small area of land sat a small wooden shack. The light from within it shone outwards, brightening up the twilight of the lake, as smoke billowed from its chimney. Saskia smiled – her mother was awake! Finally! She couldn't wait to tell her of what she had missed over the past decade: the imprisonment and death she had suffered at the hands of the wolf. Her subsequent resurrection from the Blood Queen. The world below and the savior to come… So much to impart to the one who had brought her true self into this world – the one who turned such a small, innocent child into the vile creature of the dark, she now was.

As she swam, she could sense the fear of the other creatures in this lake, as they hid in the depths, out of sight from her pure evil – as they always did and had to, if they chose to live. She would, as she had in the past, stop and kill some of them for sport, but she was too excited to see her mother than to play with a lesser being's fate.

The Black Witch had been part of this realm for a millennium, as had the creatures of the lake who dwelled alongside her in a co-existing peace. She emerged only a handful of times every century to venture up to the reality above, returning a few years later bloated and full like a gargantuan slug. Full of the flesh she had feasted on. Disappearing into the water, she would sludge her way along the bottom of the lake's basin, up to a cave entrance at the bottom of the darkest parts in the middle of this watery expanse. A part of the lake where no creature dared go near. Slowly pulling her engorged body inside, she would follow the tunnel's wide passages upward until she came out in a cavern. A cavern that was beneath her shack. Once there, she would hibernate as she digested her victims, for many years until their sustenance had run its course in her belly - When she would awaken from her hibernation, she would venture up to her shack and live in peace until she craved the next meal. But it was in the years between the hibernations ending and the future hunt above, that she had become lonely. Isolated, she craved a companion. And it was when she could bear the loneliness no more, that she found Saskia – the one she would call her daughter. She had created many with her mark, including the Black Queen, who was almost if not more powerful than she was now, but wanted one that was hers to guide and raise. She wanted a daughter. So she found Saskia, and ate away all of her goodness.

The Wolf in the Falling City

"What is this?" Gobolt asked, awash with confusion as he stared up at the full moon hanging over this desolate city, the first full moon he had seen with human eyes since being born. Each time before had brought out the beast in him, taking his memory of that night away. Now, staring up as a man to this bright rock in the sky, he couldn't help but smile.

"I guess it is different here?" the Priest posited, as he slithered a few steps further down the asphalt, looking up and down the streets which lay around them. He then turned and looked up at Gobolt. "Why did you kill that beast?" he asked as Gobolt glanced back down at him. "He was our way home."

"He deserved it and I don't regret doing it for one second. Besides, you got out of here without *that* thing to help you."

"But..." the Priest began to say, before Gobolt interrupted him

"No buts... *If* we survive. You take us the way *you* left... But we will in all likelihood not survive. Well, you may. Not putting much on my odds."

"I don't even know if there is any passage from here," the Priest said truthfully, knowing only his own realm. But this one? He had no idea what was available here.

"Then if no exit and by some miracle we make it to *her* alive… We force that cunt to take us back." Gobolt smirked. "She seems to slither through these places with ease."

"Force… a witch?"

Gobolt laughed at the Priest's doubt. "I never said it'd be easy!" he retorted.

Gobolt's blind faith that he could escape from this world, without ever being here before, was a worry to the Priest. But he soon came to realize what was happening. What his real intent was in coming here.

"What?" Gobolt asked, noticing the worried look on the Priest's demon face.

"You keep saying 'if you survive'… You're not actually planning to go home, are you?" This question made Gobolt's smirk drop.

"Whatever happens. You're safe. You're a demon, you'll be okay here. Don't worry about me. I'll get what's coming to me, I'll find Ferenc and I'll take some of these bastards with me. My life is the least of my concerns."

Gobolt's intention was simple. He would save Ferenc if he could. He would kill the two witches, if he could – but he could not have left a gateway to his world open. He could not trust any link to this realm to not be of a danger to his own world , and he could not bear the thought of that evil surviving with his seed. To birth more of the acolytes using his semen. Not again. So, if it meant he was stuck here. So be it. If it meant he could perhaps get revenge on a witch. So be it. If it meant he would die trying. So be it.

"I think we better move. I can hear something coming," the Priest said as he looked around. "Can you feel that?"

Gobolt looked down the streets at either side of them. Both looked the same as each other – both dark and both foreboding. But something... There was... Something... "Yeah… I can, I think," he said as he heard a vague rumble in the distance. "What is it?"

No sooner than he had finished speaking, that rumble quickly became louder and louder with each passing second. From far down the end of the street emanated this building cacophony.

This noise was coming from a large horde who were marching their way far down the street – toward them. Without a pause, and before they could be spotted, Gobolt raced over to the Priest, scooped up his small demon form with one hand, then bolted into an open doorway he noticed on the side of a building.

He was not comfortable running into this stone and glass monstrosity, but it was the only place he could see for him and the Priest to hide. He was also not happy picking up the demon with his hands, but he couldn't afford any delay.

Inside, trying to acclimatize his eyes to this dark, Gobolt quickly glanced around for any way for them to run, as they were still visible from the street through the glass, but the darkness had fallen thick in this place – this place away from any moonlight – from any glimpse of illumination. The priest, though, did not have the same problem. He was born in the dark and was one *with* the dark. In this shroud of night, his eyes glowed a dull hue from deep inside, allowing him perfect sight in this shadow. He scanned the area to see anything that Gobolt could not. Spotting an open doorway at the other end of the room and with Gobolt still carrying his diminutive form in his arms, he pointed. "There! There's a way through there."

"I can't see a fuck's cunt in here. Where d'you mean?!" He spoke quickly, knowing they had to act fast. The marching from outside getting nearer and nearer. The noise getting louder and louder.

Without much of a chance to consider his actions, the Priest started to fold himself into his own chest. Gobolt, now unable to carry this shifting being, dropped him to the floor. The Priest's human legs folded out the back of its demon body and landed on them as he hit the floor. Standing up out of his monstrous other half, the Priest now stood as a human, naked and cold.

"I'm sorry, I'm not fast enough in that form," the Priest explained, as he then reached into his small sack strapped around his human chest and pulled out a thin Priest's tunic.

"Fine," Gobolt spat out as quick as he could. "Hurry!"

Gobolt could hear the rustling. "What are you doing?" he asked frantically as the darkness was throwing him into a bit of a panic. Never one who felt comfortable in the dark, he had always slept with a light source nearby. Maybe due to his hidden Lycan nature and his innate fear of becoming that beast? Nevertheless, he tried his best to cover this unfounded discomfort with his brevity.

Now dressed in a thin black tunic, the Priest grabbed Gobolt's arm and pulled at it. "Come on," he commanded, as he guided Gobolt across the pitch-black foyer deeper into this building and into an open doorway on the far side of them.

"There are stairs here. Be careful," he said as they started to ascend the large stone steps in this next room.

From the outside, a loud booming roar could be heard in the distance – stopping the Priest, in mid-ascent, dead in his tracks. He could hear this was not from the marching crowd. "This can't be…" he said in a quiet panic as he heard the din. THAT roar? The roar he had heard in these realms before, was *here*?

"What… was... that?" Gobolt questioned.

The horde outside were still firmly on their march, striding down the street, heading to Parliament Square to witness the end. Their time was up and they were now allowed to be their true selves. Their demon selves. Blood soaked and with their human skins in varying states of completeness, they walked in unison and with purpose.

One of these demons who marched at the front slowed down as he smelled something on the breeze. Something he couldn't quite place. Something not of this world, or from his realm. Something unnatural even in a place as fabricated as this city. Quickly discarding this notion, the march soon continued – there were now bigger things than an errant aroma to concern themselves about.

Staring down from the first-floor window of this office tower, Gobolt and the Priest hid in the shadows, watching as they saw the long procession walk through the moonlight and onto their destination. Hundreds of them with a singular purpose.

"Where are they going?" Gobolt asked in a hush.

"I have no idea," the Priest answered. "But it can't be good."

"Could you ask them?" he posited, knowing full well it was not a good idea, but an idea none the less. "Just go down, speak to one? Demon to demon?"

"I'm not a demon like they are."

"Surely a demon's just like any other demon at the end of the day," Gobolt replied as he stared at the demonic procession below.

"You know that's not true. There are many of us. But these… They don't even have their own skin. That's all stolen from the innocent." He turned to Gobolt. "I'm not from this darkness and I'm as much like them as you are. If they knew what I was, they would probably turn on me." Gobolt shrugged as the Priest continued "And that roar?"

"You know it?"

"A leviathan… Consumer of worlds…" the Priest said blankly as Gobolt's expression grew to surprise.

"Leviathan?" he asked.

"Yes. They live in the darkness. Waiting to be called to end places like this… We are in a torment creation."

"What the fuck are you saying?" Gobolt asked. Not sure what to make of what the Priest was telling him at that moment. He had been proved wrong about this demon once before, but still could not just trust his words as truth yet. Just because he had faith in his world's God didn't absolve him from the blood on his hands.

"This place," the Priest began. "These streets. These goliath structures. They exist as a torture. For prisoners... enemies... Anyone who is chosen. Think of them like a human-sized doll house – dressed to look like a real house. Invented for the sake of one person" Gobolt tried hard to understand, but could only wonder whether Ferenc was still here and why his dead-wife was leading her charge here. "And for all intents and purposes…" the Priest continued, "this *is* a real house. But it's constructed *only* to look like one, and not to actually *be* one. And like a doll's house, it's destined to be broken and thrown away. And that is where that Leviathan comes in. I had no idea what this place was till I heard it. Then it made sense. They only exist to eat the fakery created by the demonic."

"So, this Leviathan you speak of… it's about to eat this place… Right? You know when?"

"It can't be long." The Priest pointed to the marching demons below. "But they… *they* won't be walking towards it… They'll be walking away from it."

"So… Guess we follow them, then…" Gobolt said as he got ready to leave. "Lead the way."

"There's no guarantee that the Blood Witch is even still here," the Priest said as he grabbed Gobolt's arm, ready to lead him through the dark building again. "What do we do if she isn't?"

"Simple. We die," Gobolt said with a smile, reiterating his point that this was most likely a suicide mission.

Another roar boomed throughout the sky, from the horizon. And with that goliath monster's wail, the whole world was then cast into complete darkness. The moon without notice disappeared from view. Turned off like a light. The stars blinked out with it. Everything in his view was now hidden from Gobolt's eyes as the minimal light he had relied on now disappeared from the streets.

"You've got to be fucking kidding me." He uttered.

Deep in the heart of the realm of the Black Witch, within her shack on the small island, the perpetual twilight of the land seeped through the small cracked windows inside – where Saskia sat on a wooden stool in front of a small fire place, in which crackled a few burning logs. Her face cast downwards, this moment was far from the happy reunion she had hoped for, the reunion with her creator.

"You knew he was *mine*... yet, you *hunted* him?" a grotesque and sickly voice spoke from the shadows at the far side of the room. "And, you expect me to feel proud of you for it?"

"I wanted to bring him to you as a gift..." she said weakly. Too weak for the figure in the shadows to hear.

"Speak up, child!" the voice commanded with a sternly reserved violent rage.

"I'm sorry!" Saskia looked up with blood tears welling in her eyes.

"My mark rests deep in him. I did not mean for it, but it happened." The figure moved forwards from the shadow, revealing herself in the firelight as being dressed in a heavy long black veil. One which covered her gnarled ancient face. She raised her gnarled skeletal fingers and lifted the veil – her face was as sunken as a corpse, her skin as thin as paper yet as gray as fog. "And in return he gave me these," she said motioning to her mouth, around which sat old scars. Scars the boy's blood had seared into her flesh four decades before.

Saskia looked up at the Black Witch, at her ancient and terrifying visage. A red tear fell down her child's cheek. "Why can't I get my vengeance for what he did to me?"

The witch smiled. "Whether willing or unwilling, whether you or he, you are *both* my children!"

Saskia pleaded. "He can hurt me, but I cannot hurt him?"

The Black Witch moved slowly forward in front of Saskia and knelt down, so her face was parallel to her child's. "Little one…" her voice was now soft and cracking with its age. "You would not have been killed by his hand had you not hunted him. He is a wolf and a trapped wolf will bite. When he found you, you should have left well alone. And when you died… I could feel it even in my slumber. I felt the fires burn me as it burned you. I wailed in agony as I slept. And I felt the warmth in my soul as your sister gave you the gift of life back."

"And if he comes for me again?" Saskia asked as she stared deep into the milky eyes of her terrifying mother.

"Then, if he comes for you, there will be bloodshed," came her reply. "And I will be holding the knife making the incisions."

Through a back alley, the Priest lead Gobolt through the unnatural darkness. Unable to see a thing, Gobolt now relied on the guidance of his companion. He hated putting his trust in someone else, especially a demon, but there was no other choice.

As they ran down the dirt-filled alleyway, a few streets away from Parliament Square, a light started to break through the darkness, allowing

Gobolt to see some of his surroundings – even to a limited degree. The Square was now the center of this falling world and was the only place where any light still existed. Large fires reached up at the edges of the square, casting dancing orange glows across the massed congregation of demons, who all faced the bone altar, with many more demons filing into the area from the darkness, waiting for the world to end.

The Priest guided Gobolt down behind an abandoned car as they got to the mouth of the alley. Now being able to see from the glow of the lights nearby, he looked at the metal beast in front of him for a moment in a state of wonder, before forcing himself back to the situation at hand and looked up over it. At the far end of the street they could see a few stragglers walking toward the square. These marching demons were slower than the others, and were far behind the main throng of the congregation already in wait.

"Do we follow them?" the Priest enquired, pointing to the stragglers.

Reaching for his belt, Gobolt pulled out his scimitar and split it into its two sections. He handed one of these thin deadly blades to the Priest and smiled. "You'll need this."

"I… I can't kill anyone." the Priest said mournfully as he looked at the rune etched weapon now resting in his hands.

"Then just injure them…" Gobolt said, and smiled. "Go for the legs, they don't die, but they'll stop trying to take yours."

The Priest then looked up at the street and soon noticed that far behind the last few walking demons, leading out away from the square and into the darkness, Saskia was skipping along merrily, oblivious to their presence.

"Look!" the Priest whispered, motioning to where the young witch passed by.

Gobolt caught a glimpse of her before she disappeared out of sight and, without a second of hesitation, he got up from behind the abandoned car and started to walk in her direction, keeping close to the walls, out of sight of the demons.

"Come on," were his parting words to the Priest – who now looked on in shock as Gobolt ran directly towards the enemy, with not even an ounce of fear. Since getting here, the Priest had got used to being relied on to lead the march, and did so willingly. He felt like he was earning the respect of this man who had never shown him one ounce of it before. Being the only one to see in the darkness meant he was needed. But now, with the little light from the square, Gobolt ran along the pavement, his etched curved weapon tightly in his hand – he ran in a half-crouch toward the street corner where his enemy had just skipped by.

Her sister, the Blood Queen, had released her to go home. She had been indebted to her since being cured of the death that the wolf-man cast upon her. But now, she was free. Having paid back her debt with subservience. Released to go home.

Further down the street, as Gobolt stared on, she continued skipping happily. Where she was heading did not lead to another street, or a building, but was instead a thick blanket of dark covering everything. Seemingly splitting the buildings in two as it hung down and with each second brought an end to this world, nearer and nearer to the center.

Without even slowing down, she skipped at a joyous pace into this absence of light at the end of the street.

Had she not been so wrapped up within her happiness, had she not been so distracted dwelling in the joyous expectation of seeing her mother – she would have caught the scent of the wolf and the Priest as they followed closely behind her. She would have sensed them watching as she got to the room of passages. She would have felt their hidden stares as she took her chosen aquatic being, clawed deep into its chest and dragged herself into its very being and exited this realm for her own.

But she did not sense a single thing.

Deep in the nothingness of the dark, Gobolt and the Priest peered through a glassless window within a stone building. Flaming torches cast their fiery illumination from two large golden bowls, placed on six-foot plinths at either side of the room. This room where the cage of prisoners sat, where Saskia had just disappeared through the fish creatures ripped open body.

The two large demon guards stood by, also oblivious to the two men looking in at them. One of them had just thrown the dead creature onto the top of the pile of rotting corpses, and walked back to his position next to the door of the cage.

They felt no remorse of guilt for what they did. To them, they were merely holding doors open for those of a higher class. The things they guarded were alive but did not have a valued life. They saw plants as higher than these caged things.

They also did not feel as a scimitar blade came through the darkness and sliced through both of their throats. In one violent motion, Gobolt had rushed through the entrance with a battle cry and with only two fluid and powerful arm strokes, he had cut deeply through both of the guard's necks – twice – so quick they did not even have a chance to raise their weapons. And so deep that their heads lolled back, held on by the thinnest strips of flesh, before their bodies crashed to the floor.

Standing, with a smattering of the guard's arterial spray dripping from his face, Gobolt walked over to the corpse pile and pulled down the fish creature.

The Priest hesitantly followed Gobolt's trail of death into the room. His eyes fixed on the guard's corpses. "Our Father who art in heaven, hallowed be thy name," he said under his breath. Though he had seen many die before – and been the cause of their death for most of them, he now held life – even the lowest demon life – in a much higher esteem. In his faith-filled mind, they were all God's creations to him. "Thy kingdom come, thy will be done. On earth as it is in heaven."

"This ain't heaven or earth, so quit your praying and help me," Gobolt said as he poked his blade into the ripped-out chest of the fish creature, wanting to see where Saskia went. The rotting fish smell of this corpse filled his nose, as he grimaced down at it. “Smells like a sailor’s arsehole,” he mumbled to himself.

The Priest’s hand crossed himself towards the corpses, hoping his prayers helped their eternal souls on their travels into the afterlife. He then turned and walked over to where the fish creature’s body lay. As he walked by, he glanced into the cage, seeing the many terrified creatures within, all of them looking at these two men in confusion and fear.

“What do we do about them?” the Priest asked, motioning to the cage.

“We shall deal with them in a moment. First… Where the fuck has she gone?” Gobolt asked as his blade pried open the flaps of skin on the creature, seeing only the decimated guts, sinew and bone that lay inside.

“She has gone wherever this creature had come from,” the Priest answered.

Gobolt looked at his companion with a quizzical look. “A spell?”

“It’s how we travel. How I got above. She crawled through the soul-”

“Wait…” Gobolt looked down again at the body. “A fucking witch’s Doorway? They’re real?”

Witch’s Doorways were things of urban legend. At least that is what Gobolt had thought – a story to scare the young. A rhyme which young children sang as they innocently played.

Beware, beware the Witch’s grasp, With one fair swoop, will rip your heart.

And climb on through to your very soul to kill your loved ones, one and all.

"So... we can only go back in... one of these?" Gobolt spoke softly to himself.

"...If you go through someone who came from where you need to go to, yes," the Priest continued. "But you won't be able to control when..."

"When?" Gobolt queried.

"Unless you're a witch, you can't control when you exit. You could come out in the past, the present or the future. There's no telling. When I traveled, I came out across many existences. I saw cities like this one. Cities as dust. Communities in caves, or tents. Some with sticks, some with weapons of light. There is no way to control how to exit. They, though. They have the magic."

Gripping his blade tight, Gobolt walked over to the cell door – and with one almighty swing, cut through the lock which hung heavily upon it, sending it in pieces onto the floor.

Without its bolt holding it in place, the cell door swung outwards.

"You want out?" he shouted to the prisoners. "Well get the fuck out, then." He then turned to the Priest as he walked toward the exit. "You coming?"

"Where are we going?" the Priest asked.

"If the only way out is through me, Ferenc or that bitch cunt – then she's our doorway... The when we go to can be damned." He reached out and took the unused blade from the Priest's hand.

"I'm gonna need this back if you're not gonna use it…"

"What do I do?" the Priest asked, dreading the response.

"We're gonna put that demon side of yours to good use." He smiled. "You're gonna go tell her I'm coming."

"She may not even be in this place anymore," the Priest protested.

"Only one way to find out," came the reply.

Only a few minutes later, the Priest sprinted down the asphalt of Great George Street, past all the cars and debris – on his way toward Parliament Square. In a nervous panic, his human legs carried him as fast they could, the breath in his body painful within his lungs as he breathed in the stagnant air at speed. Desperate to keep control, he exerted himself to his maximum effort as he started to approach some of the last of the demons marching into the Square.

"*The wolf is here*!" he screamed as he ran. The breath burning heavier in his lungs, he struggled to keep going. "*Tell the Queen*!" he continued shouting, as some demons turned to him in shock at his exclamations "*The wolf is here*!"

Gobolt did not know if the queen was even part of this world, or if she just traveled through. But he knew that if she was not here, then he would in likelihood never be able to find her – and his life here would soon be at its end. Though if she was, then she would not allow these demons to kill him if she found out he had followed her –

Especially as the Black Witch left her mark on him, whatever that meant. She wouldn't let the young witch, Saskia, hurt him after all. Elizabeth thought that the Black Witch had her grip on him and he would use this to his advantage as best as he could.

As the Priest sprinted down the long and dark street, he continued to shout the same warnings about the Wolf at the top of his lungs – hoping to his God that his words were heard and understood. If it failed and Gobolt was taken and killed, he would have to hope that these demons would not know that he came to their realm with him. He hoped – if that happened – that he would be able to save his own life from the same fate.

Following from behind, Gobolt strode purposefully through the throng of oncoming demons who were already advancing down the street towards him. Ones who had heard the Priest's cries and wished to capture this interloper. As they got near, he swung his scimitar with the fluidity and grace of a dancer.

As if his movements through this attack had been rehearsed many times before, his hand swung like it was being carried by the wind, on a path that it had always been intended to take, his superiority in battle high above the desperate attempts of his attackers which now stood up against him. Each blow he dealt out against these demons dispatched or maimed them with a furious and precise ease. Without even a breath lost and a snarl on his face, the fact he had one working eye did not hamper his ability in the slightest. It was a battle that none of these monsters could win on these streets, their weapons never hitting their mark and their lives being cut out of existence. If this even was an existence.

With Parliament Square fast approaching ahead, Gobolt could not see how many of these demons were now advancing on him. But he could hear the Priest still shouting ahead, still warning them. He could not see if his plan was working, if the Blood Queen had been alerted to his presence. He did not know whether they wanted to capture or kill him – he just kept slicing down each and every attack that confronted him, unleashing his brutal hell upon these damned hell spawn.

But as he fought, his body had started to become more and more exhausted, more with each body that was sent to the ground into bloody chunks. The further he got into this bloody assault, the more blood that was spilled, the slower he became. But even at a quarter of his strength and speed, he was still vastly superior in battle than any of these approaching demons.

"*The wolf is here*!" the Priest continued to shout, struggling to run much further, praying with each step for this plan not to be folly. But before he could take any more steps, a huge demon grabbed him with monstrous strength. Lifted him up like a doll and leaned into him – an inch from his face. Growling at the now cowering priest this demon spoke with hateful power. "*You are not one of us*!" he hissed aggressively as thick gloopy spittle dripped from the corners of his leathery black mouth, and down onto the priest's tunic.

As a marker for the linear passage of events, time ran differently – if at all - across all realms. Whether in the realm of the humans – which they referred to as reality – or the realm of the fire demons, or the deepest darkest realms of the below, not one hour ran the same across all infinite plains of existence. The difference between the hell which Gobolt and the Priest found themselves in and the land which they traversed from was vastly different. In this place below there was no time, so nothing to match to the worlds above. This realm had no framework of when it was, and was such, a creation out of existence with no fixed exit to a certain time.

After only a few days of being away on their mission, King James' army returned to the palace without their general in tow, without the Priest he took with him. Upon seeing this, the king had no other option but to expect that the worst had befallen them. He feared that either Gobolt and the Priest had missed the deadline for their passage home, so were stuck in whichever realm they had gone to, or had died at the hands of the Blood Queen that they chased.

He had sent some men back into the swamp, to meet with the monster. But it was no longer there. No swamp. No doorway. And without this, he had no way to save or avenge Gobolt, Ferenc or the Priest. Though ignoring the kingly order, James was silently glad Gobolt had refused to take his army with him.

So all he could do was wait. Wait for his lost men to somehow find a way home, or wait for the

Blood Queen to make an appearance and confirm their fates. But with time running differently between realms and without their passage in the swamp, the king accepted that even if Gobolt and the Priest managed to find another way out, they might not make it back within his lifetime

This forlorn royal then spent the rest of his life holding onto the splinter of hope that his men *might* return. He hoped that maybe when they came back, that the good fight could continue as before. But in his malaise, he sunk into an unescapable depression. His secret armies soon disbanded from his neglect and he spent the rest of his life in a drunken stupor until, one day during his 58th year, malaria stole his life away. Well, that's the official story.

The leech, the prisoner who had executed the monster within the swamp, had escaped the putrid confines of its captor's lair. Before any of the other captives even thought of how to escape the prison below, this leech had dragged its way up through the filth and muck, up to the forest above. As it pulled itself onto the swamp's edge and breathed lungfuls of the fresh and verdant air – the first it had tasted in years – it glanced back at the swamp – which only a moment before, was made of thick excrement, and was now starting to solidify and turn from a brown to a grayish dead hue. The one path for the other prisoners to escape from was now dying – forever trapping them below. Stuck within the putrid confines of the monster's lair, it would only be a matter of time before they turned on each other for food, before eventually starving to death, or suffocating on their own damnation.

Walking away in a daze from this now solidifying tomb, its body was withered and pale. Open sores covered its pale frame, and dripped with pus and the remnants of swamp sewerage. This leech started to notice that all of the otherworldly trees and wildlife, which once flooded this forest, now just lay dead and pale as hollow husks on the dirt ground. The weather that once changed on a dime throughout these trees, had now become a constant and was no longer the menagerie of interchanging wild seasons that it once was.

Opening the four flaps of skin on its face, it exposed its large leech's mouth and took a deeper breath in for a moment. Relishing the freshness. Reveling in its luck. Ignoring the deaths its fellow prisoners were condemned to.

All that it felt as it walked away to its freedom was a chilly breeze that ambled through the trees on this autumnal evening. The nearer it got to the edge of the forest, the more it saw the woodland life starting to bloom. Life that belonged in this realm.

Over the next few years, the forest itself would soon find its path back from the death it had suffered, as the monster was executed. It would once again be filled with all types of natural life and no traces of anything from other realms.

The world, as Gobolt and Ferenc had known it, would now be nothing but a memory to them –

for they would never return here to see anyone they knew or loved. As Gobolt was held down by a dozen demons in the other, more terrifying realm which lay below – as the Blood Queen heard word of his arrival and demanded he be brought to her – the world that they had come from had already become lost to the ages. The king was now dust in his tomb. The first battalion army were all now a thing of myth. Not one living human on earth remembered the name of Gobolt of Mythur Standing, and no one knew any more of Count Ferenc than him being the husband of Elizabeth Bathory. A cruel coward of a man who died whilst in a futile battle – but that was only amongst the living humans. Gobolt and Ferenc's names would live on for many years on the lips of the dead and within the underworld. Their names would be spoken with reverence by those who dwelt in the shadows for more than an eternity.

Emergence & Atonement

Gobolt stared from his cage. Looking upward in horror at the flayed skin of his friend, as he fought back his bubbling emotions of fury and sadness.

Now proudly displayed on the top of the hill of bodies, overlooking the bone altar on which the cocooned rested, Ferenc's empty eyes stared out blindly. He could hear screams. He could hear the cries. He could hear cheers. The words that he could hear were now just noises without any meaning. He had heard the word "Ferenc" spoken a few times, but did not know what that word meant, nor remember that he even had a name, let alone that one. Or what the meaning for the word "name" even was.

The cage Gobolt was imprisoned in was large and placed to the right of the bone altar. At the front of this altar, a still unconscious Rebecca was still tied to a large wooden stake. To the left, Elizabeth sat on her throne which had been moved here, as Leanne and Helen stood to one side, waiting attentively.

The cage itself was four meters wide and tall, made of thick steel bars. Its girth filled up a wealth of space on top of the hill made of bodies. Gobolt was shackled in huge chains, and he stared in fury at the remains of his skinned friend, hanging above.

"He makes a fine banner, don't you think?" Elizabeth grinned at the displayed Ferenc, as she walked over to the cage.

"This man..." she said, addressing the congregation loudly, whilst staring directly at Gobolt. "This man came here stop me... to stop *us*."

The crowd howled in fury along with each word.

"He came to hurt me..." she continued.

Their screams of rage grew louder.

"And has hurt *many* of you on his journey..." She motioned to the skin of Ferenc, with a grand sweeping gesture of her arm and spoke in a mock shocked and theatrical tone "He came to take my one true love away from *me*!"

Gobolt looked out to the crowd with a grimace as they commenced their chants of "*kill him, kill him, kill him".*

"Kill him?" the queen asked the crowd, before turning to Gobolt. "Do you want to die, wolf-man?"

Smiling a sadistic smile, she walked up nearer to his cage, the volume of her voice now dropping as she spoke only to him, not the crowd. "Do you want to die at my hand, do you want me to plunge my fingers into your throat and rip out your path to breathe?"

Gobolt smirked at her, knowing her plans to intimidate were futile.

"I get you think you have tricked me into imprisoning you, but what can you do to stop me? What is the plan? Do you have an amulet? A spell?" Her words drifted off as she turned to the altar, where she glanced at his bloodied scimitars, now resting against one of the bone legs. She walked over and picked one up, looking at its runes etched down the blade. "Did you think these would harm me? This primitive magic is for the lesser forms? Like those out there."

With a blade in her hand she looked to the crowd again, speaking out loud, holding it up high. "He thought he could kill your queen *with these*?!" she exclaimed with glee as she turned back to Gobolt in the cage, the crowd joining in her mockery of him.

Her smiling face suddenly dropped to a cruel grimace, as she lifted up the blade and slit her own throat whilst she screamed, *"Your trinkets have no dominion over me!"* the wound healing back up as fast as she had slit it.

"I don't have to kill you. Just have to rip you apart…" Gobolt said, pained by his shackles.

"Who do you think you are?" she snarled down at her prisoner. "You think I won't destroy your entire existence?"

"You better check with your master before you do… You know the one I mean." Gobolt staggered painfully to his feet. The large manacles that clasped his hand behind his back were very heavy and made him feel like his wrists were breaking. The chain around his neck tied him to the back of the cage itself, weighing upon his shoulders. On his feet, he took a step forward, that step was as far as the shackles would allow him to go. He started intently at the queen. "You know the one I mean, *you fettered crone's arse*!"

Her expression filled somehow with more rage. Any beauty that was on her face before, was now replaced by the ugliness of unbridled hate.

"Why don't you tell your little followers down there? That you can't hurt me… That you live in servitude of a higher *cunt*." His words dripping with his contempt for her.

Quickly steeling her temperament, she closed her eyes for a second then turned to the crowd who were still in the throes of screaming adulation.

"No, my children. We should *not* kill him even though we crave his blood," she shouted. "You see, I have a better punishment for one who interrupted us." She walked over to Rebecca who was still unconscious and kissed her on the forehead. "We have a more important task than revenge. We have my daughter! The reason we are even here! Who cares about this filth in the cage?"

Gobolt looked wide-eyed to the woman tied to the stake. *Could it be true*? He thought. *Hanna?*

Elizabeth walked to the cocoon on the bone altar and stood in front of it, looking down. She gazed with love at the pulsating and glowing mass. On the top of it was a huge mouth-like crevice. Closed yet drooling. As she ran her fingers across its lips lightly, they opened and closed – for a brief moment showing the baby below. The real Hanna. Trapped in this shell. Tendrils from every part of the inside of this cocoon burrowed deep in her small body. Her whole being plugged into this fleshy mass. Being one with it.

Turning, Elizabeth glanced left to Helen and Leanne, as she walked to the front of the altar again. "Bring out the accomplice!" Elizabeth commanded.

Up the bone steps walked a large guard, dragging the Priest with him, with one of his huge hands wrapped around the back of this prisoner's neck. The Priest's hands were shackled in front of him and he had been beaten considerably. His face was a mass of bruises and flowed blood.

"Put him in with the dog," Elizabeth ordered the guard, as he then dragged the Priest to the cage and threw him inside – locking the door behind him.

Landing with a thud onto his back, the Priest grimaced in a shock of pain.

"With the stench of humanity dripping off him, he tried to helped the wolf-man destroy us!" She continued to address the baying crowd. "A Priest of all things! An emissary of a fictitious God."

The Leviathan's roar echoed through the square with an immense power – This sound cut the crowd's noise to a hush – All turned to the darkness in awe, Elizabeth looked out towards the nothingness, which now sat at the very edge of the square. From this sheet of night, large tentacles protruded out of the solid black and flailed slowly in the air - poised to attack and destroy the last of the square. To consume the final remnants of this world.

"Soon, my beautiful. Soon," Elizabeth said softly.

The crowd continued to ecstatically cheer.

The Priest spoke in hushed and pained tones to Gobolt. "They don't know that I'm a demon," he said as he moved to sit up on the metal grated floor, his cracked ribs and bruises making this simple movement agony. Gritting his teeth, he grunted as he shuffled himself up, with his back against the bars.

"Does it even matter if they know? You're a bit fucked no matter what you are, wouldn't you say?" Gobolt whispered back. The crowd's cheers and raucousness drowned out their conversation from being able to be heard by the queen. "Even if you could get out of your shackles…" he continued, "you're still in a fucking cage!"

The Priest painfully smiled at Gobolt. "This cage can't hold my kind of demon."

"And what will you do if you get out? Pray them to death? I'm still gonna be stuck here." Gobolt said as he motioned to his large chains. The Priest now noticed the banner above the bone alter and stared in shock – seeing the fate of Ferenc. "We can't save him anymore…" Gobolt said, trying to assuage the horror they both felt. "I guess the only thing we got left to do is either die like dogs, or kill the bitch. Or both."

"We *can* still save him, you know?" the Priest said. "Dead isn't always dead in these realms.

We could try to bring him back. At least part of him."

Elizabeth then motioned to Leanne, who now walked over to where Rebecca was tied to the stake. She slapped her fake daughter hard in the face, violently forcing her out of her calming unconsciousness, back into the nightmare she had hoped was but a dream.

As her eyelids burst open, her vision was flooded with the thousands of baying demons – each awaiting her demise. Now holding a long knife up to Rebecca's throat, Leanne untied her. She pushed the knife harder, as it cut into the first few layers of her skin. Rebecca froze in fear trying to back away from the cutting blade. Leanne's demonic expression snarled at her. "Resist and I'll empty your throat onto the dirt," she said. "Go willingly and you will feel nothing."

"Leave her the fuck alone!" Gobolt screamed at Leanne.

Elizabeth cackled at this attempt by her prisoner to command the proceedings.

"Who wants to see the wolf?" she shouted into the fever-pitch crowd, who got louder in approval. "Are you ready to change?" she shouted intently at him. "We have other business to tend to. You can busy yourself with ripping up your friend."

With this, Gobolt's expression dropped. He had not thought that she had this power. He looked to the Priest in a panic. "If you can get out... Run… Take Hanna... And run…"

"Hanna?" the Priest enquired.

"Ferenc's daughter!" Turning on Gobolt's word, the priest saw Rebecca standing there. Unable to understand the situation.

Tuning back, the Priest's said dejectedly, "I won't live long enough to take anyone."

Elizabeth raised her hand and pointed it toward the cage. "Arise Lycan," she said with glee as she closed her eyes, casting her silent spell over her prisoner.

Like a punch to his face, Gobolt's head was suddenly yanked back as he screamed in agony. His veins raising up as the blood pumped through his body. Boiling in his veins. Searing his nerves with a familiar agony he always dreaded. His heart building to beat faster than it ever had could do as a human.

Gritting his teeth, he managed to look down to the Priest and spoke in a growl at him "I'm sorry I did this to you! Get Hanna and run..."

Elizabeth laughed more as she watched the pain that Gobolt was in, as the wolf started breaking through. Leanne had dragged Rebecca over to the altar where Elizabeth stood, her knife still dug into Rebecca's neck, splitting through more layers of skin as she did.

"I hope the Priest tastes nice, as it will be the last thing you will taste. But hurry... for the darkness will soon tear you limb from limb. And that will not be on my head. My mother could stop the night if she wanted."

Then, grabbing Rebecca by her hair, Elizabeth took the knife from Leanne and held it back up to Rebecca's neck, the wound there dripping blood. Not enough to threaten her life, but enough to raise a panic. Trying to struggle, Rebecca lashed out and elbowed Elizabeth in the face. Sending a shock through her body, the Blood Queen gripped the knife tighter and in a split-second, stabbed Rebecca in the arm – three times in the same area - a retaliation for the elbow, then returned the blade and pressed it hard to her throat.

"One more insubordination and your death shall last an eternity, instead of a mere moment," Elizabeth sneered.

Gobolt's body was arcing in the chains, his biceps growing then twisting. His fingers then split in two and his canine claws burst through and out of them. Bits of his human skin sloughed to the floor, as the wolf's entrance discarded them.

The Priest looked out at the Blood Queen in a panic, then back to Gobolt. Without considering his plan fully, he quickly moved his head downward and folded himself inside his chest, splitting open his tunic, his manacled hands retreating in the same path inside him. From his back, with incredible speed, the demon came forth, breaking through the back of the tunic with a scream of fury amidst emitting a bone-crunching sound.

Elizabeth saw none of this and was casting her spells over the cocoon.

With his demon arms now released from his human shell, the Priest launched himself at Gobolt, who was still screaming in agony as the wolf knocked at the door to his mind. Landing on the Lycan's transforming chest, with his demon tail hanging down to the floor, his long black gnarled arms held himself up on his companion shoulders. Leaning into Gobolt's ear he snarled, "Get your revenge if you must... But don't give your life for a girl you do not know… I will save Ferenc... I do this for you, to prove that I am God's child!"

Opening his mouth, the Priest exposed his many razor-sharp teeth with a growl, then bit down into the chain around Gobolt's neck – the strength of his bite being of such power and sharpness that it split the metal apart as easily as if it were rotten wood. The chains fell crashing to the floor, as he then crawled over the back of the emerging wolf and bit through the manacles, freeing his arms.

Crashing to his knees, free of the restraints, Gobolt cried aloud as his teeth were pushed out of his separating gums, becoming replaced with sharp canine fangs. His face started to change its shape, as his jaw cracked off then started to reset in different places. Happening as many times as he had bones within his body. Over and over again.

Elizabeth, meanwhile, held Rebecca over the cocoon which was now wide open upwards, exposing its tendrilled baby deep inside. Holding up the knife Elizabeth looked in glee at her adoring crowd. Leanne held the prisoner by her arms and felt the warm glow of fulfillment as she saw the end that was about to arrive.

Gobolt screamed in agony as his spine broke in half, then reset into a new formation.

Now at the other end of the cage, the demon Priest bit through the door lock, pushed the door open and turned to Gobolt. "NOW!" he shouted to him. "Get your revenge!"

As Gobolt looked up, his eyeballs burst outwards, the liquid inside spilled down his cheeks. Through the jelly of his burst eyes, his wolf eyes now pushed out from deep below.

Ushering any of the humanity he had left, he scrambled to his feet, roaring as his claws exposed their talons, tearing out of the cage with destruction and escape on his mind. As he ran, the Priest scampered out and over the cage, then disappeared in the opposite direction of the crowd and into the dark night.

Through the air, the wolf slashed out, his claws ripping through Leanne's head, knocking Rebecca to the ground. Before Elizabeth could react at all, Gobolt had turned on her and clawed at her chest. As his mind started to fade away, he had no idea if he could kill her, he only cared about the doorway out and about Ferenc's daughter. He didn't know how she stood here as an adult – but he had no care to find out within the fury of this predicament. All he could do was tear at her body, over and over, slash after slash, whispering under his breath the spell the Priest had told him before their capture, the spell that opened the door to her soul. This as her flesh was ripped away in a violent fury and the bone of her breast plate ripped apart, exposing her organs below.

As this beast clawed into her, Elizabeth tried to summon magic, but the intense pain drowned her into a shocked haze.

The crowd, upon seeing this attack, now started to scream in anger and crawl over themselves, heading up to the bone altar to save their queen from the wolf. But no matter how fast they ran, no matter what they planned to do, they could not stop the wolf's tirade into the organs of Elizabeth – they could not save her from the pain she screamed and flailed her arms at, trying in her weakness to beat this attacker away.

From the stairs, Helen had pulled out a long blade from a sheath around her waist and screamed toward the murderous wolf. Her demon mouth opened so far that the human mask tore in two. As she got to the wolf, her intent was short-lived as he had seen her coming – and with one single slash of his claw, knocked the weapon from her hand and tore the demon's head clean off – sending her body crashing backwards, down the bone-made stairs.

Rebecca scrambled to escape this horror, but before she could get away, the wolf leaned off from the altar, whilst his hands remained deep in Elizabeth's chest – clawing viciously inside and he bit into the back of Rebecca's jacket – pulling her towards him. She turned to this in horror as the last of his human face broke apart – the wolf's fur bursting through. Looking at her through his pain he growled, "I'm here to save you..." his words turned to a howl. Before the queen could fight any more and as she screamed a blood-filled gurgle, he turned and silenced her by tearing at her neck with his large teeth.

Gobolt hoped that if he did manage to save Ferenc's daughter from this place, that the wolf would not try to eat her. But even if it did – it would be a preferable death to the one that the Blood Queen had planned to give her.

Out of fear, Rebecca stepped back, away from the monster wolf – but as she did, a throng of demons crawled up the staircase towards her, climbing over each other to save their queen.

The wolf that Gobolt changed into was a lot bigger than he was as a human and his mind now almost totally slipped away. Everything he knew drifted into the distance as quickly as the Blood Queen bled out.

The only part left of Gobolt managed to command the wolf's next action – as it lunged at Rebecca – who was advanced upon by the approaching horde, and bit into her jacket sleeve, managing to avoid biting through her arm. With a firm grip, he dragged her toward him, pulling her back into the exposed wound which led into the passageway to another world. A passageway which was now nearly collapsing as Elizabeth's life was almost gone.

As the wolf dragged Rebecca into the open wound in the Blood Queen's chest, the world around began its ending.

The demons got to the queen too late. They attempted to follow suit and climb through her portal to chase these heathens, but the doorway had gone. All they had left was the end of this world and the Leviathan which was almost upon them. Not that they were in danger of dying – but they could not follow.

Before the darkness consumed this land, those left in the square saw the demon Priest climb up the flag banner and rip away the skin of Ferenc – then he disappeared into the night.

A Brave New World

Standing in the middle of a bustling city, an immense wolf once called Gobolt now stared out over a much different Parliament Square. The demon-filled apocalyptic one now reversed into a bright day. Elizabeth's blood still dripped from his lips as he looked around wide-eyed.

On this clear fall day, buses, taxis and cars drove around the circumference of the grassy area on which the wolf now stood, his bloodlust subsiding as the tourists and commuters traveled their needed routes on foot, paying no mind to the animal that had just bloodily crawled out of the dirt nearby, posing no threat to him.

With no capacity to understand this new environment, the wolf's eyes darted sheepishly around the area – on the lookout for any danger about to rear its ugly head. But nothing came for him, though despite the seeming safety he continued to growl in a low exhalation, in case of any threat lying in wait.

The people, though strangers to him, walked by without a second look. But there were not only people walking by, there were also a wild variety of creatures which had long dwelt in the shadows – now in the daylight with their heads held high. People with tails, people with more than two legs, incorporeal people – all these kinds were walking alongside seemingly normal humans. Walking as equals, with their own purposes to wherever they had in their schedules.

The monsters here were normal and every day. Accepted for what they were, the shadows here fully lifted across the reality.

In this wolf's mouth hung Rebecca's now bloodstained denim jacket – half stuck out of the ground below. After accepting that this place was not full of immediate danger, like the world he was just in, the wolf turned around and opened his blood-stained maw, dropping the sleeve of the jacket.

In an instant, an unmistakable aroma hit his nose. The person he dragged in with him was still here. He could still smell her. He *knew* she was important – but did not know *why*. Though he could not comprehend this information – Gobolt's command to save her remained, and was all the wolf could now focus on.

Pulling the rest of the jacket out from the hole he had crawled through, the wolf then started to dig into the dirt. Deeper, then sniffing again. Digging, then sniffing. As it dug further and further, a white shirt started to come into view through the mud – Rebecca's white and now torn shirt.

With its teeth, the wolf leaned into this exposed hole, then gently bit into a loose part of the shirt which stuck out from the ground and tugged at it. He could sense that something was still here. The smell was too strong for him to ignore. The command in his mind was loud and stern. He *had* to dig. His wolf mind did not know Rebecca, did not know Hanna nor did not know what she was or could have been. He did not know Ferenc. His mind only knew that she had to be safe.

As he pulled the shirt out of the dirt, he released his teeth, then used his snout to move aside the collar which had been folded over. As he dug his nose in, a shock of pale soft skin came into view. It was Rebecca – but during the travel from one realm to another, she had reverted to the age she had originally left this world. The wolf stared down at this barely three-month-old baby.

He nuzzled her face, and she opened her wide blue eyes. With all of her innocence displayed in her gaze, she stared up hopefully at this terrifying one-eyed beast. As they shared a silent look, she smiled and giggled softly.

Folding over the shirt's sleeves and using them like a makeshift cradle, the wolf picked up the baby with its teeth, making sure to take great care of this cargo.

He knew that he could not stay here. Even though he felt safe, he had to take this child away, somewhere isolated.

The darkness had nearly folded in on itself in the realm below. The congregation now left, having run away to avoid the Leviathan.

All that remained as the darkness crept in, consuming the remnants of Rebecca's old world, was Elizabeth laying back over the altar next to the cocoon. Her chest ripped widely open, her insides mauled and ripped to a liquid pulp.

Her dead eyes stared out at what was once her child – her last thoughts had been distressed as she saw all her plans fail. As she witnessed the avatar of Rebecca disappearing within her and simultaneously, saw the cocoon wither and die as her child's real life had left with that abomination of an avatar.

The roars of this beast now became a deafening din, as it approached the body on the altar. The body of the one who had called it into existence in the first place. The body of one who was not a demon, so could not survive its hunger.

A tentacle burst out of the dark and covered the Blood Queen's corpse – dragging it back into the midnight nothingness.

Soon, this world was no more. All that was left was the darkness the demons dwelt in, their lives now empty and without purpose, as they had lost their cause and their meaning. Having seen their Queen fall, having seen their savior disappear, they did not know what they were to do. And it would be a long time until they would find any new purpose.

As the wolf tore into the Blood Queen's chest, across the many realms to the shack which sat on the small island in the middle of the lake, the Black Witch fell down onto the wooden floorboards. She screamed in insurmountable pain as she clutched at her chest wildly.

Running over to her, Saskia tried to grab her mother's arm, to steady her and help her back up. "What is it?" she asked in a panic. "What's happening?"

The Black Witch's eyes spilled bloody tears as she sobbed angrily through the pain, as she felt her chest being ripped in two in unison with Elizabeth's fate.

"What's wrong?" Saskia shouted in terror.

The Black Witch, now in a blinding pain, shoved Saskia away from her with all of her might. The Young witch was sent flying backwards and smashed into a wooden stool. Splintering in into pieces beneath her.

Dropping to her front, the Black Witch used all of her strength to crawl across the floor to the door of the shack, not knowing where she was going, or what she was trying to do. The pain clouded her whole being and blocked out all other thoughts. Her whole body was only running on animal instinct. Her flight emotion was in full bloom, trying to escape her inescapable pain. As her hands grabbed onto the wood in front of her, to pull her body along, some of her fingernails broke backwards, this pain though secondary to the feeling of her heart splitting in two – feeling all the pain Elizabeth was actually experiencing.

Unable to crawl anymore, she rolled onto her back and emitted a loud a shrill scream as she clutched at her chest – in the realm below the Blood Queen felt her last moments torn apart – and the pain inside reached its apex.

Saskia could only look on helplessly, scared at the anger and pain the Black Witch was experiencing.

Outside on the lake, her screams echoed out and down into the water. Her pain had grown and her screams now gotten louder, until her final scream, her one terrifying final scream. One full of power and hate, one that burst the glass windows of her shack outward – sending their shards tumbling to the dirt ground below. This scream spread out and flooded the depths of the black lake. This raging cry split through the water's darkness and through the very bodies of the fish creatures that dwelled within it, liquefying their insides as it passed through their fragile bodies. And in an instant, extinguished their lives.

With the sound now gone, an unnatural silence filled the land. The bodies of these creatures had started to float up to the surface. At first only a few, but quickly became dozens upon dozens, until the whole surface of the lake was littered with their genocide.

The Black Witch lay in torment upon the floor of her now windowless shack. The pain that had ravaged her body was now just an echo within her repugnant ancient heart. In the dull hum of her hate, in the vast recesses of her evil, she vowed revenge on the wolf. She promised to all of the old

Gods that she would hunt him down and make him pay for stealing away her firstborn.

Out of the busy city, the wolf had run. Away from the people, away from the loud machines which had moved around the streets at terrifying speeds, away from the large structures which seemed so high they looked to be breaking through the skies and into another realm.

He had run over fields and through countryside. Past villages and through towns. Going as fast as he could, away from any dangers that may follow him, all to protect this small life.

With the shirt clenched in its jaw, the incubus – Rebecca – slept inside, unaware of the fear in this wolf's heart. All the horrors of her life had now gone and dissipated in the haze of her dreams.

The wolf had – where it could – stopped to find sustenance for this baby. He drank up water from a stream and dribbled it gently into the child's mouth. He chewed berries and let the child eat her fill from the mush. He tried all he could to keep this innocence safe.

Upon arriving at the edge of a thick forest, with the baby hanging from its mouth in the shirt-made cradle, the wolf felt some apprehension before making his way inside. This place carried a feeling of familiarity, but it knew no more than that. But he had to find a place to hide, so cautiously entered the thick tree line and walked into the forest itself.

Deep inside, after a couple of hours of walking through the now luscious and verdant landscape – the wolf came to a large clearing. A clearing that was once home to a monster in a swamp, but now a place where a single large willow tree stood - its branches full of autumnal blossom, a vision of tranquility and beauty. A place untouched by the hand of man.

After days of running, this exhausted wolf now slowly walked up to the base of the large willow tree. He placed the cradle on the ground with care. The vibrant green grass pushed its way up around the fabric. The baby – who had been crying for the past hour – had showed no sign of stopping. Its cries echoed throughout the trees on its journey here.

Laying down and with the baby now placed between its front paws, the wolf looked at this tearful child. Whether she cried for food, cried for drink, cried for its parents or the life that it felt it lacked – this Lycan did not know. He just moved his large head down to the baby and one by one licked her cheeks – taking her tears away from her. As he did this, the baby slowly ceased her screaming. Her piercing wails now ebbed off into the distance.

She raised her small hand out of the shirt, touched the wolf's snout and let out a small laugh. She then softly gripped his whiskers. Sharing a moment together, both this wolf and incubus were far from the people they were in the other realm. Both had lost the memories of their battles – yet both felt safe here and safe with each other.

The wolf knew that he must protect her life. He did not know why, he did not know how. But he knew this life was greater than his own. And she looked at the wolf as her parent. Her security. Her protector.

A few blossoms from the branches above now drifted downward upon them, dancing in the breeze as this wolf and child now drifted off into a mutually deep sleep.

The evil was now left far, far behind them. The danger no longer imminent… For now, at least.

Epilogue

Ten years after the wolf and the incubus slept under the willow tree... On the other side of the world... A bedside alarm rang out with a shocking volume.

The repeating tones echoed throughout this New York brownstone townhouse.

From inside the bedroom, the sheets covered this sleeping figure. This was a man, who in order to wake up, needed his alarm set at an ear-piercing volume – not that it worked here. He remained snoring under the covers as it blasted noisily.

Walking into this room a small female fish creature strode in – dressed in a fitted black suit. A Bluetooth headset in her ear, she was busy on a call. She carried an open ledger in her arms and held a steaming cup of coffee with the other.

"He'll be on time. Yes… I promise!" She placed the coffee on the bedside. "11a.m. Yup. I assure you. What else do you want me to say?" She hung up the call by tapping on the headset.

"Wakey, wakey. Time to greet the morning. Don't make me a liar, you lazy bastard." She walked over to the large curtains and opened them noisily.

The metal hooks scraped loudly, as they were pulled across the pole they rested on.

The man in the bed still didn't stir, he was busy dreaming the same dream he had dreamt every night recently. Standing in front of a God, striking a bargain with it. Reality then changed. And he lived someone else's life.

"Get up!" She kicked the mound on the bed where the man lay.

Waking with a start, the man looked wide-eyed at her. The memories of the dream slipping away from his mind – waiting to reappear the next night.

"The fuck?!" he complained.

"Breakfast will be downstairs. You need it..." she said, motioning to his cheek.

He put his hand up to his face. It was slowly blackening from an onset of rot.

"You skipped eating again, didn't you?"

He smiled at her.

She grabbed the coffee off of the bed-side table. Handed it to him. Then walked out of the room, "You've got 30 minutes," she said matter of factly.

Taking a sip of coffee, he pressed the power button on his remote control, turning on the TV. The newscasters there were talking about the latest tragedy, a school shooting. A terrible, but seemingly increasing common, occurrence. The human male newscaster spoke softly as he talked about those who had tragically lost their lives. The female newscast sat next to him – complete with green scaled skin, pointed ears and a wide razor-toothed mouth – and tried to fight back the tears in order to remain professional.

He turned off the TV with a sigh and stood up out of the bed.

Walking into his bathroom, he turned on the light, filling the mostly mirrored room with a bright glow.

Looking into the mirror, he saw his pale and tired face. Bald, bearded and undead, he stood in his nudity – seeing and believing only what he saw now. With no memory of his real past, he presumed his name had always been Deacon Sorbic and that he had always been a successful horror author.

He had no idea that, a long time ago, deep in another realm, he had been re-born as one of the undead; the final act of atonement from a dying demon Priest. His memories had been eaten away, just as fast as his flesh once was. His skin was all that was left to resurrect this man now looking at himself in the mirror. This man who was once was called Count Ferenc.

A man who would – one day – know his name again. But this would not happen until the Black Witch found him.

Printed in Poland
by Amazon Fulfillment
Poland Sp. z o.o., Wrocław

62330024R00186